"You live in Texas, I live in Montana…"

Cassie saw the unexpected glimmer of amusement in Andrew's eyes as she spoke. She tried again. "Besides, I don't even really know you."

"The lawyer I need to see is out of town for a week. Means I have to stick around a little longer than I'd planned. That gives us the perfect opportunity, if you ask me."

The humor was there, all right, sexy and dangerous. How tempting it would be to follow his lead…not to worry about the future, just to enjoy a day or two, a week perhaps, with an alluring stranger. But it was a luxury Cassie couldn't afford.

She stood, setting her lemonade on the table beside her. "Sorry, Andrew," she said lightly. "I'm not in the market to start anything new, no matter how… temporary." She saw the regret in his eyes and felt her own regret. But it didn't hurt; that was the blessed thing. Thank goodness she'd learned how to stop before she did get hurt. Before her son got hurt, too.

And so she walked away from Andrew Morris.

10639270

Dear Reader,

I've always been fascinated by Montana, with its mountains
and prairies, its rivers and ranchlands. I'm therefore delighted
to be part of this trilogy about the women of Montana—women
with hopes and passions as grand as the Big Sky state itself.
Thea, Jolie and Cassie Maxwell are Montana sisters who grew
apart over the years, as they struggled to deal with their
difficult father and their rebellious kid brother.

I hope you've enjoyed the stories of Thea and Jolie, the
youngest and oldest Maxwell sisters. After finding love with
wonderful men, and in the process learning to open their
hearts, Thea and Jolie are hoping that their sister Cassie—the
"middle" Maxwell—will have the same luck in love. Cassie,
however, has too many reasons not to fall in love. She's
determined to protect herself as well as her young son, Zak,
from ever being hurt again.

Please join me now as Cassie tries as hard as she can not
to fall for handsome Dallas lawyer Andrew Morris. When
Montana meets Texas, though, anything is bound to happen.

Happy reading,

Ellen James

My Montana Home
Ellen James

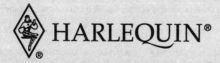

HARLEQUIN®

TORONTO • NEW YORK • LONDON
AMSTERDAM • PARIS • SYDNEY • HAMBURG
STOCKHOLM • ATHENS • TOKYO • MILAN • MADRID
PRAGUE • WARSAW • BUDAPEST • AUCKLAND

ISBN 0-373-71014-3

MY MONTANA HOME

Copyright © 2001 by Ellen Cain.

This edition published by arrangement with Harlequin Books S.A.

® and TM are trademarks of the publisher. Trademarks indicated with ® are registered in the United States Patent and Trademark Office, the Canadian Trade Marks Office and in other countries.

Visit us at www.eHarlequin.com

Printed in U.S.A.

This book is dedicated to my husband.
Robert, here's to many more Montana dreams.

CHAPTER ONE

CASSIE WARREN STARED at the drop below her with a mixed sense of wonderment and panic. She knew the tree house stood no more than seventeen feet above the backyard of freshly mowed bluegrass. And climbing up the rope ladder had been so easily accomplished—egged on as she had been by her seven-year-old son, Zak. Yet now, to her chagrin, the rope ladder had disappeared, and Cassie had no idea how she could descend to terra firma without breaking her neck in the process.

"Zak!" she called again. "William Zachary Warren! I'm not kidding. I'll count to ten and then..."

This morning had started out innocently enough—six o'clock alarm; twenty minutes of Jazzercise with her *Fit or Flab* video; a quick shower; then breakfast and some time with Zak before work. Only, that quality time with Zak had turned sour again, and mushroomed into what amounted to a full-blown therapy session—forcing Cassie to push back her first two appointments of the day and cancel lunch with her boss. Zak had withdrawn severely since the breakup of Cassie's marriage over a year ago. She'd tried everything she knew in order to reach him, to get him to express the pain and anger he kept bottled up inside. So today, when Zak retreated into his usual forlorn silence, she'd been willing to do anything to spark a response in her son. Acting on sudden inspiration, she'd ascended with him to the one place where he seemed to feel safe and at home: this old backyard tree house perched high in a venerable oak.

Once ensconced, Zak had seemed to relax just a bit, answering her attempts at conversation with guarded monosyllables. Finally she'd settled back, allowing her eyes to drift shut. She'd been so tired lately, trying to juggle motherhood with a job at Child Services that drained her emotions while scarcely paying the bills. She'd been so worried, too—worried about her kid brother, Bobby, and all the trouble he'd been in. The drunk-driving accident he'd caused…the baby daughter he'd fathered at the young age of nineteen. And then there was Robert Maxwell, Cassie's dad—an impossible man in so many ways, refusing to take care of himself the way he should…

Yet up here in the tree house, she'd left all that behind for a moment. It was so peaceful, with only the chatter of sparrows and a rustle of leaves in the warm breeze. No wonder she'd fallen gently asleep.

And meanwhile, her darling, infuriating young son had left her stranded. She knelt to peer once again at the drop below. Since he'd taken the ladder, there was only one way Zak himself could have made it to the ground—shinning down the tree trunk. Not exactly her idea of fun...

"Zak!" she hollered. "William Zachary! This isn't funny. You're in big trouble—major trouble."

At last she heard the sound of footsteps approaching on the gravel path.

"Young man," she said sternly, "you and I are going to have a very serious talk."

"I'm listening," remarked a voice. Not her son's, though. It was a man's voice, all grown up. Cassie craned her neck so she could see through the leaves. The man gazing up at her looked both gorgeous and bemused. He had rich dark hair, which this morning's Montana breeze seemed to take delight in rustling about his forehead. From this distance, she couldn't be certain about the precise color of his eyes, but his features were undeniably strong and decisive. Even perched as she was above him, he looked tall and ruggedly built—the perfect build, perhaps, to rescue a damsel stuck in a tree.

"In my day," said the man, now standing in full view beneath her, "girls weren't allowed in the tree house...because they were...girls."

Cassie tried to send down a withering look. "I don't suppose you have a ladder handy," she said.

"Not on me," said the man. "Sorry...didn't realize I'd be involved in a lifesaving attempt today."

"It's hardly a matter of life or death," Cassie began, then stopped herself. The situation was ridiculous. She considered her options. Maybe she'd just slide down the tree herself. She'd always been athletic—played soccer in high school and college. If she could bodycheck a goalie, she could certainly manage a simple tree trunk—

"I could call the fire department," the man said helpfully.

"That's for cats stuck in trees," Cassie retorted. She eyed the branch several feet below and to the right. It looked substantial enough. If she could get that far, it shouldn't be too difficult to clamber the rest of the way down...she hoped. She inched forward...

But then, quite naturally and almost effortlessly, the man began climbing toward her. He seemed to know just where to put his feet, and just which knot or branch would provide a perfect handhold. He also didn't seem to mind that he was wearing an elegantly tailored suit in slate gray, hardly the attire for scaling a one-hundred-year-old oak. Before Cassie knew it, he'd reached the tree house, pulled himself up easily and was sitting beside her. She stared at him, a bit flustered by his sudden proximity. Now she could see his eyes very clearly. They were deep brown yet with a hint of gold...a color that made her think of dark maple syrup and autumn firelight.

Cassie drew in her breath a little, dismayed at the direction of her thoughts.

He regarded her soberly. "Feeling okay?" he asked.

"Fine," she said more grumpily than she'd intended. "I just want to get down from this tree."

The man seemed to be in no hurry. He glanced around, shrugging off his suit jacket. Next he loosened his tie and settled back, resting one arm on a knee. "I haven't been up here in years," he said reflectively. "Not since I was a boy. But it's just the way I remember it. Snug and sturdy...with just enough room for your imagination. Gramps really knew what he was doing when he built it."

Cassie finally collected her thoughts. "Of course," she said. "You must be Andrew. Hannah's grandson." She paused, then went on more softly. "I can't tell you how sorry I am about your losing Hannah."

Elderly Hannah Elizabeth Rogers had been Cassie's salvation this past year. The divorce had left Cassie cash poor, with virtually no financial assets— yet the most important asset of all, a son she loved with her entire heart. She'd been determined not to ask her wealthy, domineering father for help. From long experience, she knew he would have tried to take over her life. Instead she'd moved to Billings to start a new job, a new existence.

A chance meeting with Hannah had resulted in

friendship, as well as an invitation to stay in the guest house on Hannah's property. Cassie had paid rent...not enough, she'd often protested. But Hannah would hear none of it. She'd said that having Cassie and Zak around made her feel part of a family again. And young Zak, she'd said, reminded her of her grandson Andrew when *he'd* been a boy. Andrew, the beloved grandson who lived in Texas, and who Hannah visited every six months. Except that, on this past visit three weeks ago, Hannah had suffered a massive heart attack.

Now Cassie watched the expression of sorrow and wistfulness that played across Andrew's face.

"She was a grand old lady," he murmured. "Stubborn...funny...generous. Even when it came to her last wishes. On her deathbed, she made me promise no funeral...no mourning. She insisted everyone remember her alive."

Hannah *had* been generous, especially with her time and affection. Zak had been lured from his shell by the stories she'd told him about her childhood in Montana during the Great Depression, and he'd even taken a fancy to the chocolate macadamia cookies she baked especially for him. Now that she was gone, he'd withdrawn even further than before.

Cassie stirred. "I must go find my son," she said.

Andrew gave a slight smile. "Don't suppose you'd be talking about a quiet little kid with red hair and freckles."

"That's the one," she said ruefully. "Also identified by the rope ladder he absconded with."

"If it makes you feel any better," Andrew said, "he's the one who told me where to find you. And don't worry—I loaned him a golf club and left him practicing his putt on the front lawn. That should keep him busy for a few minutes at least."

Cassie raised her eyebrows. "You play golf?" she asked. Somehow it didn't seem quite his sport. She would have pictured something more adventurous, more…physical.

"It's from Hannah's old set of clubs," he explained. "I found them in the attic when I was poking around up there just now. I'd forgotten about the golf phase she went through in her sixties till I saw those trophies and clubs."

Cassie hadn't even known about Hannah's golf phase. Of course, Cassie had never been part of Hannah's real family, just someone who had enjoyed the old woman's kindness for a time. With Hannah, things had been so uncomplicated…so different from Cassie's relationship with her *own* family. Suddenly she felt very lonely.

"Well," she said to Andrew. "I expected that you'd fly up from Dallas to settle your grandmother's affairs. I just didn't know you'd be here today. Zak and I will clear out of the guest house, of course. I've been looking for an apartment, and—"

"Relax," Andrew said dryly. "I'm not going to throw you out on the street. I barely got into town a few hours ago—I haven't even met with Hannah's lawyer yet." He settled back even more comfortably. "We've got plenty of time to sort things out." A jay alighted on a branch above, wings a smoky blue. It stared at Andrew and Cassie for a moment, then skimmed away again. The breeze brought a faint scent of lilac.

"Kind of nice up here, isn't it?" Andrew said. His gaze traveled over Cassie. He seemed to be taking his time, and enjoying it. She felt herself flush. Rather pointedly, she glanced at her watch.

"I have to get Zak to the sitter's. And myself to work—"

"It's Saturday," Andrew said. "Nobody should have to work on Saturday."

She gave him a skeptical glance. "From what Hannah said about you, *you're* not the type to take off weekends."

"She always did tell me I worked too hard," he said reflectively. "So now I'm trying to follow her advice. I'm trying to kick back."

Hannah had shared quite a few tidbits about her grandson. He had his own law practice in Dallas, he was too involved in his job, he always seemed to date women who insisted they weren't ready to settle down yet, but frankly *he* was the one with the settling-down problem....

Cassie made an effort to control her thoughts. His personal life was absolutely no concern of hers. She wondered just how long she was going to be up in this tree with him. Yes, it was undeniably pleasant, and the man was extremely easy on the vision, but still…she had a life waiting below.

"Who knows," she said, "what damage my son will manage to do with a golf club. Children are alarmingly inventive. I really do have to get down from here."

"Too bad," Andrew murmured. "But, if you insist…I'll go down first. Follow my lead, and you'll be fine."

He began descending as expertly as he'd come up. Cassie tried to do exactly what he did—putting a foot here, finding a handhold there. The ground seemed much too far away.

"You're doing fine," said Andrew. "We're almost there."

"Let me guess," Cassie muttered as she clung to the trunk of the tree. "Rock climbing's your sport." She inched her left foot downward, then her right. Her sneaker found an anchor, and she breathed a little more calmly. Andrew dropped to the ground, gazing up at her.

"Just a little farther," he said.

She finally relaxed—and that was her mistake. Her sneaker slipped, and suddenly she was flailing wildly.

"Oh no!"

"HUNKS FALLING FROM TREES? Surely, Cassie, even you can think of a better one than that."

"I've already told you, Gwen. *I* was the one who fell out of the damn tree. I landed sort of, well, sort of on top of him." She glanced over to where Andrew Morris was seated.

Andrew was getting just a tad impatient. He'd been sitting in this examination room like an afterthought for the better part of fifteen minutes, waiting for the doctor to show—turned out Cassie had rushed him to the office of her son's pediatrician.

"Right, right…you simply happen to fall into the arms of a ravishing male. Some girls have all the luck."

"Luck," said Cassie. "I don't think falling on a man and practically killing him is good luck."

Andrew's finger hurt like hell, and he was starting to feel a little light-headed from overoxygenation—he had always used deep, steady breathing to cope with stress. It wasn't so much the purple color of his finger that bothered him, nor the fact that it was now swollen beyond its normal size. No, what really bothered Andrew was the way his digit looked longer than any of the others, and it just sort of stuck out there on its own at an odd angle.

The doctor, Gwen-something-or-other, who had finally breezed into the examination room a moment ago, now slapped up some X rays and perused them.

"I mean, if you've made a new gentleman friend," she remarked to Cassie, "why not just come out and say so. No need to make up this fanciful story about falling out of trees."

The doctor was definitely getting on Andrew's nerves. Among other things, she had already given him a very *painful* painkilling shot in his hand. And, along with the fact that she treated him as if he was seven years old, she had stout blond hair that looked too big for the rest of her.

"He is *not* my gentleman friend," Cassie protested. "Please, would you just tell me how much damage I've inflicted on him?" Cassie, unlike the doctor, had hair that was just right—vivid red, cascading haphazardly down her back. She also had hazel eyes, and the merest hint of freckles across her cheekbones. She was, in sum, beautiful. Too bad that Andrew couldn't truly appreciate her at this moment. Too bad they weren't alone in the tree house, before the...accident.

He cleared his throat. "Ladies—"

"Not broken. Just dislocated," said the doc, giving Andrew an annoyingly cheerful grin. "We can be thankful for that, at least. Now, I am going to have to pop that joint back into place. Not squeamish, are you?"

He gave her a sour look.

"Tell you what," she went on imperturbably,

rummaging through a supply drawer. "Cassie'll hold your arm steady—*she's* not squeamish."

Cassie gave Andrew an uncertain look, then glanced toward the door. "I'd better go see how Zak's doing—"

"Your son's fine," said Dr. Gwen. "You know how he likes that new game on Lucy's computer. No, you stay here and help me with your gentleman friend. Right, right, you're going to tell me he's *not* your gentleman friend. But, honey, after Jeff...you really shouldn't let a good one get away."

Cassie had flushed a bright pink. "Gwen," she said in a warning tone.

The doctor came over next to Andrew with gauze, surgical tape and a splint. She gave him a conspiratorial nod. "Surely you've heard all about Jeff by now?"

Andrew stared at the lamentable condition of his finger. "Actually, I haven't," he said.

Now Cassie treated *him* to a warning glance.

"Jeff's Cassie's ex," said Dr. Gwen as she positioned his arm. "Cassie, hold on to him right there...anyway, wouldn't you know she ended up marrying Jeff even after her dad told her the guy was a flat-out loser. Of course, maybe that's why she married him. I mean, what better rebellion can you have? Elope with a man your father despises..."

"Gwen!" Cassie exclaimed, a brighter pink than ever.

"Anyway," Dr. Gwen went on relentlessly as she examined Andrew's finger, "in case you're wondering—I am a very reliable source of information when it comes to Cassie. I grew up in Paradise Corners, went to high school with Jolie…that's Cassie's older sister. Jolie pretty much kept to herself back in those days. It was the longest time before I found out we both had the same dream—becoming doctors. Well, here I am, and Jolie's practicing medicine back in our hometown. Of course, Jolie's married now, and I'm still single. Now, Andrew, dear, I'm afraid this is going to hurt like hell…and Cassie, get ready to hold as tight as you can. One…two…there! That wasn't so bad, was it?"

"You forgot to count to three," Andrew said between clenched teeth. But he had to admit the lady was good. His finger was back where it was supposed to be, and Dr. Gwen was taping it to a small metal splint. Meanwhile, Cassie kept her viselike hold on his arm. He gazed at her, but she seemed to be making a determined effort not to look back.

"Of course, you've heard of Cassie's family yourself," Dr. Gwen went on. "The mighty Maxwells, and all."

"Can't say I have," Andrew said. Now Cassie was glaring at him again.

"Goodness," said Dr. Gwen as she wielded her

surgical tape. "I thought everyone in Montana had heard of the Maxwells. They practically wrote the book on ranching. And Cassie's dad…well, *he's* practically written the book on being a patriarch. More than a little overwhelming, if you want to know the truth. I used to be scared to death of him when I was a kid, and I'd see him striding down Main Street like he owned it. The look he could give you… No wonder Cassie and Jolie and even Thea— the youngest—ended up rebelling against him… There! All set. I'll put you on an anti-inflammatory and some pain meds. Don't move that finger, and make sure you come back day after tomorrow so I can have a look. Now, Cassie, don't scowl at me like that. I didn't tell him anything he wasn't going to find out eventually." Dr. Gwen gave both of them a cocky grin, and vanished out the door.

"She kind of grows on you," Andrew remarked, observing his bandaged hand.

Cassie muttered something under her breath and dropped his arm as if she'd just realized she was holding it. "Oh, look," she burst out. "I'm sorry, I really am."

"Relax. That's about the twentieth time you've apologized. It was an accident. Could've happened to anyone."

"It was very…nice of you, trying to break my fall the way you did."

"Don't mention it." Andrew liked the way she blushed, and she seemed to do it quite a bit.

She picked up her purse and fiddled with the strap. "When I was apologizing just now, it was about Gwen, too. This was just the first place I thought to bring you. She's a wonderful doctor, but she does talk a lot—"

"So now I know you're divorced, and you have a rebellious streak when it comes to your father," he said mildly. "Hardly capital offenses."

"I *used* to have a rebellious streak. Not anymore." She sighed. "I don't know why I'm explaining. What do you say we get out of here?"

It seemed an excellent idea to him. A few minutes later they were out on the sidewalk, beneath a brilliant blue sky. Dr. Gwen's office was in downtown Billings proper. The building was a converted Victorian on an old-fashioned street, tree-lined, with other old houses that had been turned into offices or duplexes. Cassie's son, seven-year-old Zak, walked ahead of them, his head bowed as if he was deep in thought. Cassie gazed at him worriedly.

"He's an okay kid," Andrew said.

"Yes, he is. He's wonderful. But he's...quiet."

"A lot of kids are quiet," Andrew said.

"He didn't used to be this way," Cassie muttered. "It's only been since...since the divorce."

The infamous divorce. He gathered that it was

still a big part of her life. "How long ago?" he asked.

"Over a year. So, Andrew," she said determinedly, "have *you* ever been married?" She couldn't have made it more clear that she wanted to change the subject.

"No. Hannah always told me I was missing out."

"All depends on who you're married to," Cassie said grimly. And then, as if concerned she'd directed the conversation to herself again, she gave him another glance. "How's the finger?"

"I'll live."

"I really am sorry—"

"There you go again," he said. "Apologizing."

She gave an exasperated shake of the head. "You have to admit the whole thing's been highly unfortunate."

He didn't know what to think. It wasn't every day that a beautiful redhead fell into his arms—and dislocated his finger in the process.

"Why are you smiling?" Cassie asked suspiciously.

"No reason." He found, surprisingly, that he was feeling pretty good. He didn't know if it was because of Cassie Warren, or the unexpected turn of the day. Cassie, however, didn't appear to share his optimism. She gazed at him for another moment, and then her expression grew shuttered. She might as well have put up a warning sign: Keep away. Don't get too close.

She called to her son. "Zak, the car's over here. We're going home." And then she turned to Andrew one more time. "At least—it's home until Zak and I find an apartment. We'll clear out just as soon as we can."

Andrew felt a stirring of disappointment. And that, too, was unexpected.

CHAPTER TWO

"WHY IN HELL did I have to be right-handed, anyway?" Andrew grumbled. He was attempting to undress himself, and not doing a very good job of it. His splint kept getting in the way of things like buttons and buckle. At last he was down to the basics—not that sitting around in his underwear was ordinarily his idea of a well-spent afternoon.

After the encounter with Dr. Gwen, he'd had Cassie drop him off at his hotel. He'd had in mind getting cleaned up and taking care of business here in Billings. Only, his hand had started to hurt again, and all he really felt like doing was stretching out and catching a game on TV. The childproof container on the pain medication proved even more of a challenge than his pants. But finally he managed to down a couple of the big white pills and flick on the remote. The Rangers and the Dodgers—baseball perfection. He had box seats for all the Texas home games, but rarely had time to go.

He smiled a little grimly to himself as he lowered the sound with the remote. His grandmother had often accused him of using his career to avoid solving the personal problems in his life. Problems—according to Hannah—such as his lack of a wife and children. Those were the only things that really mattered, she'd told him. Love...family... What was he afraid of? she'd asked him. Did he think there was too much potential for hurt, too much possibility of loss? But the past doesn't have to repeat itself, she'd told him.

The irony of her remembered words made Andrew restless. He clicked off the game, stood up and began to pace around the hotel room, a space too small and confining. He'd had the option of staying at his grandmother's house, where the surrounding acreage gave a sense of openness and freedom. So why *hadn't* he stayed there? Was he really still running away from all the old memories?

"Crazy," he muttered to himself. He'd hit the far end of thirty-five. After all this time, he should have gained some perspective. Some peace.

In Texas, at least, the shadows always seemed more remote. A background of darkness always there, but muted somehow. Distanced, as if he was watching a storm from very far away. In Texas it was easy—much easier—to go about his life. Keeping busy with work that mattered to him, seeing women he genuinely liked even if the relationships never went anywhere.

In Montana it was different. Time seemed to play tricks on him here. He'd be thinking about something inconsequential, and then, without warning, the years would seem to vanish, falling away and leaving him unprotected. Leaving him a kid again. And he would see the whole damn thing play over again in his mind, every detail as vivid as if it were happening right at that instant. Every sound, every whisper of pain.

So he'd stayed away. It had been up to Hannah to fly out and visit him. Sometimes she'd complained about it, but he knew that deep down she'd loved all the fuss and bother and adventure of her trips. She'd arrive in Dallas with far too many suitcases, take over his apartment and deluge him with the everyday dramas of her own life. On her last trip, she'd been full of stories about the boarder she'd taken in at her guest house. A vulnerable, red-headed woman who had a seven-year-old son.

Now Andrew stretched out again on the hotel sofa and clicked the game back on. Usually baseball could keep him occupied for an hour or two. But the image of lovely Cassie Warren kept intruding. The guarded look in her eyes, and then the dismay on her face when she'd fallen—quite literally—into his arms. Dislocated finger and all, it had been a rather intriguing experience. He smiled a little…a real smile this time.

The painkillers were making him drowsy, and he closed his eyes. The sound of the game drifted over him. And, for the moment at least, the old memories faded away.

WHAT WAS IT you were supposed to do with spaghetti? Throw a piece at the wall to see if it would stick? Ridiculous, of course, but Cassie never had been a whiz with pasta. Whatever help she could get...

She eyed the piece of spaghetti dangling from her fingers, and considered the wall beside the stove. Exasperated, at last she shook her head. Maybe she just should have chosen a frozen casserole and been done with it. But when you'd inflicted bodily harm on a man, you needed to make it up to him somehow—a home-cooked meal seemed a good way to go.

Cassie stirred the sauce simmering on the stove. There didn't seem any way she could mess *that* up. All she'd had to do was open the jar. A familiar guilt stirred in her. She'd never been much of a cook, which was fine when you were on your own. But when you had a son to raise, surely you ought to provide him with nourishing, lovingly prepared meals. You shouldn't rely on the local fast-food joint and the freezer section at the grocery store. But Cassie, usually so exhausted from her job, did exactly that.

So maybe this evening would help motivate her. If the spaghetti was successful, maybe she'd try a lasagna or a pot roast next. Feeling inspired, she went to the base of the front stairs and called up to her son.

"Zak...Zak! Dinner's almost ready. Wash your hands and come down."

The guest house remained determinedly quiet. Cassie waited another minute, and then climbed the stairs. She poked her head into Zak's room. He was sitting cross-legged on the bed, an oversize book spread in front of him. Cassie knew which one it was—an illustrated history of medieval castles that he'd chosen from the public library. Lately he seemed fascinated by stories of knighthood. At any time, Cassie could find him carefully turning the pages of that volume, and studying the pictures. Maybe she ought to feel grateful that Zak liked books at such a young age. Except that a book was like everything else in Zak's life these days—another excuse to retreat, to hide. Cassie longed for disorder, chaos, noise...all the ordinary signs that a little boy lived here.

"Zak," she said now. "Mr. Morris will be here any minute. I want you to get ready and come down."

Zak continued to turn the pages as if she had not even spoken. She battled a growing frustration.

"Zak—" She heard the way her voice sharpened, and she tried again. "I think we've caused Mr. Morris enough trouble for one day. Let's at least provide a pleasant evening for him.''

Zak finally raised his head and stared solemnly at her. ''I'm not the one who fell on top of him,'' he said.

''A mere technicality. If it hadn't been for you taking off with the ladder, *I* never would have fallen...'' She gave Zak a stern glance. ''And, by the way, you haven't had your punishment for taking the ladder.''

''Okay. I'll skip dinner,'' Zak said, and he buried his head in the book again.

Cassie gazed at her son. ''You don't get to choose your punishment,'' she said firmly. ''You'll wash your hands, and come downstairs, and you will be exceedingly polite to Mr. Andrew Morris when he arrives.'' With that, she turned on her heel and marched downstairs before her son could respond— or ignore her.

Back in the kitchen, Cassie found that the sauce had splattered. Cursing under her breath, she wiped the stove and then checked the spaghetti. Now maybe it was too soggy. The casserole in the freezer was starting to seem like a very good idea.

But then the doorbell rang. Cassie felt suddenly, unaccountably nervous. She hurried out to the hall, glancing in the mirror as she went. Perhaps she should have worn something less casual than jeans and her embroidered Mexican top. And she could have brushed her hair at least one more time—

She was behaving for all the world as if she'd invited Andrew Morris here on a *date*. It was nothing of the kind. It was an apology dinner, as simple and uncomplicated as that.

But when she reached the front door, somehow she couldn't bring herself to open it.

ANDREW RANG the doorbell again, then stood back to survey his grandmother's guest house. In the dusk it looked like something out of a storybook—the kind of cottage you'd expect to find deep in a magical forest somewhere. It was two stories high, with dormer windows and vines growing up a trellis. It had been built almost fifty years ago, when both his grandparents had been young. Back then, they'd used it as mother-in-law's quarters for Hannah's mom—Andrew's great-grandmother, a very independent and outspoken lady who'd lived to the impressive age of ninety-three. Andrew thought of his family enduring generation after generation in Montana. He had been the one who'd broken with tradition by moving away to Texas.

His gaze wandered back to the door. He was about to ring the bell a third time when at last the door swung open reluctantly. Cassie Warren stepped forward—and in the dusk she, too, seemed like someone from a storybook. Long red hair, a wariness in her hazel eyes, her skin beginning to take on the beguiling flush that highlighted her freckles.

"Before you apologize again," he said just as she was about to speak, "no more apologies."

She gave a shrug. "I constantly seem to be disrupting your life. I mean, when I called you at your hotel earlier, I could tell I'd woken you up—"

"I don't usually fall asleep in the middle of the day," he said. "Your doctor friend prescribed some pretty potent pain medication. But I'm glad you woke me."

She treated him to a disbelieving glance. "Well, please come inside. I'll warn you, though, I'm not the greatest cook—"

"You're doing it again," he said. "Apologizing."

"Sorry," she said, and then she laughed. It was a very pleasing sound. "Okay, okay," she said. "Enough. It's just not every day I maim someone."

He proffered a bottle of white wine with his good hand. "Just to show there are no hard feelings," he said.

She took it from him, surveying the label. "Very nice, indeed," she murmured. "You have excellent taste, Andrew. Thank you."

She stepped aside, and he entered the guest house. It looked a lot different than the last time he'd seen it. All the fussy details had been stripped away— carpet pulled up to reveal the pine floors, light curtains replacing the frilled drapes and valances, walls whitewashed over the yellow he'd never cared for.

"The place is better," he said. "Your influence?"

"Hannah was open to suggestions," she said diplomatically. "If you'll excuse me, I'll just finish up dinner. Make yourself at home." She vanished into the kitchen, leaving him at loose ends. He wandered around, thumbing through a book without even reading the title, glancing at a painting without actually seeing it. Then he heard a bang and a muffled exclamation from the kitchen. He crossed to the kitchen doorway.

"Need some help?" he asked blandly.

Cassie had pulled something from the oven. It had landed on top of the stove, and now she was giving it a dour stare.

"Burnt," she pronounced. "This means just ice cream for dessert, instead of ice cream and...apple betty."

"Wonder why they call it that," he said. "Apple betty."

"I'm sure I wouldn't know," Cassie muttered. "Who am I trying to fool, anyway? I hate to cook."

"So why do it?" he asked. "You could have sent out for pizza, and I would've been just as grateful."

"Right. Men *say* that, but they never really mean it. Deep down, they all want some beautiful, big-chested blonde who can whip up a batch of brownies to boot."

It was an image that gave pause, to say the least.

Cassie sighed. "I didn't mean *all* men. Just a lot of them—including my ex-husband. Not that he ever found the blonde of his dreams. He just always gave me the impression he was looking. And after hearing Gwen spill the beans, you know all about how my dad warned me against Jeff, and how I went ahead and married the guy anyway." She gave another sigh, explosive this time. "What *is* it about you that makes a woman run off at the mouth?" Very purposefully, she got busy with some salad tongs and lettuce.

He liked watching her as she moved around the kitchen. She pulled a strainer from the cupboard and plopped it in the sink. He took it on himself to drain the pot of spaghetti over the strainer. It was a little awkward with his taped finger, but he managed. Cassie stood beside him watching.

"Don't tell me *you* know how to cook," she said.

"I do eggs," he told her, "as long as they're scrambled."

A few minutes later everything was on the dining-room table. Cassie sat down, then jumped up. "I'll be right back," she said. She went up the stairs, and he heard the murmur of her voice.

A short while afterward a door shut rather forcefully and she came down again. She didn't look happy. She looked peeved. "My son," she said, "will not be joining us for dinner. You know one of the most aggravating things about parenthood? Sometimes you just give in, even when you know you should make a stand.''

Andrew tried to look sympathetic, but his experience with parenthood was pretty much nil. He and Cassie started in on the spaghetti. His bandaged hand did pose something of a problem. He tried twirling spaghetti noodles around his fork with his left hand.

''I should have thought about that,'' Cassie said ruefully. ''But, don't worry—no more apologies.''

A little practice, and maybe he could get used to this left-handed routine. At least he got a taste of the spaghetti. ''It's good,'' he said.

She gave an unexpected smile. ''Surprisingly…it is, isn't it?''

He wished Cassie Warren would smile more often, but she seemed to be a person burdened with unspoken concerns. Now and then she glanced in the direction of the stairs.

''You're worried about the kid, aren't you?'' Andrew said.

''Zak hasn't always been like this,'' she said quickly. ''As I already told you, it's just been since the divorce. I thought he was getting better. But then, after losing Hannah—he really loved her, you know.''

''I can believe that,'' Andrew said in a quiet tone.

Cassie folded and refolded her napkin. ''You'd

think I could figure out what to do with my own son," she said. "My job is supposed to give me some expertise, after all."

Right...the job that kept her busy even on Saturdays. "What do you do for a living?" he asked curiously.

"I work for Child Services," she said. "That's why I moved here last year—to take the job. I'm a field agent of sorts...a troubleshooter, too, you could say. Basically, I work with families who've been referred to court for one reason or another. I gather evidence to help decide what's best for the children involved. It's wonderful work—and terrible at the same time. I see things that break my heart. Impossible situations...and I have to make impossible decisions." She stopped, and gazed at him with perplexity. "You ask a simple question, and I give you a dissertation. Trust me, I'm not usually like this. Here...have some more wine." She refilled his glass.

"Sounds like your work means a lot to you," he said. "Why apologize for that?"

She grimaced. "So I'm doing it again... apologizing."

"It's my guess," he said, "that the ex-husband really shook your confidence."

She seemed to stiffen at that. "Jeff Warren is not worth *anyone* losing their confidence. He's a...he's a damn SOB." With that she stood regally, and took the dirty plates into the kitchen. She reappeared a few moments later with two dishes of vanilla ice cream, and slapped one down in front of Andrew.

"Getting mad feels good," he observed.

"Yes, it does," she said ruefully. She glanced toward the stairs one more time. "But the reason my ex *really* makes me mad is the way he treats Zak. Promising to visit, and then not showing. Not calling when he says he will. No wonder Zak tries to shut down his emotions. He's scared of getting hurt all over again."

It sounded to Andrew as if Cassie Warren had a very complex life. Too bad he wasn't going to find out any more about the complications. He was going to get his business done in Montana—wrap up Hannah's affairs—and return to Texas as soon as possible. That meant he would probably never see Cassie again.

But, for now, he was sitting here across from this beautiful woman, eating ice cream. Andrew had learned how to enjoy the moment. He knew it was indeed possible to block out the past and the future, and simply savor the present.

Cassie seemed to be relaxing a little, too. She leaned back in her chair, turning her glass around. "Forget about me," she said. "Let's talk about your romantic troubles, Andrew. From what your grandmother said, you've had plenty of them...plenty of women, at least, who've wanted you to tie the knot. Apparently, though, you're not the knot-tying sort.''

''That's what she always said.''

Cassie gave him a shrewd look. ''Tell me, have you tried dating any divorcées? A lot of the time *they* don't want to tie the knot. They've already done it once, and found that quite enough.''

''Meaning,'' said Andrew, ''that you don't intend to get married again.''

''That's exactly what I mean.'' Cassie stopped playing with her glass. ''I'm going to check on Zak. Be right back.'' She stood and headed for the stairs. Andrew watched her go. She moved with a natural, unaffected grace. He wondered if she realized how attractive she truly was.

When she came back down a few moments later, she looked troubled. ''He fell asleep,'' she said softly. ''Right next to a book about knights in armor. I can't figure out if he wants to be a knight, or be rescued by one.''

She didn't sit down again, even though she hadn't finished her ice cream—or her wine. Andrew decided the message was clear: the evening had ended. He stood.

''Thanks for the invitation,'' he said.

''Thanks for coming,'' she said after an awkward pause. ''It seems strange you staying at a hotel instead of at your grandmother's house.''

"Guess I like the idea of neutral territory," he said.

Cassie studied him. "You don't give anything away, do you?" she murmured. "I practically told you my life story tonight, but you're as much a stranger to me as when you walked in the door."

A stranger…somehow he didn't like the sound of that. Unable to explain the impulse guiding him, he stepped nearer to Cassie. With his good hand, he gently ran a finger over her cheek. Her skin was soft.

She drew in her breath. "Andrew…"

He heard the warning in her voice. Feeling that stir of regret, he stepped away again. "Don't worry, I'm not getting the wrong idea. That's what you want me to say, isn't it?"

"Something like that." Suddenly brisk and businesslike, she led him to the door. "Good night, Andrew."

"Good night." His rental car was parked out on the driveway, waiting to take him back to his empty hotel room. The prospect didn't seem inviting. Maybe that was why he acted on impulse again. He turned to Cassie and took her into his arms. And then he kissed her.

Her lips were soft, too. She tasted sweetly of vanilla. And, after an initial, very brief attempt to pull away, she kissed him back. Her hands moved up to his shoulders. He was looking forward to whatever might happen next.

He didn't count on what did happen, however. There was a slight scuffling sound. With a gasp, Cassie broke away from him. They turned at the same time. And there, facing both of them, was Cassie's seven-year-old son, Zak…gazing at them with a solemn, unreadable expression.

So much for a romantic mood.

CHAPTER THREE

CASSIE EASED OFF the gas. The road she was traveling happened to be well maintained, and she could have safely gone ten miles faster. But she always slowed down at this point. She always dreaded returning home.

Young Zak seemed to feel no such reluctance. He strained against his seat belt, sticking his face out the window as if to smell the ranch air. Cassie had known that smell for as long as she could remember—a potent aroma of cattle and rich red earth, prairie grass and wildflowers. She considered turning the car around and heading straight back to Billings. But she had come here for Zak. Despite all his efforts to hide his emotions, she knew that he loved Walking Stones Ranch.

Cassie slowed her Toyota a bit more, prolonging the moments before she would need to confront her family. But just then a figure appeared on the horizon—a large, broad-shouldered man astride a powerfully built horse. The image of man and steed seemed to shimmer in the bright morning light. Cassie heard Zak draw in his breath. And, as she pulled over and got out of the car, Zak scrambled out to stand beside her.

The figure drew nearer, Stetson shading his weathered face. He was, of course, none other than the boss himself—Robert Maxwell Sr., owner of Walking Stones. Cassie's stomach tightened, and she felt all the old familiar emotions roiling inside. Defiance, anger, fear...love and worry. Her father's bay mare came to a halt on the verge of the road. Robert Maxwell remained in the saddle, callused hands resting on the horn, hazel eyes surveying Cassie with neither welcome nor approval. She tried to think of something diplomatic to say.

"Dammit, Dad, you're not supposed to be galloping around on a horse! You want your heart to give out right here and now?"

Robert Maxwell stared at her for a long moment. And then the grim lines of his face rearranged themselves into the semblance of a smile. A sardonic smile.

"Glad to see you, too, Cassandra."

No one else called her that. She might as well have been ten years old again, a scrawny insecure kid wearing a too-big name. Now she tried again.

"Seriously, Dad. What does Jolie have to say about you disobeying doctor's orders?"

"Your sister has plenty of patients without me," he said dismissively. And then he focused on his grandson. "Hello there, Zachary."

"Hello," Zak answered in a small voice, gazing awestruck at the old man. Hero worship...that was probably the best term for what Zak experienced whenever he was around his granddad. Robert Maxwell was one of the few people Zak had responded to since the divorce—and that was why Cassie made the drive from Billings every three or four weeks. She would do anything for her son, even come home to Walking Stones.

Robert Maxwell Sr. fished in a pocket of his weather-beaten dungarees, producing an apple. He leaned down to hand it to Zak. "Here. Snowdrop's been waiting for you."

Zak took the apple and held it out cautiously to Snowdrop—so named for the pure white triangle on her forehead. The mare observed perfect manners, snuffling the fruit from Zak's open palm. The little boy grinned for the briefest instant, and Cassie felt a brief surge of gratitude toward her father. She knew he'd pocketed that apple especially for Zak, especially for this moment.

"Zachary," said Robert, "by now your aunt Thea's figured out I made my escape, and she's about to come chasing me down. You want to head her off?"

Zak nodded, and went racing off in the direction of the ranch house. Cassie watched him go, then turned back to her father.

"Dad—"

"Hold on. Before you start lecturing me about my heart, I've got something to say to you." He swung down from the horse almost as nimbly as he had twenty years ago, when Cassie was a child. He took off his hat, revealing hair still thick, still reddish despite the streaks of white at his temples. Cassie studied his face, looking for signs of improved health. His complexion didn't seem too bad today...

"Stop looking at me like I'm about to keel over," he grumbled. "And just listen. You and Zak are going to move here and live with me. No more arguments."

Her feelings of warmth and sympathy vanished. "I can't believe you're starting this again—"

"You won't take money from me. You won't take help. You keep talking about your damn independence. But all you're doing is hurting your own son."

Cassie struggled not to lash back at him, not to say anything at all. But *he* always knew exactly what to say. He knew where her vulnerabilities were. With Zak.

She found herself agonizing all over again. Maybe she was doing the wrong thing. Maybe trying to build a home for herself and Zak was a hopeless dream. Maybe she should sacrifice all her hard-won independence and move back to Walking Stones. For Zak's sake...

She was saved further turmoil by the appearance

of a vehicle on the road. A heavy-duty, mud-splattered Land Rover with her sister Thea in the driver's seat and Zak on the passenger side. Thea came to a stop, got out and gave Cassie a hug. Cassie hugged back somewhat awkwardly. Ever since finding the love of her life in Rafe Rafferty, the local deputy sheriff, Thea had gained a happiness that seemed to embrace the whole world. She and Rafe lived in Paradise Corners, but they were both enthralled with the house they were building on a piece of Walking Stones land. They hoped to move into their new home soon—a home they would no doubt fill to overflowing with their love, hopes and dreams. Cassie felt a stirring of envy. No wonder her younger sister was so happy these days. This new, exuberant Thea was very appealing—but also a little overwhelming at times. For years, Cassie and her youngest sister had shared a relationship of prickly politeness—and at times, outright conflict. Cassie was still trying to get used to the new openness. After all, Maxwells had never been known for their geniality.

Cassie stood back and surveyed her sister. Thea's lustrous black hair was cropped short, as befitted a woman who'd devoted her life to ranching. Usually she wore cowboy boots, jeans and a work shirt, but today she had on her Sunday dress, the one that made her eyes look a deeper blue-green than ever.

"Stunning," Cassie said in all sincerity. "The

folks at First Methodist won't be able to keep their eyes on their hymnbooks.''

''That's because they'll be staring at you,'' Thea said, sounding a bit awkward herself now that the enthusiasm of her initial greeting was over. ''They only get to see you once a month—our bona fide city girl, come back to Paradise Corners.''

''I'm not going to church today,'' Cassie protested.

''Oh, come on, you know it reminds you of old times,'' Thea said. ''You and me sitting in the back of the choir, tossing spit wads at the boys.''

Cassie smiled in spite of herself. There *had* been a time—very long ago—when she and Thea and Jolie had been close. Before their mother had died...

Now Thea approached their father. ''You know what Jolie said, Dad. Lots and lots of taking it easy. You're going back to the house, and you're going to sit down and rest while Beth brings you breakfast. And no, there won't be any eggs and bacon. Just oatmeal.'' Thea sounded almost as commanding as the old man himself. He gazed at her sourly, then climbed back on his horse.

''I'm riding back,'' he told her. Then, with a muttered comment about how much he despised oatmeal, he loped off again.

Thea shook her head. ''I don't know what to do— and Jolie doesn't either. He won't listen to us. Jolie stops by whenever she can, and I'm over here working all day, but we still can't seem to control him. Beth tries to make sure he eats right, but then she'll find him down at Grizzly's Diner, eating a steak." Beth Peace was the Maxwells' longtime house-keeper. If *she* couldn't keep Robert in line, what hope was there for the rest of them?

"He drives me crazy," Cassie said. "But...I don't want to lose him." The words popped out before she could stop them.

"Yeah," said Thea. "I'm kind of fond of the old guy myself. Go figure." The two sisters shared a glance that bespoke all the years with their father. Defying him, fearing him, longing for his approval, and now worrying about him.

Thea was the first to shake herself from the reverie. She glanced toward Zak, who'd clambered out of the Land Rover and was now squatting to poke a stick in the ground. Thea hauled Cassie a short distance away.

"Okay," she said. "Out with it. Ever since Gwen called Jolie and told her the news, we've been dying to ask you about it. Who's this new boyfriend you've got in Billings?"

Cassie stared at her sister. "What on earth are you talking about? Why would Gwen—"

"Oh, come on," Thea said impatiently. "Gwen called Jolie to discuss a patient referral or some such, and your name happened to come up. Gwen told Jolie all about how you brought some devastating hunk into her office yesterday because you'd broken his finger—''

''Dislocated,'' Cassie said. ''Not broken. For crying out loud, at least get the details right.''

''So tell me the details,'' said Thea. ''Who is he? How long have you known him? When are we going to meet him?''

Cassie groaned. ''I can't believe this, I really can't. Why did I ever choose Gwen as Zak's pediatrician—''

''Don't change the subject, Cassie. Who is the guy?''

Cassie moved to a place where she was sure Zak would be out of hearing range. Thea followed. Cassie knew there was no getting away from it.

''I hate to disappoint you,'' she said, ''but I only met Andrew Morris yesterday. He's Hannah's grandson from Texas, and he's only here to settle her estate. I, well, I fell out of a tree and landed on top of him…'' Cassie stopped when she saw the way Thea was laughing at her. ''Okay, okay, so it's not the best way to make an impression on a man. But I didn't *want* to make an impression.''

''So, tell me,'' Thea said as soon as she could control her mirth. ''Is he really as much of a hunk as Gwen says?''

''Yes, he's gorgeous. Satisfied?''

Thea looked thoughtful. ''So that's the end of the

story. You break his finger—sorry, you dislocate it—and you just walk away from the guy. Too bad.''

"I did the decent thing," Cassie found herself saying. "I invited him to dinner to make up for all the trouble I'd caused.''

Thea perked up. "Dinner…hmm. Sounds romantic.''

"It wasn't," Cassie protested. "Zak refused to come down to eat, which left me alone with Andrew—''

"Like I said. Romantic." Humor danced in her sister's eyes again. Cassie glared.

"The food was mediocre. Growing up around Beth's gourmet offerings, nobody in this family has ever learned to cook a decent meal. Me included—''

"Did you kiss him?" Thea interrupted.

Cassie felt her skin heating up. Silently she cursed the fair Maxwell complexion that betrayed every emotion.

Thea nodded. "Was it a hot kiss?''

"It hardly lasted at all," Cassie muttered. "Zak showed up, and believe me—that put an end to things.''

"This is all very, very interesting," Thea pronounced. "Jolie and I have been hoping you'd find someone.''

"I haven't *found* anyone. I met a man. I dislocated his finger. I kissed him. End of story!''

Thea didn't look convinced.

FOR THE SECOND TIME in two days, Cassie entered a doctor's clinic. This one, however, was on Main Street in Paradise Corners, Montana. And it belonged to Cassie's older sister, Jolie.

Cassie sat in the waiting room while Jolie attended to a Sunday emergency—a little girl who'd sprained her wrist after pretending to parachute out of a swing. Half an hour later, Cassie watched as Jolie ushered child and parent out the door with efficient care. The little girl's tears had dried, and now she seemed proud of her exploit.

Jolie was very good at what she did. She could have stayed in California, specialized and be driving a Mercedes by now. Instead she'd come back to Montana to attend to ordinary, everyday scrapes and sprains and bruises. It should have made her *seem* ordinary. But it didn't. Whenever Cassie was around Jolie, she still felt stirrings of the old half-resentful, half-admiring sense of intimidation. The sense that she could never measure up to Jolie…never be as smart or pretty or accomplished. Cassie sighed. Would she ever escape the trap of her childhood emotions?

Now Jolie sat down next to her, unbuttoning her white lab coat. She, too, wore a Sunday dress underneath. Her long hair, with its tendency to curl, was strawberry blond, her eyes a striking shade of blue.

''You know, as long as I'm at work, I could take

care of a dislocated finger or two,'' Jolie said in a deadpan voice. Cassie glared at her. It seemed she was doing a lot of glaring today.

''Very funny. I'm glad Gwen saw fit to share the whole humiliating episode with you.''

''Oh, I'm up on everything,'' said Jolie. ''Thea gave me a call this morning and told me about the kiss. So, just how serious is it with you and this Andrew?''

Cassie raised her head. ''I only met him yesterday, for goodness' sake—''

''Fast work,'' Jolie said approvingly. ''Maybe he's the one...''

The problem was, Jolie as well as Thea had recently found happiness in love. Ever since Thea had married Rafe, last Valentine's Day, and Jolie had walked down the aisle with Matt Dawson in June, the two sisters seemed to think Cassie should do the same.

Granted, Matt and Jolie's ceremony had been a small, private affair, attended only by family and a few close friends. Their father's ill health and their kid brother's troubles had precluded a larger celebration. Jolie had insisted on that and for once, all three Maxwell sisters had agreed. But even so, Jolie had made a lovely, radiant bride. Thea had been equally lovely—and equally radiant at her wedding in February. Now the two of them kept hinting that Cassie needed to find a bridegroom of her own.

"Jolie," Cassie tried again, "you forget that I've already been married once. I'm not looking to do it again."

Jolie gave a dismissive wave. "Jeff doesn't count by anybody's calculation. You need to find the real thing."

"I don't believe in 'the real thing,'" Cassie said. "Don't forget—I married Jeff to rebel against Dad…etcetera, etcetera. I've never been one for romance."

"Nonsense," Jolie said inelegantly. "Sure, part of you wanted to thumb your nose at Dad. But you really *were* in love with Mr. Jeff Warren, aka His Royal Blondeness. I remember—you thought he was the most wonderful man in the world. So…you made a mistake. So…you try again. And this time you do it right. Who knows, this Andrew guy could be the one."

"I'm not trying anything again. And I certainly didn't come here to talk to you about Andrew…or love…or…"

"Relax," Jolie said, propping her feet on the windowsill and settling back more comfortably in her chair. "Don't get in a tiz. What did you want to talk about?"

Cassie stared out the window. She knew the sights of Main Street so well she could have cataloged them in her sleep. Grizzly's Diner across the way, with the beauty parlor right next to it. Dillon's Feed and Tack down the way, no doubt advertising another special on bran mash. The Lone Wolf and the Silver Spur…all too familiar, all making her feel claustrophobic. She just wanted to get in her car and floor the gas pedal back to Billings. But for Zak's sake…

"I guess I want to ask your advice," she said grudgingly.

"Don't overwhelm me with your enthusiasm," remarked Jolie. "But maybe I'd better make a record of this. Cassie Warren, actually wanting her big sister's advice. Who would've thought. All those years you complained I just wanted to boss you around…"

"Are you finished?" Cassie asked with exaggerated patience.

Jolie gave a conciliatory grin. "You always take things too seriously—that's why you're fun to tease. But I'll stop. Just tell me the problem."

Cassie tapped her nails on the sill in a restless rhythm. "Dad's at it again. Wanting me and Zak to move to the ranch house, and live with him. He thinks it's the best thing for Zak. And maybe he's right. Maybe Zak needs more stability than I can give him on my own. I can just picture what Zak is doing right now. Tagging along after his grandfather, or having Beth make a fuss over him. It's exactly what he needs."

Jolie was all seriousness now. "What do you need, Cassie?"

She closed her eyes for a moment, seeking clarity. But none came to her. "I don't know...I just don't know! Jeff racked up so many debts before our divorce, I'm lucky I walked away with the clothes on my back. After that, I promised myself I'd give Zak a home—a real home. Living in Hannah's guest house, I've been able to start saving for a down payment. I've done pretty well, I think—"

"I'm not the one you have to convince," said Jolie. "You're still trying to prove something to Dad."

Cassie gazed out the window again. "If I move back home, he'll just take over my life. That's his way. Always has been."

"You know," said Jolie, "Thea's the one you should be talking to about this. Before Rafe came along she spent all those years at the ranch, trying to carve out some independence for herself at the same time. Ask her how she did it. Maybe that'll help you with the decision."

Cassie didn't say anything at first. Thirteen years ago, she'd eagerly left the ranch to attend college in Bozeman. Jolie, too, had left home for college. Thea, on the other hand, had stayed at Walking Stones. She'd always insisted that she loved ranching, and that she couldn't imagine any other type of work. But staying home had put her in an unenviable position between their father and their kid brother. Thea had pitted herself against Robert Senior's formidable will, and at the same time she'd tried to be a surrogate mother as well as sister to Robert Junior. She would've been totally justified for harboring any resentments against Cassie and Jolie for leaving her to deal with the two difficult Maxwell men. These days she never complained, but still…

"Talk to Thea," Jolie repeated.

"I can't," Cassie burst out. "I just…I just feel guilty about all the time I've spent away. And I'm sure deep down she must still resent me for it."

"So you think she won't give you an unbiased opinion," Jolie said astutely. "You think she'll tell you to come back so you can put your time in with Dad, too."

"She'd have every right to ask that," Cassie said.

Jolie straightened. "Listen, Cassie. I've had my own share of guilt for leaving Thea here to be family caretaker. And maybe that's part of the reason I came back to Montana. I wanted to make it up to her somehow. But she made a choice to stay—and it was the right choice for her. You just have to decide if it's right for you. I can't give you the answer, and, in the end, I suppose Thea can't, either."

That left Cassie right back where she'd started. Confused. Uncertain. Wanting with all her heart to do what was right for her son. But feeling that something inside her would die if she lost the independence she'd struggled so hard to attain.

Jolie glanced at her watch and stood up. "We're gonna be late for church. We'd better get moving."

"Oh, no. I'm not up to going to church in Paradise today—"

Jolie gave another grin. "Did you just listen to yourself?"

"Okay, okay, very funny. But you know how I feel about this. When the Maxwells show up at First Methodist, they're on display. And right now I just don't want to be...on display."

"Honey," said Jolie, "you won't be the one giving the show this time. Our kid brother is going to try talking to Megan again, and we're all going to be there to lend support. I think it would mean a lot to him if you were there, too."

Cassie wasn't so sure about that. But, like everyone else in her family, she had a major soft spot for Robert Maxwell Jr.

Church it was going to be.

CHAPTER FOUR

THE MAXWELL CLAN filled up two entire pews at First Methodist Church. Cassie's attention strayed from the sermon as she sent a glance down the row of faces next to her. Robert Sr. sat in his customary seat next to the aisle, as if ready to make an exit at any time. He always gave the impression that God would have to wait on his schedule, not the other way around. Beside Robert Sr. sat young Zak, looking a little sleepy-eyed by now. And, next to Zak, sat Beth Peace, her eyes on the minister. Thea and her handsome husband, Rafe, took up the last seats in the pew. Thea didn't seem to be paying much attention to the sermon, either. She kept turning to gaze at her husband. He gazed back just as adoringly. Someone ought to censor those two.

Cassie didn't have to turn around to see who sat in the pew behind. Jolie and her own handsome husband, Matt Dawson. No doubt *they* were doing the adoring bit, too. Next to them would be Lily, who'd just turned fifteen, and ten-year-old Charlie, Matt's kids from his first marriage. Cassie heard some whispers and a muffled laugh, and then Jolie's voice shushing. It had been tough going at first with teenage Lily, but Jolie had won over both her stepchildren big time. She'd acquired a family as well as a husband.

And, of course, at the very end of the pew, right behind Cassie, would be Robert Maxwell Jr. Nineteen-year-old Bobby, trying to deal with the terrible troubles he'd caused this past year. The drunk-driving accident that had left his best friend, Dan Aiken, seriously injured…the volatile love affair that had left him with a baby daughter and a girlfriend who had declared categorically that she wanted nothing more to do with his charming unreliability.

The congregation stood to sing a hymn. As the organ music swelled, Cassie unaccountably felt her throat tighten. The gold and ruby and turquoise of the stained-glass windows seemed to waver through the tears that rose to her eyes. She told herself fiercely to get a grip. What was wrong with her? Just because she was surrounded by her family…the family that she wanted to embrace and escape all at the same time…*that* was no reason to start blubbering.

Cassie managed to get herself under control. The service ended, and the Maxwells filed out with the rest of the worshipers. The blue Montana sky stretched overhead, clean and brilliant, while a breeze stirred through the aspens beside the little

white church. It should have been a time of peacefulness and contentment. But one of the congre-
gants, Megan Wheeler, was walking away quickly,
long auburn hair flying behind her. She carried a
blanket-wrapped bundle protectively against her
body. Bobby hurried after her.

"Shucks," murmured Jolie by Cassie's side. "I
thought he was going to wait for the moment to be
a little more opportune."

"He can't wait," said Thea on Cassie's other
side. "Megan's making her getaway."

The three sisters watched as Bobby caught up to
Megan and began talking to her earnestly. They
were too far away to hear what was being said, but
the body language was more than eloquent. Megan
stood stiffly, angled away from Bobby, still holding
her baby close to her body. Cassie knew how much
the girl had been through this past year or
so…loving Bobby, believing he loved her, giving in
to his charm. She'd been terribly hurt at his first
reaction to her pregnancy—his blustering denial of
responsibility. Later—much later—he'd tried to
make amends. He was still trying. But who could
blame Megan for refusing to trust him?

Now Cassie studied Megan's regal bearing. Over
the past months she'd changed from a shy, hesitant
girl into a confident and independent young woman.
Jolie could be credited for a lot of that. When Megan
had run away from her abusive father, Jolie had

taken her in, offered her a roof and a job. Now Megan lived with Jolie and Matt, and still worked at the clinic. Although she saw her mother and her little sister, Lisa, quite often, she never talked about her father who was serving time in prison. And, with Jolie's help, she'd won a scholarship to Montana State University in Bozeman. She'd be starting school very soon...starting a new life. A life, perhaps, that would not include Bobby.

Megan's face had turned stony and implacable. She listened to Bobby for another moment. He made wide gestures as he spoke, no doubt promising grand reforms. Megan, clearly, was not impressed. She simply walked away from him...more slowly this time, as if she knew that Bobby wouldn't follow her. He didn't. He just stood gazing after her, a look of despair on his face. And then, rather belligerently, he glanced at the people who had been watching him with covert interest. He strode off in the opposite direction from Megan.

"We have to go to him," said Thea.

"He needs some time to himself," said Cassie. "She just shot him down all over again."

"He wants our help, whether or not he'll admit it," said Jolie.

And so it was that Cassie found herself propelled between her two sisters, off in pursuit of the kid brother they all loved.

They found him on the slope behind the church.

He stood with his head bent, his elbows planted on the whitewashed fence surrounding the graveyard. It was a stance evocative of despair and frustration, two emotions that Bobby'd had good cause to suffer of late. Not only had he apparently lost Megan, but his best friend was in a wheelchair. Dan Aiken had regained some movement in his arms, but no one knew if he would ever walk again. No wonder Dan's family was threatening to sue for millions of dollars...no wonder Bobby looked so downcast.

Cassie's natural instinct was to hang back for a moment, allowing Bobby some time to collect himself. That was what *she* would have wanted in his situation. But Jolie and Thea just kept nudging her along with them.

At last, it seemed, Bobby could no longer ignore his sisters' approach. He raised his head and frowned at them. As always, what struck Cassie the most about her brother was the resemblance...his striking similarity to their mother. Beautiful Helen Maxwell, gone now fifteen years but still so fresh in Cassie's mind. Bobby had Helen's wavy black hair and fair skin. He also had her very intense dark eyes.

"What do you want?" Bobby muttered, glancing from Thea to Cassie to Jolie.

"We want to help," Thea said in the soft voice she reserved for the brother she'd practically raised ever since their mother's death.

"We're your sisters," Jolie said, her tone more

brisk but nonetheless unable to disguise her affection.

Cassie said nothing at all, sensing Bobby's emotions. Stubbornness, unease, a restlessness—the very same emotions she had known at Bobby's age, when she'd been all of nineteen.

"Guys, just give me a break—all right?" Now her brother was trying to sound careless, nonchalant. He wasn't succeeding.

Thea stepped toward him, resting a hand on his arm. "What did Megan say, Bobby?"

"Hell, what do you think?" he retorted. "She told me to get lost all over again. No surprise. No big news."

"Bobby," Jolie said, "maybe you're moving too fast for her. Pushing for too much, without giving her reason to trust you."

He turned away without answering. Cassie had to admit that maybe Jolie was right. Not so very long ago, Bobby had asked Megan to marry him. She'd flatly refused. He'd asked her again—she'd turned him down again. She'd told him that she didn't believe one word of his love, his declaration that he was ready to be a husband and a father. "Grow up, Bobby Maxwell," she'd said witheringly. "Grow up, but just leave me out of it." And today, if Bobby had actually proposed again…fact was, Megan already had too much practice saying no to him.

"Bobby," Thea said, her voice still gentle, "you

know what's really still eating at Megan, don't you? The way you reacted that day—the day you learned she was going to have a baby. So what you really need to do is convince her somehow that, well, that you really *are* ecstatic about the whole thing.''

''It's more complicated than that,'' Jolie said thoughtfully. ''It's Bobby's entire history that has Megan running scared. Somehow we have to convince her that he really has changed—''

''Don't you think,'' Cassie said, ''that this is between Bobby and Megan, and there's not a whole lot we can do about it?''

''That,'' said Jolie, ''is a cop-out.''

Cassie gave a sigh. So maybe Jolie was right about that, too. But their kid brother's ''entire history'' really was a complex snarl. His teenage years of drinking and rebelling against every possible sign of authority, especially if the sign happened to come from their father. It didn't seem likely that three sisters, no matter how well meaning, could sort out Bobby's problems.

Driven by that unaccountable restlessness, Cassie pushed open the gate to the little graveyard. She was drawn almost against her will to the granite headstones at the far end. They were just a bit bigger and grander than the ones surrounding them. Even in death, the Maxwell clan had always needed to proclaim its preeminence. Cassie stopped before one of these Maxwell monuments. *Helen, beloved wife and mother...* How inadequate the words seemed. They didn't capture any of Cassie's memories: Helen's liveliness and irreverence, her ability to stand up to her dogmatic husband without ever giving a doubt of her adoration for him.

Cassie's fingers curled against her palms as the old emotions raced through her, among them the grief and anger first experienced by a sixteen-year-old girl who'd lost her mother. *Why did you leave us? If only you'd stayed here, alive and well...surely then Bobby wouldn't have made such a mess of his life. Surely then I wouldn't be so confused, wondering all the time about my own life...*

Cassie took a deep breath. Impossible, of course, to expect that her mother would have been able to soothe every hurt, calm every fear. Now that Cassie was a mother herself, she knew that much for certain. But still the protests and the longings rose within her.

She'd hardly noticed that her sisters had come to join her.

"Will you look at that," Thea murmured.

"Sometimes Dad shows a soft spot," Jolie said, "in spite of himself. He was carrying those flowers earlier this morning, trying to hide them from us."

Cassie gazed at the flowers that had been laid fresh on her mother's grave. Daisies and violets with a few sprigs of sweet william. They had been Helen's favorites. She'd always liked to say that the

Maxwells had gotten too far above themselves, with their taste for roses and orchids. *She* would stick with the simple blooms...violets and daisies. It seemed that her husband, Robert Maxwell Sr., had not forgotten.

"Sometimes," Cassie said in a low voice, "he can really get to you."

"Talking about me behind my back?" came Robert's gruff tone.

Cassie gave a start. Robert Sr. had appeared at her elbow, young Zak in tow. That would teach her not to get lost in her own thoughts.

"Hello, Dad," Jolie said, apparently unperturbed. "Now and then we do admire your better nature."

"Surprised you even think I have one," Robert grumbled. "I know Cassandra doubts it."

Cassie was starting to get that claustrophobic feeling, the one she got around her family.

"Dad, this is hardly the place for Zak," she muttered. She took her son's hand. "We're going back to the ranch—"

"Running away," Robert said disapprovingly. "Just as always, Cassandra. And this is a fine place for my grandson." He took Zak's other hand. The little boy went willingly with him, slipping away from Cassie. "It's too bad," Robert said to Zak, "that you never knew your grandma. She would have thought *you* were the best thing since glazed doughnuts."

"Doughnuts," Zak echoed with a quick, shy grin. "Really?"

Something twisted inside Cassie—a love for her son so boundless that it hurt. But there were other, less admirable emotions, too: jealousy and resentment. Worry that she could all too easily lose Zak to her father's power and charm. Sadness at the fact that her father had never lavished on her the love and approval he gave to Zak. She glanced back at the gate, automatically judging the distance of her escape. A few strides, and she could be out of here, away from everything. Away from her father...

But then she saw Bobby. Her brother had stepped just inside the gate. He, too, was watching Robert and Zak. The expression on his face was shuttered, as if he was doing everything he could not to feel— not to care. Cassie could guess what he was thinking. Once upon a time, he had been the much-indulged Maxwell heir. In their father's eyes, he had been unable to do any wrong. All expectations had been high. Until, of course, Bobby had started rebelling against the expectations. After that, his fall from grace had been swift, indeed.

Now Cassie gazed at her brother, and could imagine his own jealousy and pain. Robert Sr. had a new heir in whom to place his hopes, it seemed: William Zachary Warren, a Maxwell in everything but name...

"Zak," Cassie said more sharply than she'd intended. "Come along. We're leaving."

"I don't want to go," Zak answered solemnly.

That earned him a glimmer of a smile from Robert. Cassie's fingers clenched again.

"We're not going back to the ranch, after all," she said as calmly as possible. "We'll head straight back to Billings."

"I thought you were going to stay all day," Thea said, drawing her eyebrows together. "I've planned a big family dinner for us."

"That's wonderful of you, but—"

"I was counting on it myself," Jolie said. "Seems like we never get the chance to be together."

"Next time," Cassie said in a light tone. "We'll plan on it then."

"You're always telling me that," Thea said, the slightest hint of exasperation in her voice. "We'll plan on it…we'll do it later. Dad's right, Cassie. You're always running away. But I wish you wouldn't anymore. I want…I'd like it if we could be a real family for once."

Cassie stared at her younger sister. "A real family," she echoed, not as steadily as she would have liked. "Oh, we're that, all right. We have all the requirements—wounds that won't heal, pain that won't be forgiven…"

Thea gazed back, her own expression tight. "Are you implying, Cassie, that *I* haven't forgiven?"

"You'd have every right to be angry at me still. Because you're right, aren't you? I *did* run away all those years ago. I left you with…with everything." Cassie made a wide gesture. Only then did she collect herself, stopping before she could say too much. Her son was glancing with far too much interest from one sister to the other.

"Come on, Zak," she said, holding out her hand.

"Wait," said Jolie. "Just stay, Cassie. We need time together—all of us. Isn't that true, Dad?"

He didn't say anything, just stood there holding Zak's hand and regarding Cassie with a look of disapproval. And that was when she knew she could not possibly stay—not for another minute. Not for another second.

"Zak, come here. We're leaving."

"I don't want to go. I want to be with Grandpa." And her young son burst into tears.

Robert shook his head, still gazing at Cassie with that look of utter disappointment. Now she felt truly desperate. Maybe she was a terrible mother, but she couldn't seem to help what she did next. She grabbed her son's hand and hurried him away from his grandfather. Zak cried the entire time.

She felt like crying, too.

IT HAD TAKEN less than twenty-four hours for Andrew Morris to become completely fed up with the splint on his right hand. The thing made even the most rudimentary of activities damn near impossible, so that tying a shoelace, starting the car, even eating a submarine sandwich became near feats of heroism. It also seemed to fascinate everyone who saw it. Andrew couldn't count the number of times he'd been compelled to explain the tree-house incident—until, finally, he'd had enough of the sly winks and knowing nods he'd receive when the "redhead falling from a tree" reference was revealed.

So it was with absolute calm and resolve that he untaped the blasted splint and tossed it into the garbage. So what if his finger still hurt like blazes. He was through being a spectacle. Without the splint, running his new table saw was a glorious experience. It had been nearly twelve years since Andrew had had time to work with his hands. After finding that Hannah's lawyer had unexpectedly been called out of town for most of the next week, Andrew had done some serious soul-searching about what to do with the hole in his schedule. Of course, he could fly back to Dallas to catch up on the Connell casework. But somehow, jumping back into his workaday grind hadn't seemed so compelling. What *had* seemed compelling was the cupped and twisted decking on his grandmother's back porch. Couldn't let that go untended, if he wanted to help the resale value of the house.

Sunday afternoon, then, and he was having a fine time chalking lines and surveying and measuring those water-damaged boards. Time stretched out in front of him. The shadows of the past had receded, even here in Montana. He felt the late-summer sun warm on his back as he knelt on the porch.

The sound of a car turning into the driveway disturbed his reverie about wood screws and planking. He looked up, surprised to see Cassie Warren's little hatchback. She climbed from the driver's seat, and her son bolted out the passenger side. He was dashing away from her when she called his name in a warning tone.

"Zak!"

He skidded to a halt. She went over and talked to him in a low, intent voice. Mother and son faced each other. Both had their arms crossed, and both wore stubborn expressions. After a moment, the kid gave a shrug, followed by a reluctant nod. He whirled and sprinted to the oak at the back of the yard. In a matter of seconds he'd clambered up the now-replaced rope ladder and disappeared into the tree house.

Cassie shook her head wearily. Head bowed, she walked toward the guest house. But then she happened to glance up, and saw Andrew. She stiffened, the look on her face revealing that she'd much rather avoid him. He couldn't say he liked having that effect on a woman.

After a moment she came toward him. "Hello," she said too politely.

"Hello."

She studied his right hand. "Amazing," she commented. "Your finger healed overnight. Why, you don't even need that splint anymore."

The sarcasm wasn't lost on him. "Miracles do happen," he said agreeably. He sat back and took a long, enjoyable look at her. She was wearing a sleeveless blouse, a skirt that swirled pleasingly around her legs and sandals that showed she'd painted her toenails a bright cherry red. Her toes *made* him smile.

She crossed her arms and gave him a severe look in return. "I really wish you wouldn't do that," she said.

"Do what?" he asked.

She flushed. "Check me out," she said. "You seem to be…considering possibilities."

He thought about the kiss they'd started last night. That was what it had been—the merest of beginnings. Too bad he'd be in Montana only another week or so…

Once again the flush was making her freckles stand out in a very alluring manner. "Andrew," she said in a repressive tone, glancing toward the tree house at the end of the yard.

"He can't hear us from all the way up there," Andrew said helpfully.

"Nonetheless..." She took a step away, as if about to leave. He didn't want her to go. But something told him he shouldn't feel this way. Something told him to put some distance between them, as he always did with women.

"Didn't expect you back so soon," he said, straightening.

Her face got a closed look. "Let's just say that things didn't go as expected with my family." She stopped, as if thinking over her statement. "Actually, things did go as expected—only more so."

"Sounds mysterious," he commented.

"Oh, there's nothing mysterious about the almighty Maxwells," she said a bit grimly. "They have a long history of thinking they own the world, and everything in it."

"Interesting," he said. "You talk about them as if you don't belong to them at all, as if you're not a Maxwell yourself."

She looked disconcerted, but then recovered. "I suppose that's one of the hazards of being a lawyer," she said dryly. "You pick up on the subtleties other people miss. Well, I'll let you get on with whatever you're doing."

He definitely didn't want her to go.

"Those are some pretty comfortable deck chairs over there," he said. "And I'll even make you some of my grandmother's famous lemonade."

She almost smiled at that. "Right. You'll open a

can of the frozen stuff, add some water and stir. Hannah always made her cookies from scratch, but not her lemonade.''

''So, are you game?''

She hesitated, glancing once again toward the tree house.

''Who knows,'' Andrew said, ''maybe some lemonade will lure him down.''

That seemed to do the trick. ''All right,'' she said. ''I'll stay...for a little while.''

A little while was fine.

CHAPTER FIVE

THE LEMONADE WAS COLD and tart. Cassie cradled her glass in both hands, telling herself she'd already spent enough time here on the porch with Andrew. Five minutes, to be exact. She glanced at her watch again.

"Relax," said Andrew.

Relax...that was the one thing she *didn't* seem able to do. Not with her family, not with her job, not with her son—and certainly not with Andrew Morris.

All she had to do was look at him to find her heart rate quickening, her skin heating up. If being calm was her goal, she'd chosen the wrong company. But that didn't stop her from looking. He sat in the chair across from her, legs stretched out casually, the Montana breeze once again playing with his thick dark hair. Faded jeans suited him. So did his Texas Rangers T-shirt.

She forced herself to glance away, taking another sip of lemonade.

"Must have been pretty bad with the family today,'' he remarked. ''Somehow I get the feeling you're pretty wound up.''

She grimaced. ''It shows that much? Believe me—nothing you want to hear about.''

''Try me,'' he said.

Now she gave him a suspicious glance. ''Andrew, I can't believe you have nothing better to do—''

''Actually, I don't. I'm all ears.''

A gorgeous man who actually wanted to listen to her family escapades…too good to be true. But Cassie found herself giving the abbreviated version.

''My father wants me to move back home, to Walking Stones Ranch. He says it's the best thing for Zak. I've been thinking maybe he's right. After all, Zak adores his grandfather. His grandfather adores him right back. But today, well, today I looked at my nineteen-year-old brother, and remembered how Dad used to spoil and indulge *him*. After my mom died, it seemed that the Maxwell sun rose and set with Bobby, who was four at the time—and that was just too much pressure for one kid to handle. So when he reached his teens, Bobby started rebelling. He started drinking, and messing up every way you can think of. And, dear Lord, I don't want the same thing to happen to my son. I don't want him to bear the weight of all the Maxwell hopes and dreams, and then see him doing anything he can to escape.'' She took a deep breath. ''So today I dragged my weeping child away from his grandfather, and felt horrible for doing it. But I *had* to do it. There. Is that enough for you?''

Andrew swirled the lemonade in his glass. ''It was quite an earful,'' he said.

He hadn't heard the half of it. No way was Cassie going to tell him the rest—the mixed emotions elicited by her sisters, or the way she'd longed all her life for her father's unconditional love and approval. No, that was not conversation for a warm summer's afternoon, when you were sitting next to a man who happened to take your breath away every time you glanced in his direction.

''You're still thinking about it, aren't you?'' he said.

''What…?'' She spent a few seconds too long gazing into his eyes. Deep brown with that shot of gold…

''Against all your instincts, you're thinking about moving back with your father. Because the guy still intimidates you. Even though you grew up and left home a long time ago, he's still the one you measure yourself against. And you find that you don't measure up—not by his standards, and not even by yours. It bugs the heck out of you.''

She stared at him. ''How could you possibly know—''

''Don't forget. Hannah used to talk about you a lot. But you're not the only one with a larger-than-life dad.'' He sat up a little more in his chair, gazing out across the lawn with an expression Cassie didn't know how to read. She studied his profile.

"So, you, too," she murmured. "What's your father like?"

"He died when I was nine years old."

The words were stark and harsh against the summer air.

"I'm sorry," Cassie said inadequately.

"Funny thing is, I remember everything about him." Andrew spoke almost as if to himself, gazing into some distance only he could see. "They say children forget, especially when they lose someone at such a young age. But I remember even the small details. The old boxing gloves he hung on to, years after he'd won Golden Gloves. The way he was embarrassed to admit he liked tea instead of coffee. The way he and my mom used to sing together. They sounded terrible."

They sat in silence for a long moment. Cassie sensed the tension in Andrew, as if he, too, had left so much unspoken. She knew what it was like to lose a parent, and to find the pain of it surprising you at unexpected times. But she knew that any words she could offer would sound trite or false. And so they remained in silence.

At last Andrew stirred, setting down his glass. Cassie felt suddenly awkward. "I'll go now."

He gazed at her. "Don't."

"Why not?" The question came almost in a whisper.

He gazed back at her somberly. "I don't know," he said. "I'd just like you to stay."

"That's not a reason at all." She found herself faltering, battling a fear she couldn't explain. Andrew continued gazing at her, his expression brooding.

"You don't want this any more than I do," she murmured.

"Fact is," he said reluctantly, "I'm attracted to you."

She clenched her glass. "Andrew, I really don't like where this is headed—"

"Maybe we don't know where it's headed."

She saw the unexpected glimmer of amusement in his eyes, and that only made things worse. It was as if he'd silently said, *You're getting too serious about this. Let's enjoy each other...without anything serious at all.* Unfortunately, he only seemed more handsome and appealing than before.

She tried again. "You live in Texas, I live in Montana. Besides, I don't even know you, anyway."

"Hannah's lawyer is out of town for almost a week. Means I have to stick around a little longer than I planned. That gives us a perfect opportunity, if you ask me."

The humor was there, all right, sexy and dangerous. How tempting it would be to follow his lead…not to worry about the future, just to enjoy a day or two, a week perhaps, with an alluring stranger. But it was a luxury Cassie couldn't afford.

She stood, setting her lemonade on the table beside her. "Sorry, Andrew," she said lightly. "I'm not in the market to start anything new, no matter how…temporary." She saw the regret in his eyes, and felt her own regret. But it didn't hurt, that was the blessed thing. Thank goodness she'd learned how to stop before she *did* get hurt. Before her son got hurt, too.

And so she walked away from Andrew Morris.

ZAK HAD DECIDED not to come down from the tree house. For the moment, Cassie was respecting the decision. The boy had already gone through enough turmoil for one day. He'd dried his tears, and he'd retreated into dignified self-control. Cassie had walked across the lawn to visit him briefly in the tree house, taking him a snack and a few comic books. Cowardly, she'd chosen a time when Andrew was no longer on the porch.

Now, here she was, alone in the guest house, Sunday afternoon turning into Sunday evening. She wandered from room to room, unable to settle down. It was no use trying to concentrate on the files she'd brought home from the office. It was no use trying to read the novel she'd been meaning to start. It was no use trying to clean out the kitchen cupboards, a job long overdue. She felt almost as restless as she had back at Walking Stones—back at Paradise Corners. Was there no escape to be had at all?

At last, however, she had to admit that this restlessness was different. This unease had less to do with her family, and more to do with Andrew Morris. She was attracted to the man. Much too attracted. If she felt like this after only a couple of days...

"He's leaving," she whispered as if weaving a protective spell around herself. "Going back to Texas. Soon...very soon."

The words didn't help. Nothing helped. She simply could not sit still. And so, finally, she resorted to her time-honored cure for all ills: she drew a bubble bath.

It was supposed to be a guaranteed soother. Extra bubbles, with a supply of magazines and that novel she'd been meaning to read. But this time even the bath failed her. She kept picturing the most absurd—and sensual—scenarios. Andrew running the sponge over her bare back...Andrew settling into the bubbles across from her...

"For crying out loud!" she exclaimed. She exited the tub with a splash of water, grabbed a towel and then her most demure terry-cloth robe. She cinched the belt firmly. These fantasies were ridiculous, and the product of simple loneliness. The truth was, she hadn't even dated since the divorce. She certainly wasn't going to count that miserable disaster with Phil What's-His-Name, the accountant who'd taken her to a Schubert piano concert and then fallen asleep during the performance. Cassie had been so tired *she'd* wanted to fall asleep, too. So, no, that didn't count as a date. And that brought Cassie back to her problem: sheer loneliness. No wonder she was fantasizing about Andrew Morris.

She paced around the guest house again, her bare feet padding across the wooden floors. Down the stairs, then up the stairs again, pausing at the window beside the landing. Rather guiltily, she poked her finger between two slats of the blind and peered across to Hannah's house. She knew she was hoping for a glimpse of Andrew, but she couldn't seem to stop herself.

What she saw did nothing to reassure her. He'd come back out to the porch. Zak was there with him. Her young son looked rapt, kneeling beside Andrew. The two of them were gazing into a metal toolbox as if it held the wonders of the world. Andrew took out a screwdriver and passed it along to Zak, who held it reverently. Next came what appeared to be a clawhammer. That was the object of some discussion. Then it, too, was held carefully by a solemn Zak.

Cassie allowed the blind to fall shut again. She leaned her forehead against the wall and gave a soft moan of dismay. It was one thing to be fantasizing about Andrew Morris. It was quite another thing to allow her son to get close to a man who would be leaving town first chance he got.

Zak had already known far too much loss in his short life. And it was up to Cassie to protect him from any more.

ANDREW KNOCKED on the driver's-side window of Cassie's hatchback. At first it seemed she was determined to ignore him. But then, after he'd knocked again, she rolled the window down slowly.

"Morning," he said. "Sounds like you've got a little trouble there."

She gripped the steering wheel. "The damn car—" She glanced at Zak sitting beside her in the passenger seat, and seemed to think better of her choice of words. "The car won't start," she said with forced calmness. "I've got to drop Zak at the sitter's in about five minutes and get to work, and the da—the car just won't start."

"Let me give it a try," Andrew said.

She looked as if she wanted to argue with him. She also looked very appealing this morning, even though she'd pulled her hair back and was wearing a business suit.

"I've known my way around a car or two," Andrew said encouragingly. Somehow he got the feeling she didn't want to be beholden to him in any way. But at last she swung open her door and climbed out.

"This is very decent of you," she said, using her too-polite voice. It was probably a good thing he didn't act on his desire to reach over and loosen her hair. Instead he slid in behind the wheel.

"Morning," he said to Zak.

"Morning," the kid answered back, as if trying out the word. Andrew turned the key and got a feeble response.

"Any symptoms?" he asked Cassie.

She looked disgruntled. "It's been running kind of rough. And I've been meaning to get it into the shop, but I thought if I could just delay a little while longer—"

"I grant you absolution," Andrew said gravely. She leaned down and frowned at him through the open window.

"I really do believe in taking care of one's vehicle," she said.

"Hey, I'm not disputing it. But why don't I give you a ride in my car, and you can worry about yours later. Otherwise you'll be late."

He'd said the right thing, apparently. "Thank you," she answered.

In short order, the three of them were tooling through Billings in his rental.

"Did you specifically ask for a convertible?" Cassie asked wryly.

"No, but when they mentioned it as one of my choices, how could I turn it down?"

"I see your point," she said. "There's something about a convertible that makes you feel..."

"Reckless," he supplied.

"Yes. And..."

"Adventurous," he suggested.

"That, too." She sounded wistful. "Sometimes I wish Zak and I could just take off on a trip. Just the two of us. No problems, no worries except choosing a destination every morning."

The little boy in the back seat remained silent. Maybe Andrew wasn't an expert when it came to the under-ten crowd, but it seemed to him that most kids would start talking a mile a minute at the thought of a car trip. Young Zachary Warren was something of a puzzle.

They dropped Zak at his sitter's. Cassie gave her son a kiss on the cheek, but he quickly ducked away from her. She gazed after him unhappily, then climbed back into the convertible. After they'd been driving again for a few minutes, Andrew spoke.

"Parenthood, I take it, is something of a challenge."

"Oh, you could say that. Especially when your son thinks everybody in his life is going to end up leaving him...and he has good reason to think that. And all you want to do is make sure he doesn't get hurt again..."

Andrew knew he was getting onto some treacherous ground here, but he went on anyway. "I take it you're not just talking about my grandmother. I assume Zak's father's the real problem."

Cassie flashed a look at him. "Oh, no, we're not going to get started about my ex. I'm absolutely not going to talk about Jeff," she said with determination. "Enough's enough."

"Right, if I find out too much, I might actually know you," Andrew murmured. "I can see how that'd be a problem for you."

Cassie folded her arms in that defensive way she had. "You haven't exactly been Mr. Forthcoming," she said acidly. "Let's talk about *your* love life, Andrew. Isn't there somebody back in Dallas?"

He thought about it. "There was Grace. I argued a case against her—that's how we met. We stayed together about six months."

"That's a record, based on what Hannah had to say about you," Cassie said dryly. "But obviously Grace is in your past. I'm talking about someone current. Isn't there anybody?"

Now he made a right turn. "Marianne," he said grudgingly. "She's fairly current. We only broke up six weeks ago."

Cassie chuckled a little. It was a nice sound, low and easy on the ears. If he'd known that telling her about his personal life would bring on the mirth, he would have brought up the subject a while ago.

"Sorry," she said. "It's just that, well, you're so exactly the way Hannah described you when it comes to women."

"Go on, what terrible things did Hannah have to confess about me?"

"It's silly," Cassie muttered. "It's just—she said that if I ever met you, I had to make certain that I didn't fall for you. She said you weren't the settling-down type, and she said Zak and I needed the settling-down type. I'm embarrassed I even brought it up. Because I wouldn't even think about falling for you in the first place—" She stopped. "For goodness' sake," she grumbled. "I'm just trying to reassure you, Andrew. I have no designs on you."

It wasn't too flattering, knowing that his grandmother had thought him a bad risk. But Hannah always had been refreshingly honest. He came to a stop at the address Cassie had given him, and she made herself busy with her briefcase.

"I'm sure you're glad this conversation is over," she said. "And I really do thank you for the ride."

He came around to open her door.

"Thank you," she said again.

"You're welcome."

Neither one of them seemed able to move. They just stood there on the sidewalk, gazing at each other. Cassie was the first to glance away.

"You really know your way around this town," she said as if searching for some neutral topic.

"I grew up here. I didn't move to Texas until college, when I was eighteen." But the subject of his travels in life wasn't the one intriguing him right now. "Cassie..."

She gave him an almost desperate look this time. "You're not actually thinking about the other night, are you?"

He was thinking about it, all right, picturing how it would be to take her into his arms and continue what they'd started. Cassie held her briefcase against her as if that would somehow stop his thoughts.

"Please don't," she said firmly. But he could tell she was thinking about it, too.

"Good*bye,* Andrew," she said somewhat fiercely now. "Thank you, but—goodbye." She made it sound final, as if she hoped never to see him again. And then, briskly, she left him, her briefcase swinging with an air of purpose.

Too bad they couldn't spend the whole day together. And too bad his grandmother was right... when it came to women, he was a lousy risk.

CHAPTER SIX

CASSIE WALKED SLOWLY up the driveway. A co-worker had dropped her back home after what had been a very long day. Even her briefcase felt heavier than usual. But she knew what really weighed upon her: the thought of Andrew. Somehow she couldn't get him out of her mind. The way he looked, the way he spoke…

And, as if she needed reminding, here he was now, leaning under the hood of a car. *Her* car. Cassie stopped and observed him…what she could see of him, anyway. Long, jean-clad legs, a very nicely jean-clad posterior.

She made a sound somewhere between a groan and a laugh.

"Hello there," came Andrew's muffled voice.

"Hello, indeed." She walked around the hood, and now observed the car parts strewn on the ground. Not precisely on the ground, however—they were arranged neatly on an old towel. Andrew did seem to have something of a method to his madness.

"Don't panic," he said cheerfully. "I'm rebuilding your carburetor."

"I see," she said, her own tone rueful. "Didn't have anything better to do, I suppose."

He straightened, wiping his grimy fingers on another old towel. He winced a little, as if he'd forgotten about his sore finger. Then he gazed at her, looking immensely satisfied. "What can I say? Your carburetor was crap."

She stared at him, unable to speak for a moment. How could a man look so attractive with a smudge of motor oil on his face? She had an overwhelming desire to lift her hand and touch his cheek...

"Where's Zak?" he asked.

She gave a guilty start, and finally managed to find her voice. "Janice—the sitter—she took him to his swimming lesson. I thought swimming would help him gain a little confidence, but so far the jury's out." She knew she was overexplaining, but now she couldn't seem to stop.

Andrew leaned against the car. "So, let me get this straight," he said. "You and I are actually alone for the first time in our acquaintance."

She tightened her grip on her briefcase. He smiled. "Hand me that socket wrench, will you?"

She didn't trust him. But she set down her briefcase and handed over the wrench.

"First," she said, "I fall on top of you. Now you're rebuilding my carburetor. What next?"

"Makes you uneasy, doesn't it?" he said as he

bent over the engine. "Feeling like you're beholden to me somehow."

"Believe me, I'm grateful," she said quickly. "But you just should have let me take my car into the shop."

"This is more fun," he said. "Besides, you've obviously been avoiding the mechanic."

Cassie sighed. "If you must know the truth, my budget has been a little tight. But I had it all planned out. The car just needed to hang on another three months—"

"I hear what you're saying," he remarked seriously. "You don't like some guy you hardly know thinking he can rebuild your carburetor. But, hey, I'm not taking it personally. You hate the idea of any man trying to manage your life. You had enough of that with your dad."

Cassie battled chagrin, right along with an unwilling acknowledgment that Andrew spoke the truth. "Just how much did your grandmother tell you about *me?*" she asked.

"I've figured out a lot of it on my own," he said. Still looking pleasantly engrossed, he squatted and fiddled with some of those loose car parts.

Cassie unbuttoned her suit jacket. Then, a second later, she shrugged it off altogether. Now, in her short-sleeved blouse, the warm, late-afternoon air felt much more comfortable. She used her folded arms as an impromptu hanger for her jacket.

"Andrew," she said, "you really must have something better to do than work on my car."

He considered his grandmother's house for a moment. "Plenty of repairs waiting for me," he admitted. "Can't sell it the way it is."

"Maybe you don't have to sell it," she said, speaking offhandedly. "I do know one thing—Hannah always hoped that you'd move back to Montana."

He stared at the house another long moment, a shadow seeming to come across his face. "No," he said, his voice oddly brusque. "I'll never move back."

It occurred to Cassie again how little she really knew about him. Beneath his easygoing manner there seemed to be something forbidding, something that warned her not to get too close. She'd seen a glimpse of it just now, even though it took him only a few seconds to regain the casual facade. He was back to rebuilding her carburetor—slightly favoring his bad hand.

Since he seemed determined, she wondered why she just didn't leave him to the job. As usual, she'd brought files home from the office. Now, before Zak returned from the pool, she had a perfect opportunity to catch up on her paperwork. Instead, she lingered beside Andrew.

"I don't get a chance to do this kind of thing much anymore," he told her. "Always too busy."

"What kind of cases do you handle?" she asked curiously.

"Environmental, mostly. Lately a lot of my work involves negotiating agreements for land preservation."

"Wow, I'm impressed," Cassie said.

"Don't be. It involves a lot of meetings where people sit around too long and forget how to come to the point."

"Meetings...I suffer through enough of those myself. Speaking of which, I have one tomorrow morning, first thing, and I really have to get ready for it." She'd come up with a good exit line. Now all she had to do was...exit. But somehow she continued to linger, watching as Andrew fit pieces of things together and took them apart again. It was fascinating.

"Don't get too scared," he said. "There's a chance I know what I'm doing here."

"I don't doubt it," she said dryly. "Well, thanks again, Andrew. I really do have that work to do." Another exit line. This time she was going to act on it. Reluctantly, she moved away from the car.

"Don't go," he said.

She gazed at him. "I don't..." She didn't get a chance to finish. Because what happened next came so naturally. He stepped toward her. She waited, her heart giving a slow, steady beat. The air around her seemed to grow still. Andrew stood close to her now, regarding her with the slightest of smiles. Then, with one finger, he tilted her chin. And he kissed her.

His lips were as warm as the summer afternoon. They explored her mouth with the lightest, most leisurely of touches. He kissed her as if they had all the time in the world to indulge. Cassie followed his lead, taking it slow, savoring the moment, savoring his nearness. It felt so right to be with him. So inevitable. How could she have fought it—how could she ever have thought it would be wrong? Now what she wanted was to have his arms around her, to know a closeness even more elemental. His body next to hers...

It took her a few seconds to realize the reason he didn't hold her. His hands, covered with that motor oil. She smiled, even as the kiss continued, and heedlessly she dropped her jacket on the ground so she could run her own hands across his shoulders. Oh, yes, it all felt so right, the heat of the sun seeming to spill through her. If they could just stay like this always. No darkness, no shadows. Just this summer afternoon, and Andrew's touch, and the warmth enveloping her.

Unfortunately, it had to end. The two of them had to breathe, if nothing else. They stood together, Andrew's head bent, his cheek resting against hers.

"I've wanted to do that," he murmured, "since the first minute I saw you in the tree house."

"I've wanted it, too," she said.

"Seems like we're in agreement, then."

"About this...yes." She moved slowly away from him. "I wish there wasn't anything else to think about," she said, her voice so low it was almost a whisper. But she knew he could hear her.

"Maybe we don't have to think about anything else."

"Maybe you don't, Andrew," she said softly. "But I do. And that leaves us...just about nowhere, I think." The words held a bleak finality she hadn't intended. But she'd given herself another exit line, and this time she took it.

Only later, looking into the mirror, did she see the smudge of motor oil on her own cheek. She put her fingers to it, closed her eyes, and felt a surge of longing so strong that it hurt.

A FEW DAYS LATER, Zak stood in the middle of the small apartment, clutching his castle book. "Please take me home."

Cassie knelt beside him. "Zak, *this* is going to be home from now on. Or at least until we find a house. I've told you how much our down-payment fund has grown. We've saved and saved—"

Zak's face started to turn red with distress.

"I've told you," Cassie said gently. "Hannah's guest house can't be our home any longer. Mr. Morris needs to sell the property."

Tears shimmered in Zak's eyes, although he was making a valiant effort to contain them. Cassie felt her heart ache. She gathered her son close, oversize book and all.

"Honey, I don't want to move, either. But we've both known this day was coming. Ever since—" She stopped herself. Ever since Hannah had been gone, she'd been about to say. But she wouldn't remind Zak of that. "We're going to have a wonderful time here," she said with determination. "We're so lucky this place became available right now. It's much closer to Janice, and to my office—"

Zak, no longer able to control himself, began sobbing. Cassie felt answering tears smart at her eyelids.

"Honey, it'll be all right," she murmured. "Home is wherever the two of us are. The park is so close by, and we'll have wonderful times."

"Can we get a dog?" he asked with a hiccup.

"Not right away," Cassie said. "They don't allow pets here. But when we find a house to buy, of course we'll have a dog—"

Zak slipped away from her. Tears continued to trickle down his cheeks. He sat on the floor, opened his book and stared unseeing at the pages. Cassie ached all the more for him. And, meanwhile, the voices of doubt assailed her. *If you move back to the ranch, Zak will have his grandfather. He'll have a tree house built especially for him—Robert Sr. will*

*see to it. He'll have his very own dog—Robert Sr.
will see to that, too. And he'll have a family surrounding him. How can you measure your independence against all of that?*

For one long, terrible moment, Cassie felt like the
most selfish person alive. How, indeed, could she
deny Zak all that her father would offer? What kind
of mother *was* she?

But then the other voices had their say...the
voices of reason. *If you move back to Walking
Stones, your father will overwhelm your son. He'll
expect too much, hope too much. Your father's love
doesn't come without a price. In the end, it will only
hurt Zak, just as it hurt you, Jolie, Thea and Bobby.*

Cassie took a slow, deep breath. She felt a much-
welcome calmness take her over. "Come on, Zak,"
she said in a firm voice. "We're going to walk down
to the ice-cream store and get ourselves something
to celebrate. How many kids can say they live only
two blocks from an ice-cream store?"

Zak still didn't answer. He just lifted his tear-
streaked face and gave Cassie a mutinous glare. He
couldn't possibly understand that she was doing
what was best for him. That hurt, too, but she
couldn't let it stop her.

"Come along, son," she said, making clear she
would tolerate no refusal. And at last he came to
stand beside her...and he walked silently with her
down the street.

ANDREW WASN'T IMPRESSED by the shabby moving van parked in the driveway. He'd been in Montana less than a week, and already he'd driven Cassie out of house and home. He wondered what his grandmother would have said about this.

Cassie came out of the guest house carrying a box of dishes. Before she could protest, Andrew took it from her.

"Explain to me again," he said, "why you're doing this."

Cassie gave him a stern look. She couldn't really pull off the look, though, in her shorts and denim shirt and baseball cap. She looked like somebody who should be out enjoying the last of the summer, maybe dangling her feet in a stream, or fishing, or tossing around a baseball. Instead, she was busy vacating the premises.

"I've been looking for an apartment for weeks," she said with exaggerated patience. "Of course I grabbed the right one up when it came along. It's clean, it's reasonable, it's in a good neighborhood."

"You don't have to move out," he argued, not for the first time. "I haven't sold the place yet. Until I do, you're welcome to stay on." He paused. "It's what Hannah would have wanted." He thought that might make Cassie reconsider, but it didn't seem to have any effect on her.

"Hannah was a very dear and wonderful person," she said. "I miss her a great deal—so does Zak. And that's just one more reason why we need to make a fresh start." She went back into the guest house, came out with another box. Andrew took this one from her, too, and placed it in the van.

"The kid's pretty upset, I gather. That's why you're not letting him see any of this."

"Zak," said Cassie, "just happens to be spending the day with Janice and her nephew. Janice always likes to have Zak around when she's baby-sitting her nephew. The two boys entertain each other." She marched back to the guest house. Andrew followed.

"You're damn stubborn," he said.

"I am told that particular quality runs in the Maxwell family. Andrew, you're doing it again. You fixed my car. And now you're helping me move."

He couldn't deny it. Cassie Maxwell Warren seemed to have a lot of loose ends hanging around—and he seemed to be making an effort to help her tie them up.

Bad idea, he warned himself. *A beautiful woman with a complicated life…stay away.* He knew all about messy lives, messy families. He didn't need any more.

But somehow that didn't stop him.

"You're running away," he told Cassie.

Her face turned pink underneath the baseball cap. "I despise it when people say that. It's such a convenient accusation."

"I kissed you, and now you figure you'd better get the hell away from me."

She turned even more pink. "If you think one kiss from you is going to have that kind of effect...or even *two* kisses..." She looked completely exasperated now, and grabbed another box. Andrew appropriated that one, too.

"You'll hurt your hand," she said.

"Nonsense. The thing's practically as good as new."

She didn't argue. She picked up a basket of laundry, and together they went out to the van.

"If you're not running away," Andrew said, "then you'll let me take you and Zak out to dinner tonight. Moving-day special."

"Thanks very much," she said in her too-polite voice. "But I'd planned to order in pizza and rent a movie for the two of us." She paused. "I suppose you'll tell me that if I'm not running away, I'd invite you for pizza, too."

"I didn't say anything."

"Andrew..." She gazed at him very seriously now. "I'd like to make this something of a clean break. The truth is—Zak *is* fragile. He desperately needs some stability. I need to get him settled into his new life as soon as possible. School will be starting, he'll make new friends...I just need to ease the transition, that's all."

Andrew slid the box into the van. What she said

made sense. A clean break...but he didn't seem to be listening to logic at the moment.

"I'll be in town a little while longer," he said.

"That's just it." Now her voice had an edge. "You'll only be here a little while. Zak has already gotten too accustomed to you. He seems to like you. Frankly, I don't want him to get any more attached."

The kid liked to hang around him, he'd noticed that much. Another complication, he told himself—one he didn't need.

"Guess you're right," he told Cassie.

"Of course I'm right," she said sharply. But she looked displeased. "You know," she burst out a second later, "if the circumstances were different—if I were younger, if I didn't have a son—sure, why not? Maybe it would be just fine to take one or two weeks, and have a grand and wonderful time with you until you go back to Texas. But it's not like that." Back she went to the guest house. Again he followed.

"Cassie..."

"Dammit, Andrew."

He took her in his arms, and held her the way he'd wanted to all day.

"Dammit," she repeated. But then it was a very long moment before she said anything else. She clung to him, molding her body to his. This was what he needed. From everything he could tell, she needed it, too.

She leaned her forehead against his chest. "Why, Andrew?" she whispered.

"I don't know," he murmured, running his hand down her back. "It's just the way it is."

"I don't want to feel this way."

"Maybe there are worse things," he said.

She lifted her face to gaze at him. "For me, right now...there couldn't be anything much worse. Don't you understand?"

Apparently he didn't. He'd learned not to think too far ahead. Somehow that helped him not to look too far back into the past. But Cassie Warren seemed to judge every event by its effect on some distant, unknowable future. Maybe having a kid did that to you.

"I have to go now, Andrew. And I really do want to make this a clean break."

"Meaning," he said, "that I'd better not show up at your apartment."

For just a second, she pressed her forehead deeper against his chest. But then she left his arms.

"Goodbye."

CHAPTER SEVEN

ANDREW FIGURED he'd filled his rental convertible to capacity. Two brand-new sawhorses took pride of place in the front passenger seat, while several one-by-sixes jutted out the back. A visit to the local hardware store had also netted him a chop saw, a portable drill, reinforced work gloves, the ultimate in cushioned knee pads, a couple of pounds of screws and his favorite purchase of all: a crowbar-style tool aptly known as a tweaker. Somehow he'd managed to load everything into the car, make the necessary tie-downs with bungee cords and cruise out of the parking lot.

Fortunately for the car's shocks, it was only a short drive to Hannah's house. Andrew would have given a lot right now for his grandfather's old '52 Ford pickup. He eased his way into the driveway, turned off the engine and contemplated a thoroughly enjoyable afternoon of home repairs.

He also contemplated something else: the oak at the end of the yard, where the rope ladder was drifting back and forth as if nudged by the wind. But there wasn't so much as a whisper of a breeze. It was a particularly calm, hot day.

Andrew climbed out of the car and walked along the gravel path toward the oak. He stood beneath it, craning his neck to look upward. There seemed a wary silence above him. He tested the ladder with his hands, then climbed up. When his eyes reached tree-house level, somehow he wasn't surprised to find a small redheaded boy crouched there.

Young Zak quickly swiveled until his back was turned to Andrew. He drew his knees up and clasped his arms protectively around them.

"Hello there," Andrew said. Zak said nothing. Andrew climbed into the tree house, then sat down in as comfortable a position as possible.

"Didn't see your car," he remarked. "Guess somebody dropped you and your mom off…and your mom's down at the guest house right now, cleaning out a few last things."

Zak hunched his shoulders over his legs.

"Then again," Andrew went on, "could be your mom's not here. Could be she doesn't know you're here, either."

This, at last, elicited a response. "So?" mumbled Zak in a half-scared, half-defiant voice.

"Could be she's worried about you," Andrew said. "Not knowing where you are, that type of thing." He fished his cell phone out of his shirt pocket and flipped it open. "Let's give her a call."

"No." Still scared, still defiant.

Andrew considered the matter. The right thing to do, of course, was call Cassie. If he knew anything at all about her, at this moment she'd be frantic. But something told Andrew to wait just a minute or two—some instinct not wholly familiar. What did he know about kids, anyway? Yet, even so, he waited. The silence of the summer afternoon drew out, undisturbed by birdsong or rustle of leaves.

"What I wonder," Andrew finally remarked, "is how you managed to slip away from your mom. That would take some doing."

Another silence, followed by a grudging response. "Swimming class," said Zak succinctly. "Locker room, back door."

Andrew nodded thoughtfully. "I'm beginning to get the picture. You make your escape—and meanwhile your mom's out by the pool, expecting you to show."

"Not Mom. Janice."

Right—the baby-sitter. "So Janice is waiting for you," Andrew amended. "When you don't come out of the locker room, *she* gets frantic and calls your mom, who gets frantic, too. Definitely time to put her out of her misery." He pressed a button on the phone. Cassie, despite her stated intention never to see Andrew again, had been obliged to leave her cell number with him. He'd envisioned perhaps the need to deliver stray mail to her. It hadn't occurred to him that he'd need to deliver her stray son.

He'd punched another few buttons when Zak swivelled around and spoke again, the words tumbling out in a rush.

"I hate that class. I can't swim, and everybody makes fun of me. And I'm not going back, ever."

Andrew paused diplomatically. "Pretty good scrape you've got on your knee there."

Zak drew his eyebrows together. "I fell down. Tripped, sort of."

"On the way here, I take it," Andrew remarked. "Moving a little too fast."

"A little," Zak said reluctantly.

This time around, Andrew keyed in Cassie's number all the way. "You want to do the talking?" he asked.

"Maybe you'd better," Zak hedged.

"Maybe so."

The phone call revealed exactly what Andrew had expected: one very worried mother of a seven-year-old. At this very moment, she was out canvassing the streets.

"I was working my way over to Hannah's," Cassie said rather grimly. "Somehow I had a feeling…well, anyway, I'll be right there."

Andrew gave Zak a glance. The kid looked quietly unhappy underneath all the freckles.

"Tell you what," he said into the phone. "I have

a better idea. I'll bring him over to your apartment. We'll meet you there.''

''And why,'' said Cassie, ''should I agree to that?''

Andrew thought it over. ''It's a guy thing,'' he said.

''A *guy* thing…'' The pause on her own end of the line was potent. But then, her voice clipped, she gave him her new address. ''I'll be waiting,'' she said, and then she hung up.

Andrew folded the phone and slid it back into his pocket. ''Guess we'd better get a move on,'' he told Zak.

''Guess so,'' Zak answered manfully.

Andrew climbed down first, then Zak. At the car, however, Andrew realized he didn't have room for even one small boy. He lifted out the sawhorses, one at a time, afterward starting on the one-by-sixes. Zak ran to take hold of one end of a board. Andrew was about to tell him no, then stopped. By balancing the board at the center, he could let Zak help without putting too much weight on the little boy. Preserving dignity was important to a kid—Andrew knew at least that much. Together they got the lumber out of the car, and then Andrew allowed Zak to carry the bag of screws.

''Are you fixing up the house so you can live here?'' Zak asked.

''Not exactly. I'm fixing up to sell.''

Zak gave him an accusing stare. "Are you going to sell the tree house, too?"

Andrew rubbed his jaw, wondering why he suddenly felt guilty. "It's sort of a package deal," he said. "Main house, guest house...tree house. Several acres, too." He sounded like a real-estate ad.

"Great," Zak muttered disparagingly, climbing into the passenger seat. He wasn't forthcoming on the drive to his new home, providing only monosyllables to Andrew's attempts at conversation.

Cassie was waiting at the front of the apartment building. Apparently calm, she waited for Zak to get out of the car. Then she knelt in front of him and looked him straight in the eye.

"William Zachary Warren," she said in a firm, even tone, "do you realize how terrified I've been?"

He gave an uncertain nod, uttering a single word in a wavering voice. "Mommy." And then the tears started trickling down his cheeks.

Cassie enveloped him in a fierce hug, her eyes shut tight. The expression on her face was so revealing, so evocative of love and pain, that Andrew felt like a trespasser. He had no right to be here. And yet he remained where he was, unable to move, as if reluctant to break a spell. Another scene appeared before his mind's eye: himself, only a few years older than Zak, sobbing, too, his own mother holding him, trying to make him forget...only he had never forgotten.

Andrew did turn now, his intent simply to get back into the convertible and drive away. If he tried, he could still have that pleasurable afternoon of home repairs. Nothing on his mind, no shadows from a long-ago past. It would just take some trying...

"Andrew's gonna fix my knee," came Zak's watery voice. Cassie drew back and observed the wound in question.

"I'll fix it," she said.

"It's a guy thing," said Zak.

Cassie stared at her son with dismay as well as the beginnings of exasperated amusement. "Very well," she said. "If it's all right with Andrew." She gave him a wry glance.

"Okay by me," he said after a moment. He could tell the afternoon of home repairs was fast receding.

Some soap and water, some antiseptic, a Band-Aid. The scrape on Zak's knee was soon dispensed with.

"Not so bad," Andrew said.

"Sure," Zak said. "But Mom overreacts to this type of thing."

The kid sounded thirty years old. Andrew couldn't say he envied Cassie the task of parenthood. Now he watched as she gave Zak some cookies and milk, and settled him onto the couch. The kid was asleep practically by the time his head hit the pillow. Clearly he'd had enough adventure for

the day. Cassie stood beside him for a moment, gazing. Then she gestured to Andrew, and he followed
her to the minuscule kitchen. He supposed it was
about as much privacy as you could expect in a
place the size of a pocket handkerchief.

"Andrew," Cassie said formally, "I'm sorry we
put you through all this—"

"No problem."

She gave a shudder. "When Janice called and told
me she couldn't find Zak—if only I could tell you
what I felt...but there's no describing it, really. The
fear that goes through you..."

Now he regretted even the minute delay before
he'd called her.

She pushed a hand wearily through her hair. "My
crazy job," she murmured. "Another Saturday at
the office, when I should have been with Zak."

"It's not your fault," he told her.

She gave a rueful laugh. "Andrew, when you're
a mother, particularly a single one, *everything's* your
fault. You can't help feeling that way, anyway. How
about a soda? It's the best I can offer."

He settled on cherry-vanilla soda. He and Cassie
sat at the small kitchen table across from each other.
Today she'd allowed her red hair to hang loose, and
her tailored shirt couldn't disguise the hint of curves.

"I know what you're thinking," she said, frown-
ing at her own can of soda. "You're thinking this

apartment is ridiculous. Okay, so it's small, but it *is* clean. And this is a very safe neighborhood."

"I wasn't thinking about that at all," he said. She lifted her face, and her skin turned that beguiling shade of rose.

"Andrew, you're not going to start…just don't, all right?"

It was a little late for that, but he took another swig of cherry vanilla.

"Anyway," she said with determination, "I've gone over and over it in my mind. This apartment is terribly small, especially compared to all the space Zak would have at the ranch, but it's right for us. And just because Zak ran back to Hannah's house first chance he got—" She groaned, propping her head in both hands. "Just listen to me, trying to convince myself that I have it all under control. Well, after the stunt Zak pulled today, obviously I *don't* have it under control."

Andrew didn't say anything. Not for the first time today, he realized he was no expert.

"At first moving to Billings seemed the perfect solution," Cassie said in a low voice. "Zak and I would be able to make a fresh start, and we'd be close enough to the ranch for regular visits. Jeff promised to visit regularly, too. I thought it would all work out, but then Jeff didn't visit, didn't call, and Zak started to get way too quiet. And my job…it was supposed to be a dream job, helping kids and families. Except that after some of the court cases I've helped set in motion, I wonder if I've helped *anyone*. And what's the use of trying to solve other people's problems when I can't even help my own son?''

Andrew decided it was still too soon to speak. He figured Cassie was only letting her guard down like this, confiding in him, because she'd just had a stressful time of it. She'd probably regret it later.

''Your own work, Andrew…do you ever have any second thoughts about it? Any misgivings?''

Maybe she was already regretting it—maybe that was why she was turning the conversation on *him*. He stalled for time, glancing around. He saw attempts at making the apartment homey here and there: a bright yellow-and-green towel tucked into the handle of the fridge, an old-fashioned Dutch-boy cookie jar presiding on the counter next to spice and flour tins decorated with cows. Yet the place still had an aura of impermanence, no doubt because it had been built with temporary lodgers in mind.

But she'd asked about his work, and he did have an answer for it.

''Misgivings,'' he echoed. ''Yeah, I have those. Like you, I thought I was going to go out and solve the world's problems. Only it hasn't exactly turned out that way. I work with my clients to save a piece of land here, a nature preserve there, but too many compromises get made in the process. Too much quibbling all around.''

''Do you ever think about quitting and doing something else?'' Her voice was intent.

''Sometimes, sure.''

''Well, *what* do you think of doing?'' she asked almost impatiently now.

He smiled a little. ''Cassie, I'm no oracle when it comes to career change. I've tossed around a few ideas, that's all. When I was a kid, I thought I wanted to be a forest ranger. The notion still has its attractions, I'll admit, but it's not exactly practical.''

''You don't strike me as the kind of man who'd be stopped by matters of mere practicality,'' she murmured. ''And you *would* look good in one of those forest-ranger outfits. But that's beside the point. You don't have a family to support, Andrew. You can afford to take chances.''

''Unfortunately, I happen to like being my own boss,'' he said. ''I probably wouldn't do too well being part of a big government organization, taking orders from higher-ups.''

''You could do something else—anything you wanted,'' she argued.

Anything he wanted…if you were going to day-dream about endless possibilities, you had to think about the future quite a lot—not his strong point. He'd gotten his law degree, plunged into his own practice, built up a certain success, but had let it all stop there. He could almost hear Hannah's voice, chiding him. *Where's your imagination, Andrew? Don't you want more? Isn't your success just a bit hollow?*

"We were talking about you, Cassie," he reminded her. "Something tells me you're the one who wants a change."

"As if I haven't put Zak through enough turmoil already, but, yes, I do want something better. Something impossible—to spend more time with Zak—but still have my independence." She shook her head. "When I was growing up, everyone thought my sisters and brother and I were so lucky. To have a wealthy and powerful father who took care of everything, but there's an enormous price to pay for that. It's no wonder that each of us rebelled, one way or another. To be myself, to be free of a father who thinks *everyone* should obey him…it seemed so important to fight for that. It seemed more important than anything in the world…until Zak came along…"

"Maybe you being independent," said Andrew, "is exactly what Zak needs."

She didn't look convinced. Clearly he wasn't helping her solve any of her problems. And maybe he was about to add to them.

"Zak told me he hates his swimming class."

She looked startled. "That's the word he used— he *hates* it?"

"Pretty much an exact quote."

She lifted her shoulders in perplexity. "I thought he wanted to go. I thought it was helping him—how could I be so wrong?" She frowned. "What else did my son confide in you? Am I going to find out he doesn't actually like Parcheesi or chocolate birthday cake?"

"We didn't get that far," Andrew said. "I think you're still safe when it comes to Parcheesi. Probably when it comes to chocolate cake, too."

She stood restlessly. "It's all right for you to joke, but he's my son. And if he's going to confide in a stranger instead of me—"

Andrew knew his cue when he heard it. He was still persona non grata as far as Cassie Maxwell Warren was concerned. He stood also.

"Something tells me you'd like some time to yourself," he said.

"I am grateful you found Zak—"

"He found me," Andrew told her. It was the wrong thing to say. Her expression grew shuttered.

"He needs to learn that everything to do with Hannah is over. Goodbye, Andrew."

She had a habit of saying that to him. But maybe, in the end, it was the only thing to say.

CHAPTER EIGHT

THE DOG WAS ONLY a puppy, but already it was oversize. It had big fuzzy feet it kept tripping over, and large fuzzy ears that pointed inquisitively straight up. It didn't seem to need much sleep. Over the past hours, it had followed Andrew all around Hannah's house—up and down the stairs, out onto the porch, back inside again. At last Andrew sat down on the floor. The puppy climbed on him and tried to lick his face.

"Look," Andrew told it. "You and I both know this was a mistake."

The dog seemed to have some idea about climbing onto Andrew's head. Andrew held the squirming bundle of brown fur and contemplated the error of his ways. He had no good explanation for what he'd done yesterday. Driving along in the convertible, he'd spotted this stray pup. He'd stopped the car...

Okay, maybe that part he could explain. Out here on the edge of town, people often found abandoned dogs. It was reasonable to stop and do something— get the dog, take it to the local animal shelter.

Now Andrew came to the part that didn't make a

whole lot of sense. He'd stopped for this particular
mutt, but he hadn't taken it to the animal shelter.
Instead he'd brought it with him to Hannah's house.
Then he'd made another trip out for puppy food.

"A mistake," Andrew reiterated. "Big one."

The pup finally settled down and began gnawing
on his shirt. Their acquaintance had now been something less than twenty-four hours. Andrew had to
admit that part of him, deep down, regretted he
wouldn't get to know the dog better. When you
made a mistake, though, best thing you could do was
correct it as soon as possible.

The puppy gazed up at him with trusting brown
eyes.

"Look," Andrew said. "It's not like I'm taking
you to the pound. That pet-adoption center I
called—they know what they're doing. Before you
know it, you'll have a house with a white picket
fence and two kids to play with."

The dog chewed his shirt some more. This wasn't
getting any easier, so Andrew stopped delaying. He
packed the puppy into its brand-new carrier, complete with blanket and water bowl. Only a few
minutes later he was in the rental convertible, tooling down the road from Hannah's house, the dog
carrier in the front seat beside him. In just a little
while he'd be out of this fix.

He hadn't counted on complications. One complication, to be exact: a small redheaded boy walk-

ing along the sidewalk toward him. Young William Zachary Warren scuffed along at a slow pace, his head bent, his gaze focused on the ground. He wore a T-shirt and shorts, and had a rolled-up towel tucked under his left arm. It didn't take much guessing to figure out the kid had hightailed it from swim class again.

Andrew pulled over just about even with the kid, and got out of the car.

"Hey there, Zak."

Zak tried to give an appearance of nonchalance. "Hey." He wasn't very successful.

Andrew leaned against the passenger door of the car. "Think maybe your mom's a little worried about you again?"

Zak shrugged. "Janice'll be along pretty soon," he mumbled.

Andrew nodded thoughtfully. "Guess she's wise to you by now. Pretty clever of you to give her the slip twice, though."

Zak allowed himself a look of moderate pride. "This time I went out the front door of the locker room. I don't think she was expecting that."

"Probably not," Andrew said. "I guess we can wait for her here. She'll see us."

Zak's look turned unhappy. "Maybe we could hide," he suggested.

"Maybe. But I'd hate to have Janice and your mom worried like they were before."

"How come I still have to go to that stupid class?" Zak asked.

Andrew rubbed his neck. "Swimming," he said, "is a useful thing to know."

"You know how to swim?"

"Learned when I was about your age," Andrew said.

"Did anybody pick on you when you couldn't do it right?"

He searched for the right words. "Nobody picked on me about swimming. But there's always something else to worry about."

Zak regarded him with interest. "Like what?"

He could give the boy some pat answer. Instead he found himself telling the truth. "When I was nine years old, after my father died...I didn't talk much. And I got picked on for that."

"How'd he die?" Zak asked solemnly.

"Car crash."

Zak seemed to think this over. "My dad's not dead, but he doesn't come to see me. So sometimes I get scared *he* had a car wreck or something, and he really did die, but my mom won't tell me. But then I talk to him on the phone, so I know he's okay."

Andrew was thinking this over when a whimpering sound came from the front seat of the car.

"What's that?" Zak asked, trying to peer around Andrew.

Now would be a really good time to lie, and say something inventive about engine noises. But the whimper came again, and Zak darted to the car.

''What's that?'' he said, staring at the dog carrier as if he couldn't believe his eyes.

The jig was up, Andrew supposed. He opened the car door, and then the door of the dog carrier. Gently he lifted out the bundle of squirming brown fur. Zak's eyes grew wider than ever.

''Want to hold him?'' Andrew asked.

Zak nodded, seemingly incapable of speech now. His swim towel dropped unnoticed to the ground, and the next second he held the bundle of fur in both arms. The puppy licked him enthusiastically.

The unhappy look on Zak's face was gone, vanished as if it had never been. It had been replaced by another look: one of complete, uncomplicated joy.

Andrew had made a big mistake, all right.

It SHOULD HAVE BEEN a perfect day. The sky was the color of polished blue marble. The air was just right, summer warm but not too hot. The grass was a rich, luxuriant green. The park bench was comfortable, conducive to the stretching out of legs. Cassie had come here for lunch, hoping for a little serenity while she read some work files. But she was simply too keyed up. Finally she slapped the folders onto the bench beside her, and uttered a particularly vivid curse.

"Glad to see me, I gather," came a voice beside her. Not just any voice. A deep sexy masculine voice belonging to Andrew Morris.

Cassie almost dropped her peanut butter and jelly sandwich. "Andrew—how did you find me?"

He sat down next to her. "The receptionist at your office was very forthcoming."

Cassie made a mental note to have a serious discussion with Linda. No doubt, though, Linda had been swayed by Andrew's sheer gorgeousness. Right now, for instance, Cassie wanted to say something withering to the man, but nothing occurred to her. All she could do was gaze at him, taking in the sight of him like someone long deprived of nourishment. Yet it had been less than one day since she'd seen him. Yesterday, to be exact—after her son had once again run away to Hannah's house. And that was when Andrew had introduced Zak to one small puppy. Zak had been thrilled ever since—and Cassie had been thoroughly exasperated.

"Andrew," she finally managed to say in a strict tone, "I'm not really in the mood to see you."

"I figured as much. That's why I brought some peace offerings." He opened the sack he'd brought with him, and took out two wrapped packages. Each one was adorned with a jaunty bow. Cassie studied them suspiciously. "What's this all about?"

"Just open them," he said.

Muttering a protest under her breath, she nonetheless opened the first package. It contained a rawhide chew bone. "Very funny," she said dryly.

"Open the other one," he urged.

She tore off the wrapping paper. Inside was a miniature doghouse, painted a bright cherry red.

"I realize," Andrew said very gravely, "that I *am* in the doghouse."

Cassie didn't know whether to laugh or cry. On the one hand, she admired a man who cared enough to pick up a stray puppy. On the other hand, she deeply regretted that Andrew had introduced her son to the dog.

"Andrew," she said, "if only you hadn't told Zak you were putting the dog up for adoption. And if only Zak hadn't gotten the bright idea he could be the adopter."

Andrew's look grew rueful. "Guess I didn't think it through."

"You know how impossible this situation is!" she burst out. "We live in an apartment. We simply *can't* have a dog."

He seemed genuinely regretful. "Never should've let the kid see that puppy. Should've just driven on, made it to the adoption center. The dog would be long gone by now. Instead..."

"Instead," Cassie finished up, "instead, my son will be devastated if you let someone else have that dog. He's demanding visitation rights, and how on earth am I going to say no to that?'' She paused. ''Do you know he even has a name for the dog? He couldn't believe *you* hadn't come up with one yet, so he did you the favor.''

Now Andrew looked curious. ''So, what's the name, anyway?''

Cassie sighed. ''Arthur. The dog's name is Arthur. I don't know how you feel about that.''

Andrew settled back. ''As in King Arthur. Kind of a grand name for a puppy, but I bet he'll grow into it.'' He took something else out of the sack and handed it to her. Gourmet yogurt, followed by a cranberry-almond bagel.

''Andrew, did you come here to bring me lunch? I have lunch. A perfectly acceptable lunch—''

''I came to apologize,'' he said. ''Lunch is just a side benefit.''

She eyed the bagel. It was from the best shop in town, and finally she gave in. She took a bite. ''Let me guess,'' she said. ''You brought some of their special deluxe cream cheese, too.''

He reached into the sack and produced a small tub of cream cheese and a plastic knife. ''At your service,'' he said.

She sighed again. ''Thank you, Andrew. This really is very magnanimous. But it doesn't change the fact that I'm upset.''

"Eat first," he suggested. "And then be mad at me."

He was truly infuriating, but Cassie couldn't resist the cream cheese, either. Andrew ate his own bagel, cinnamon raisin, and a container of cherry yogurt. Cassie's yogurt was a delicious peach.

"Who's baby-sitting the dog right now?" she asked reluctantly. "Puppies are pretty much a full-time proposition, you know."

"I'm finding that out," he said in a wry tone. "It's kind of hard to tear up floorboards when you have a dog that wants to eat your shoelaces. But I shut him in the utility room for an hour or so. Just hope he doesn't destroy it while I'm gone."

"Zak asks about him every other minute. What are we going to do—"

"For now," said Andrew, "why don't we just let your son come over and keep the dog company? How about six o'clock tonight, dinner provided?"

She wanted to stay mad at him, but was finding it difficult. "You've already provided lunch. Dinner's too much—"

"I'll order pizza," he said. "What's your favorite topping?"

"Mushroom and black olive," she said, sighing. "And Zak likes pineapple."

"See you at six," he said. He gave her the lightest, most alluring of kisses—and then, before she quite knew what was happening, he was walking away from her across the park.

That little stray puppy of his wasn't Cassie's only problem by far.

CASSIE STOOD on the porch of Hannah's house and watched as Zak rolled joyfully in the grass with Arthur. The late-evening light spilled over them, casting them in a warm mellow gold. An ache filled her, a longing so intense she hardly knew how to express it. If only she could see her son like this always…if only she could protect him from ever being hurt again…

She sensed rather than heard Andrew come to stand behind her.

"They seem to get along," he murmured.

Cassie nodded. "I haven't seen Zak like this since, well, since I can hardly remember. Even on the ranch, he always seems to hold something back. But now, with that puppy…he hasn't even glanced at the tree house today. He hasn't needed to hide. I'm so glad—and so scared at the same time."

Andrew didn't say anything for a long moment. Then he moved forward to stand beside her.

"Cassie," he said, "I know I've created some major complications here. But somehow we'll make the dog his—"

"It's more than the dog," she said in a low voice. "Don't you see? My son feels safe around *you*.

That's why he keeps running back here. He's made you into some kind of...some kind of male role figure.'' She took a deep breath. "I'm sure that's a complication you don't want, but it's happened.''

He paced restlessly along the porch. "Maybe we're both overreacting here. Maybe the kid doesn't really see me like that—''

"You're a hero to him,'' Cassie said. "He's only ever had one other hero...my father.'' Suddenly she felt very tired. Ever since the divorce, she'd been trying so hard to control her life. Yet, the more she tried, the more everything seemed *out* of control.

"We'll figure something out,'' said Andrew.

She gave him a sharp glance. "There's no 'we' here, Andrew. My son...my responsibility.''

"Maybe accepting a little help now and then wouldn't be a sign of weakness,'' Andrew suggested.

"So far,'' Cassie said dryly, "your idea of help hasn't simplified matters any.''

"Funny how one little pup can cause so much havoc,'' Andrew said, gazing out at Zak and Arthur. The expression on his face was almost brooding— as if he had withdrawn into himself, to someplace Cassie couldn't reach. Andrew had given her that feeling before, the impression that he knew all too well how to distance himself.

At last he stirred. "I'm going through some of Hannah's stuff. Want to keep me company?''

She hesitated, glancing out at her son again.

"He'll be fine," said Andrew. "I don't think you have to worry about him giving you the slip."

Reluctantly, she had to agree that Andrew was right. At this moment, Zak was exactly where he wanted to be. And so she went with Andrew through the house, past the remnants of pizza on the kitchen table and across the foyer to the living room. Here were the fussy details that Hannah had favored in home decor: the sofa with its ruffled skirt, the clutter of porcelain figurines, the lamps with their elaborate shades. Cassie and Hannah had often joked about the differences in their decorating styles, Cassie's theory being that less was more. However, right now she found the fussiness oddly comforting. She sat down in an armchair and watched as Andrew knelt before a cardboard box. He took out a loose pile of photographs, then a stack of yellowed pages.

"My grandmother was a packrat," he said. "Sorting through everything is going to be quite a job. I told my mother I'd do it, though. No sense in her having to deal with it."

"That's the first time I've ever heard you mention your mother," she said. "And, come to think of it, Hannah didn't talk about her, either."

"Yeah, well, the two of them didn't get along too well. They weren't even on speaking terms these past few years. I tried to be a sort of mediator, but that didn't work out. Both of them ended up telling me to butt out.''

Cassie couldn't help feeling puzzled. ''Hannah was always so kind and generous with Zak and me. Somehow it doesn't fit, her holding a grudge against her own daughter.''

''Families are funny that way,'' Andrew said, taking out another sheaf of paper and flipping through them. ''Sometimes it's a lot easier to tolerate strangers than your own flesh and blood.''

Cassie shrugged. ''Maybe you're right. When it comes to my own family, sometimes we have a hard time just being civil to each other. Any idea why Hannah and your mom didn't get along?''

''It goes back a while…a very long while.'' Andrew didn't offer any more information, and Cassie got that feeling again—the sense that he'd withdrawn to some unreachable place. Yet he went on sorting through the box, making inconsequential remarks now and then about his grandmother's habit of saving everything she'd ever owned.

Suddenly impatient, Cassie stood. ''It's time for me to leave, Andrew. If I can tear my son away from that puppy, I'll be on my way home.''

He came to stand beside her. ''Still mad at me, aren't you?''

''No, of course not,'' she said too quickly.

''Where you're concerned, Cassie, I don't seem to do anything right,'' he murmured.

"Don't be ridiculous."

"Can't help wanting to get something right..."
And, with that, he took her into his arms and kissed
her.

Oh, he did *this* right. He knew just how to touch
her, just how to place his lips on hers. As if at his
bidding, desire and yearning cascaded through her.
If only she could make *this* moment last forever...

"Mom!" called Zak's voice from the kitchen.
Cassie pulled away from Andrew, her breath coming
erratically. Without another glance at him, she hurried across the foyer.

"Yes, honey, what is it?"

"Arthur is hungry," her son announced. "Can he
have some pizza?"

"No food from the table," Cassie said automatically, her thoughts completely elsewhere.

"He can have a dog biscuit," said Andrew, fol-
lowing her. *He* sounded calm enough. He opened a
cupboard door, pulled out the box of biscuits and
allowed Zak to complete the honors. Zak knelt on
the floor with the puppy.

"It's time to go home," Cassie said, still speaking
automatically, still not daring to look at Andrew. To
her surprise, Zak didn't argue.

"Okay," he said. Cassie, thrown by her son being
so amenable, ended up saying exactly what she
shouldn't.

"You can come back tomorrow to see Arthur—

if it's all right with Mr. Morris.'' Now, at last, she
did look at him, and she saw the unspoken answer
in his eyes. Regret and wanting, all at once.

It was the wanting that scared Cassie the most.

CHAPTER NINE

STRANDED.

Cassie's first reaction had been to yell in frustration. Her second reaction had been simply to take charge of the situation. So it was that she found herself talking on her cell phone to Dr. Gwen.

"Let me get this straight," Gwen said over the air. "You're stuck in some podunk little town out in the middle of nowhere, and you called *me?* Why not ask that gorgeous hunk to come to the rescue? You know the one I mean."

Cassie took a deep breath. "Gwen, this is not a matter for Andrew Morris."

"Right, right," Gwen said. "You're a hundred miles from home, your car won't start, the local mechanic can't fix it until tomorrow, but you don't want the least little bit of help from a gorgeous hunk."

Cassie took another deep breath. "I'm asking *you* for help. If you could just get over to Janice's by six and pick up Zak, I would be immensely grateful. Janice would love to have Zak spend the night, but she's got a date—"

"Lucky Janice," Gwen said dryly. "Look, I'll be perfectly happy to spoil Zak rotten tonight. I'll feed him ice cream for dinner, and keep him up late watching old Jerry Lewis movies. But that doesn't change the fact that you're missing a grand opportunity here. Play the damsel in distress...call the hunk."

"Gwen," Cassie said with strained patience, "I will have *no* distress if you'll just pick up my son."

"You can count on me," Gwen replied cheerily. "But I'm telling you, you're making a big mistake. Being self-sufficient only takes you so far. I'm sure Jolie and Thea would agree with me on this one."

"What on earth do my sisters have to do with this—"

"I talk to Jolie quite often these days. She's referred me a couple of cases, and she always asks for an update on your love life."

Cassie grimaced. "Believe me, it's not necessary for you to update *anybody*—"

"I enjoy my conversations with Jolie," Gwen said virtuously. "But that's beside the point. The way Jolie tells it, both she and Thea agree that the hunk is a promising prospect for you."

"Jolie and Thea haven't even met Andrew," Cassie protested.

"Well, whose fault is that?"

Cassie felt like yelling again. "Goodbye, Gwen," she managed to say in her most civil tone.

"And...thanks." She folded up her cell phone, telling herself that she ought to feel relieved. Yes, it was highly inconvenient that once again her car had failed her. She'd come to Elk River—the little town north of Billings—to conduct interviews for one of her cases. Her work was done, and she certainly didn't care to spend the night here—she wanted nothing more than to be home right now with her son. But she knew that Zak would be in very good hands with Gwen. And the car would surely be fixed tomorrow. This whole thing was nothing more than a temporary annoyance.

But she still felt restless and out of sorts. The fact was, she *had* wanted to call Andrew. He'd been the first person who'd popped into her mind. She'd longed to have him come to her rescue. And that was exactly why she *hadn't* called him.

Now Cassie walked slowly down the main street of Elk River. The town, admittedly, had a pleasing quaintness: storefronts embellished with Victorian gingerbread, old-fashioned lampposts lining the sidewalk, across the way a grassy park complete with a pavilion and ornate wrought-iron benches. If only she could relax and enjoy these unexpected moments to herself. She had a whole night with nothing to do...in a way, it was a gift. A time-out from her stressful and busy life. Why couldn't she just be grateful for it?

She tried to relax. She tried to stop and enjoy the

sight of children riding their bikes down a quiet street…a tiger-striped cat sunning himself lazily in a shop window…a young couple walking hand in hand…

Loneliness. That was the emotion that pursued Cassie as she quickened her pace. It seemed to fill her with an ache that could only be avoided by motion and action. She turned a corner and saw the sign for the Elk River Lodge. With relief, she went about the business of inquiring for a room and checking in. The motel could not be considered luxurious, but it was clean and well kept and it wouldn't strain her budget too much. Yes, she really ought to be enjoying herself. Except that now the loneliness had returned full force.

She tried remedies. A sandwich at the café on Main Street. A stroll through town. A movie on TV, once she got back to her room. A nap to catch up on much-needed sleep. But nothing worked. She couldn't concentrate. And she couldn't drift off to sleep…couldn't escape the sense of emptiness deep inside her…

At last she dozed. When a knock came at the door, she sat up on the bed feeling disoriented and out of place. It took her a second to remember where she was—Elk River, Montana, too far away from home.

The knock came again, firm and insistent. She padded to the window, pushed the curtain aside and peered out. What she saw made her heartbeat accelerate.

Andrew. Andrew Morris was standing outside her motel room. The emptiness inside her seemed to vanish, replaced by a surge of pure uncomplicated joy. He was here. She had wished for him in the secret, silent spaces of her heart, and he had come to her.

He glanced toward the window, and their eyes met. Almost guiltily Cassie allowed the curtain to drop, cutting off her view of him. She did not answer the door. Feeling this happy to see him was dangerous...much too dangerous.

"Hello, Cassie." His voice carried clearly through the flimsy door. She curled her fingers against her palms, but she had to open the dratted door.

She tried to gaze at him coolly. "Let me guess," she said. "Dr. Gwen."

"One and the same," he said. "She gave me a ring, let me know you were in trouble. When I got here, it wasn't too difficult to find Tom down at Tom's Garage. Told me he recommended this place to you, so..."

"So you found me," she finished up for him. Her heart was still beating too hard, too fast, and she leaned against the doorjamb to hide her nervousness. "Well, Andrew, as you can see, I'm *not* in trouble. I have everything completely under control. I'm very sorry that Gwen pulled this little trick on you. Making you drive all this way—''

''That convertible tools along at a pretty good clip,'' he remarked. ''Even on country roads.''

She silently cursed Gwen. A little loneliness was far preferable to *this*...the way she felt when she was near him...the hope and the need and the desire...

''Andrew,'' she said, perhaps too forcefully, ''this really has been a big mistake. You can see that, can't you?''

He glanced behind him. ''Nice little town,'' he commented. ''I've never been up this way before. As long as I'm here, might as well take advantage of a little sight-seeing. It's only seven-thirty—still plenty of light left.''

''Just like that,'' she murmured. ''Suddenly this is a sight-seeing opportunity.''

''Not exactly sudden,'' he admitted. ''Dr. Gwen was the one who pointed out the opportunity aspects.''

Cassie groaned. ''I could strangle her—''

''Have dinner with me first,'' Andrew said.

She stared at him. Unfortunately, the man *was* gorgeous. But his appeal was far greater than mere physical appearance. The true allure was the force of his personality, the combination of strength and gentleness she sensed in him.

"I already had a sandwich," she said, still trying to resist.

"Was it enough?" he asked.

"No," she had to admit.

"Come with me, Cassie." His voice seemed to hold unspoken promises.

She was still wavering when the phone rang. She hurried across the room and grabbed the receiver.

"Hello?"

Cassie listened as the gentleman on the other end of the line spoke in a rambling, convoluted manner. His message was simple enough, however. After a few moments she put down the receiver and turned to face Andrew.

"Very interesting," she said. "That was Tom of Tom's Garage. Told me he'd decided to work a little late tonight, what with Reanna—that's his wife—still tied up for another hour or so down at the church bazaar. But that's beside the point. Tom tells me he's figured out exactly what's wrong with my car. He says it looks like some dang fool went and rebuilt the carburetor and gummed up the dang thing. That's a direct quote, by the way."

Andrew looked extremely discomfited. After a long moment, he seemed to have only one word to say. "Dang."

Cassie couldn't help smiling. "Don't feel too bad. I know your intentions were good."

He rubbed his neck. ''The way I look at it, now I really do owe you dinner.''

A recklessness seemed to be taking Cassie over. Would it hurt to indulge a little—to enjoy his company this one evening? Surely it wouldn't...

''Okay. I'll have dinner with you, Andrew.''

HALF AN HOUR LATER, Cassie and Andrew were seated in Elk River's premier restaurant: The Trout. It was rustic in the extreme—plank tables, mugs of beer on the bar, a jukebox, even a few pinball machines in the corner. Yet the place also served a surprisingly fine vintage wine. The bottle had been uncorked, and Cassie's glass filled alongside Andrew's. They had ordered two plates of blue-corn enchiladas. The food arrived promptly, and it, too, was surprisingly delicious.

''A toast,'' Andrew said, ''to people who actually know their way around a carburetor.''

The wine tasted sweet and cool. ''So you're not a mechanic,'' she said. ''There are worse things in life.''

''You don't understand,'' he answered. ''A guy wants to know carburetors.''

''Oh...I see. It's a *guy* thing.''

''I'm serious,'' he said. ''Too much lawyering in my life. Not enough work with my hands.''

''You can always stay in Montana,'' she said

lightly. "You can work on Hannah's house, and get better acquainted with carburetors."

Almost instantly, she sensed the way he distanced himself. His voice became carefully emotionless. "Maybe I'll start getting some use out of my hands, but it won't be in Montana," he said.

She wondered why she'd brought the subject up at all. Was she trying to picture a future with him? Certainly she wasn't *that* reckless. But somehow she couldn't let the matter drop.

"What's wrong with Montana?" she asked. "You grew up here, after all—"

"Right." The word carried a tone of finality, but the wine seemed to have loosened Cassie's tongue.

"Maybe I do understand," she said. "I keep trying to get away from the place I grew up, too. I haven't rejected the whole state of Montana, but still, I have such a hard time whenever I go back to Walking Stones. Somehow the ranch makes me feel as if I'll lose everything I've gained. It makes me feel like a kid again. Powerless..."

"That's a good word to describe it," Andrew said quietly. "Powerless. Nobody wants to feel that way."

She studied him across the table. "What is it?" she asked, her own voice soft. "What happened here, Andrew? Does it have something to do with Hannah and your mother? You said they didn't get along..."

He seemed to be staring off into some distance only he could see. "No, it wasn't them. In the end, they were powerless, too." There was such a bleakness in those words that Cassie drew in her breath. What pain was Andrew hiding? How far back did it go? All she had were questions—no answers.

He stirred, as if shaking off some burden. And then he gazed at her across the table. "We're here…tonight. Why think about anything else?" he asked.

Why, indeed…

They ate, and drank more wine, and lingered until the sky outside had turned completely dark. And afterward they walked down to the river itself, where dock lights glittered on the water and happy summer voices drifted on the air. A child's laughter, another child calling in response. Cassie walked hand in hand with Andrew, and never had a summer's night seemed so magical to her.

"Today," she said, "I couldn't even appreciate how beautiful this place is. I just felt so wrapped up in my work…so oppressed by it. The thing is—this is one case that's actually going well. I came here to talk to a man and a woman who want to adopt their niece, a little girl who lives in Billings. From everything I can tell, it will be the best thing in the world for her. She'll have a stable home at last. But all I could think about was me not giving a stable home to Zak—"

"Hey," Andrew said, stopping to face her. "You're doing a great job with Zak. Why do you keep doubting yourself?"

She struggled to find the answer. "Because... because I can't afford to make mistakes where my son is involved. And so I have to question every step I make. Right now, for instance, I should be home with him, instead of...here with you."

"Maybe," Andrew said, "you use your son as something to hide behind."

She stiffened. "That sounds terrible!"

"No. It sounds human. Some guy really hurt you, and you've decided no one else is ever going to do it again. Zak gives you the perfect excuse to keep me at arm's length."

She was angry now. Pulling her hand away from Andrew's, she walked rapidly away from him. Unfortunately, he caught up to her.

"I knew this was a mistake," she muttered. "Agreeing to dinner, agreeing to *anything*. Talk about people who keep others at arm's length— you're the master at that, Andrew. I tried getting close to someone at least once. Maybe Jeff was a colossal mistake, but I thought I loved him, and I gave my marriage everything I had. And I got Zak out of the whole miserable mess, and that's really something! But you—you're determined not to make a mistake even once. So who are you to criticize me, dammit?" She was quite out of breath by now, what with trying to move away from Andrew and treat him to a tirade at the same time.

"Finished?" he asked in a reasonable tone.

Suddenly she felt deflated. "Yes…I'm done accusing you. Your personal life is entirely your own business. Why I would even think about getting involved—"

"Hannah thought I'd never gotten over my father's death. She told me that was why I wouldn't let anybody get close to me. She said that, deep down, I was still a nine-year-old kid who'd just had his dad taken from him without warning. Maybe she was right, even though she never knew what really happened. Nobody knew."

Andrew uttered these words simply, starkly, but Cassie felt the pain behind them.

"Andrew…what happened?"

He didn't answer. He just took her into his arms. They held each other, there beside the river. Cassie closed her eyes and buried her head against his shoulder. His arms tightened around her. The moments passed unheeded.

"Cassie," Andrew murmured at last, his voice taut. Again she answered without speaking, lifting her mouth to his. The longing and desire inside her fanned toward flame. She knew what would happen tonight…had known, perhaps, since the first minute she'd seen him standing outside the motel-room door. And so, still silent, she slipped out of Andrew's arms. She took his hand and began leading him in the direction of the motel.

It didn't take long for them to get back to the Elk River Lodge. Continuing to take the lead, Cassie drew him toward her room.

"Cassie, are you sure?" he asked, his voice low. He fished a key out of his pocket and held it up. "I have my own room. I checked in before coming to see you. I figured it was better that way."

She marveled at her own sureness. "You figured wrong," she said. She turned her key in the lock and pushed the door open. And then, so there would be no doubt whatsoever, "I want you to make love to me, Andrew. I don't want to question it, or analyze it, or—"

Then she didn't say anything at all as his lips found hers.

CHAPTER TEN

ANDREW PUSHED the door shut as he and Cassie entered the motel room. They were now secluded in their own private world. He hadn't planned on this…well, perhaps that wasn't entirely accurate. He'd thought about making love to Cassie Maxwell Warren practically from the moment he'd first seen her. She was beautiful and desirable…

He drew her close, gathering her hair into both hands. Their bodies pressed together, he could feel the rapid beating of her heart.

"Andrew," she whispered against his mouth. "Andrew…" When she pulled away, it was only to reach up and start working on his shirt buttons. He got his own ideas about Cassie's buttons, but she shook her head.

"You first," she said with a tremulous smile. She seemed a little surprised at her own daring. Yet, by the time she'd helped him to slide his shirt off, she'd gained confidence. Without hesitation, her fingers moved to the zipper of his jeans. He liked this new, brazen side of her. He liked it very much.

"Shoes," he murmured.

"What...?" she asked distractedly, still working on his jeans.

"Got to get the shoes off first."

Her cheeks flamed, but she gave him a bold glance. Then she knelt to untie the laces of his sneakers. He couldn't let her do that on her own. Together they tossed the sneakers into a corner of the room. His socks followed in short order...the rest of his clothes shortly thereafter. Cassie's gaze traveled over him.

"Oh, my," she whispered.

He wanted to do some looking of his own. And so, still working together, he and Cassie took care of her blouse and skirt. They landed in the corner with his own things. The underclothes had to go, too, as soon as possible.

Cassie was blushing again in the light from the bedside lamp.

"What is it?" Andrew murmured, gathering her hair again in his hands. Soft, silky...abundant.

"It's embarrassing," she muttered. "When I got dressed this morning, how was I supposed to know—well, when you're not even *dating,* you don't have the most exciting underwear in the world—"

Her underwear was fine, but he wanted it off. "Don't worry," he said, his voice husky. "You won't be needing it." He slid her briefs down her legs, felt her tremble at his touch. But at last she was revealed to him, all of her…even more beautiful and desirable than he had imagined. He knelt before her, kissing gently…touching gently.

She drew in her breath, burying her fingers in his hair as he pressed himself closer to her. "Andrew, you don't have to…"

"I want to," he murmured, and then proceeded to show her exactly what it was he wanted to do.

Her breathing grew more ragged, but still she held herself back. "Andrew," she gasped. "I can't—"

"Yes," he said. "You can." He moved his tongue against her, showing her what could happen next. And, at last, she allowed it to happen, crying out with abandonment, her body pulsing against him. He smiled.

Afterward she sank down beside him, burrowing against his chest as if to hide herself.

"It's never been like that before," she whispered. "I feel…"

"Good," he suggested.

"Ashamed. That I could forget myself like that—"

"Isn't that what it's all about?" he asked. "Forgetting yourself?"

"I don't know. I told you…it's never been like that before…"

Maybe there was a whole lot more for both of them to discover. "We've only started," he said. "Come to bed with me, Cassie."

She gazed at him, her lips parted, her cheeks flushed. "I like the way you say that," she whispered.

They kicked the blanket aside, their limbs tangling together on the sheet. Andrew smiled again. "I want you to know," he said, "that I am having a very good time."

"So am I," she confessed. And then, even more brazenly than before, she opened her legs to him. "I think, after…well, I'm ready, Andrew. I want you so much."

It was clear that they were both in a hurry now. But part of him still held, regretfully, to reason.

"I didn't bring anything," he said. "Any protection. Wasn't thinking ahead, I guess."

"It's all right," she told him, drawing him even closer. "I never went off the Pill…Andrew, please…" Her breathing had quickened yet again, and so had his own. No words were necessary now. He rose over her, covering her. And then, reading the welcome in her eyes, he moved inside her. She clung to him, her fingers pressing into his back as she urged his rhythm. His own need had overtaken him, but he slowed just a little. He wanted Cassie's desire to build again, didn't want her to hurry past it. He gazed into her face, saw her eyes widen.

"Andrew…not again…"

"It can happen…" His voice was strained from holding back. But then Cassie arched against him, calling out in wonder and pleasure, and holding back was no longer required.

Afterward they lay tangled together for a very long moment. Cassie's breathing gradually slowed, and so did his own.

"Twice," she said in a voice filled with wonderment. "I didn't know it could be like that—"

"Then you haven't known the right kind of men."

Her hand traveled down his chest. "I haven't known that many," she said self-consciously. "The first time was just plain awful and embarrassing. This boy I met my first year of college…and he really was nothing more than a boy. Nineteen years old, and so worried about proving he was a man… Why am I telling you any of this?"

He wanted to hear more. He wanted to know all about beautiful, desirable Cassie Maxwell Warren. "So the first time was bad," he said. "But repeat performances usually are better."

"Not with that guy," she mumbled. "Like I said, it was always so serious. An act of concentration. A performance. We broke up after six months. I think it was because we never laughed together. Funny…I never realized that until just now."

He smoothed her hair back from her face. "Who came along next?"

She sighed. "My ex, if you have to know the truth. And it was always solemn with him, too. Jeff took himself very seriously. He expected *me* to take him seriously, too. And that is the grand sum total of my experience. Precisely two lovers in my entire life…before you. Now you know the truth. I'm sure you can top my record.''

He wasn't thinking about past lovers in his own life. He was thinking only of the one in his arms. ''Nothing can top this,'' he murmured.

''I don't believe you—''

''Believe, Cassie.'' He bent his head to kiss her neck.

''Andrew…you're not already imagining…''

He was imagining, all right, but he could take his time. ''We have all night,'' he said. ''No need to rush.''

He felt her relax in his arms. They dozed a little, talked some more.

''Andrew,'' Cassie whispered. ''The women you've known…''

''No one like you,'' he said. ''Trust me.'' He propped himself on one elbow and smiled down at her. She looked very lovely in the lamplight, her skin creamy, her red hair fanning out on the pillow. ''Cassie,'' he said gently, ''tell me what *you'd* like.''

She glanced away uncertainly. ''I don't know what you mean.''

''Think about it. If you could have anything from me right now…do anything…what would it be?''

Suddenly she smiled a little. "There *is* one idea—but it's silly."

"Tell me," he said.

"This is crazy, Andrew. But if you want to know the truth, not too long ago I had this fantasy about you and me…"

Now he was the one who smiled. "A fantasy. I like the sound of that."

"It had something to do with a bath." She spoke in a rush, as if so embarrassed she had to get the words out fast.

"This is sounding better and better," he said.

"Anyway," she went on determinedly, "when I checked in, I didn't have any of the stuff I needed. Toothbrush, etcetera, etcetera. So I got a basket of toiletries from the front desk. And there was some bubble bath included…"

Now he was grinning. "Show me, Cassie. Show me what you want."

She gave him a severe look. "You think this is amusing, don't you?"

"We're supposed to be having fun," he reminded her.

She kept trying to look stern. "All right, you asked for it." She slipped away from him and went toward the bathroom. His gaze followed her. That hair cascading down her back, and then her very enticing bottom…he was sorry when she disappeared from sight.

He heard the bathwater run, heard Cassie adjusting it. Then she appeared again, walking unselfconsciously toward him. This view was perfection, also: the round fullness of her breasts, the sweet curve of her belly...

She took his hand and led him into the bathroom. The tub already foamed with bubbles. Cassie climbed in and slid down into the water, giving him a provocative glance.

"Join me," she said.

He didn't need a second invitation. He, too, slid into the warm, fragrant water, facing her. Cassie reached over and shut off the tap. Then she reached for him. She ran her soapy hands across his shoulders, traced her lips across his cheek.

"This is a first for me," he murmured.

"I'm glad," she murmured back. "It's a little cramped in here, but I'm sure we can do some experimenting..."

She proved to be very good at experimenting. Now her hands moved under the water, finding him. He gave a low groan.

"Cassie..."

"Want me to stop?"

"No," he managed to say.

"Just lean back," she instructed. "Let me take charge."

If this was her idea of taking charge, he never wanted it to end. Her fingers worked magic, sliding over him, surrounding him, goading his response. When he didn't think he could take much more, she straddled him wantonly and guided him inside her. The water in the tub sloshed, threatening to spill over. Neither one of them paid any attention at all.

A LONG WHILE LATER they lay in bed again, their bodies still damp from the bath and from the heat of their lovemaking. Cassie rested in Andrew's arms.

"Three times," she whispered in disbelief. "Who would've thought *three* times…"

"Care to try for a fourth?" he asked.

She laughed softly. "Maybe later. Right now I just want to be with you."

That was what he wanted, too.

ANDREW HADN'T EXPECTED to sleep so well. After all, when you were in bed with a beautiful naked redhead, sleep was the last thing on your mind. But it seemed he and Cassie had finally exhausted themselves.

When he woke, morning sunlight was filtering through the curtains of the motel room. He turned to find Cassie, but she wasn't beside him in bed. He sat up, glancing around. The room itself was empty. She wasn't here.

He checked the bathroom, but no luck there, either. She'd gone.

Andrew told himself that it didn't necessarily mean anything. Maybe she'd slipped outside for a walk before breakfast. But, even as he dressed, he sensed that the emptiness in this room had a finality to it.

He went to the front desk, and learned that Cassie had checked out well over an hour ago. He took out his own motel key and studied it. He hadn't used his room, hadn't even seen it. He didn't regret paying for it, though. The only thing he regretted right now was Cassie's absence.

He went down to Tom's Garage. Tom, it seemed, had finished the job on Cassie's car late last night...something about his wife, Reanna, being tied up at that dang bazaar, and Tom needing something to do until she came home. Andrew only half listened until Tom got to the part about Cassie collecting her car and driving out of town.

Yeah, there was a finality to the whole thing.

CASSIE CHOSE HER VENUE with care. When you'd slept with a man...when you'd experienced the most intense, overwhelming lovemaking you could imagine...you couldn't face him the next day in just any setting. Particularly when you were going to tell him that you could never see him again.

The Rimrock Mansion in Billings seemed Cassie's safest choice for an encounter. The sandstone mansion had taken its name from the Rimrocks, the striking cliffs bordering the city. It had been lived in for generations by one of Billings's most prominent families, but was now a history museum. Surely among the relics and memorabilia of a long-ago past, Cassie would be able to state her case to Andrew in a careful, emotionless manner.

He arrived promptly at five-thirty, as she'd requested over the phone. The museum wouldn't be closing for another hour, giving her plenty of time to get this difficult task over with. She watched as he purchased his ticket in the front office, then crossed the foyer toward her. He looked disgruntled.

"What are we doing in a museum?" he asked.

She couldn't say anything at first. All she could do was gaze at him, remembering last night. Those magical hours when she had let go of every worry and fear, reveling only in the feel of his skin against hers. Never had she known such sensuous pleasure and closeness. Her breath caught in her throat, just remembering it. But, with morning, all the worries and fears had come rushing back. The magic could not possibly have lasted forever.

"Hello, Andrew," she said at last. "Thank you for…coming." They were the only two patrons in the place, this near to closing time. She'd hoped for that. She wanted a neutral setting, but one that would allow a modicum of privacy, as well.

He studied her, the expression in his dark eyes

unreadable. "You ran out on me, Cassie," he said. "Guess I wasn't expecting that."

She glanced away. "I'm sorry about that. I know it wasn't the best strategy—"

"I didn't know we were dealing in strategies. I thought what happened last night came pretty naturally."

His words stung. He had a right to reproach her. It would have been so much better if she could have stayed, and said goodbye to him at the motel. But she had been, quite simply, afraid. Terrified, even…knowing that if she had stayed, and waited for him to wake up next to her, and looked into his eyes…knowing that if she had allowed that to happen, she'd still be there in bed with him, all reason lost.

Now she turned quickly and entered the drawing room of the museum, where overstuffed Victorian couches and chairs displayed themselves behind a red velvet rope. The sense of history comforted her a bit. When Andrew followed her, she was able to speak in a calm, rational tone.

"I think we both know that last night was… temporary. A one-time thing." Her cheeks flamed as she remembered that there hadn't been anything one-time about last night. But she hurried past that detail as quickly as possible.

"The point is," she went on, "we both know it's not something that can last—"

"You keep speaking for both of us," he said. "It might be a good idea, Cassie, to ask what *I'm* thinking."

This wasn't going at all as she'd planned, but she nodded reluctantly. "All right, Andrew, give me your take on the situation."

He looked more disgruntled than ever. "I don't have a take. I didn't expect what happened to happen—didn't expect to feel the way I did. It wasn't a business deal. I don't have graphs and plans and damn pie charts plotting my next move."

"That's it exactly," she said, her voice brisk. "Neither one of us has a plan. But I need to have one, Andrew. I have a seven-year-old son. I can't just do unexpected things, and then see where they lead me—especially when I know they're not going to lead anywhere." She walked quickly across to the grand dining room, with its cut-glass chandeliers and massive rosewood table. The heavy brocade draperies gave her a stifled feeling. Maybe this setting hadn't been such a good idea, after all.

"You're doing it again," Andrew said behind her. "Using your son as an excuse to hide from me."

"It's not an excuse. Zak is a very vulnerable little boy who's already had too much loss in his life. He can't bear any more—"

"You're the one who's vulnerable," Andrew said in a low voice. "You're the one who can't bear any more loss. So you're dismissing what we had last night.''

She clenched her hands. ''You're the one who's hidden yourself away! I don't know what happened in your past—something terrible, from the little you've said so far—but Hannah was right. You've used it to deaden your own emotions. When your family buried your father...something else got buried, too. Hope and love and faith in the future. That's what I'm guessing, anyway.''

He didn't say anything to that. Maybe she'd gone too far. But the truth had to be acknowledged here. They stood silently, side by side, not looking at each other. And at last it was Cassie who spoke again.

''You have to see, Andrew...it's better this way. Both of us admitting that last night was a mistake. That we can't pursue something that has nowhere to go.'' She ventured a look at him, and she saw the sadness in his face. And she also saw the way he had closed himself off from her.

''Maybe you're right,'' he said. ''Maybe there is no future for us, Cassie. But last night...that wasn't a mistake. Not in any way.''

CHAPTER ELEVEN

"DID YOU KNOW that dogs lower your blood pressure?" Seven-year-old William Zachary Warren gave his mother an accusing stare. And then, after a significant pause, "Mom, what's blood pressure?"

Cassie thought it over. "Blood pressure," she said, "is what goes up when you're having a stressful day."

Zak got a long-suffering look, and continued perusing his latest acquisition: *American Dog Magazine.* Carefully he turned a page. "Did you know that dogs teach you responsibility?"

"I'm glad to hear it," she said.

"Having a dog is like having a built-in burglar alarm," Zak told her, turning another page.

"That's very interesting."

"A dog," said Zak, "is man's best friend. It says so right here."

In the past, Cassie had always been grateful that her son loved to read. Right now, though, all she could do was gaze at him with every bit of love in her heart. Too bad love couldn't tell her what to do. Last evening, she and Zak had experienced a stormy hour or two over the dog issue. Zak had announced his idea of a solution: he and Cassie should take Arthur and go live at the ranch with Grandpa. After all, Grandpa had already agreed that Zak could bring Arthur along. How did Zak know? Why, he'd talked to Grandpa on the phone about it. He'd called from Janice's house. Janice hadn't minded….

Janice, perhaps, didn't realize quite what a fix Cassie was in. That seemingly innocent call from a boy to his grandfather had already resulted in unwanted repercussions—such as Cassie snapping at Zak last night, and then feeling guiltier than ever. Her son wanted to be at the ranch.

Now Zak was gazing at her stubbornly and silently. His eyes were very clear, very indignant.

"We'll have a house of our own someday soon," Cassie told him. "Very soon. We'll have a dog then. Two dogs, if you want."

"I want Arthur," Zak said, very solemn as he turned the pages of his magazine.

Cassie silently berated Andrew for ever having acquired that dog in the first place. Andrew had made her life so much more complicated than before! It didn't matter that she'd vowed never to see him again. The mere fact of his existence needled and provoked her. And, if she were to admit the truth…she missed him. It had been only two days since she'd last seen him, but it felt like forever.

Zak had retreated even further into his magazine,

his shoulders hunched defensively against Cassie. A wave of loneliness swept over her. Too restless to sit still, she moved to the living-room window. Like everything else in this apartment, the window was too small to really let in the world outside. Now that she thought about it, the whole place made her claustrophobic, but she kept coming back to the irrefutable fact that it was all she could afford. If she had any hope of ever financing a house for herself and Zak, she had to economize.

She was still gazing out that window when she saw Andrew's convertible pull to a stop outside. She saw him climb out of the driver's seat. He was carrying a squirming brown puppy.

Cassie's muffled exclamation drew her son's attention. Instantly he was at her side, peering out the window, too.

"Arthur!" He ran to the front door, yanked it open and bounded from view. Cassie hurried after him. Her loneliness had been replaced by another emotion: quick cold anger. How could Andrew be doing this to her? She'd explained to him precisely why they should never see each other again. She'd told him that her son's emotional health was at stake. Yes, Zak would suffer a little pain now, but that was far preferable to a lot of pain later. So what was Andrew thinking? Showing up completely against her wishes...with the blasted dog in tow!

Outside, she found her son kneeling on the strip

of grass in front of the apartment building. He was oblivious to anything but the puppy licking his face. Andrew stood to one side.

"Hello," he said gravely to Cassie. "Before you get mad, I actually do have a good reason to be here."

She wanted to yell at him. Instead she just looked at him, taking in every detail. The laugh lines crinkling the corners of his eyes, the strong line of his jaw, the breadth of his shoulders under that Texas Rangers T-shirt. Oh, yes, she'd missed him.

"Can we talk?" he asked in a low voice. "It's pretty important."

She glanced toward her son, who was now lying in the grass, the dog on his chest. No matter how she might feel about the long-term necessity of avoiding Andrew and his dog, she didn't have the heart to deny Zak this short-term happiness. She considered her options. The apartment complex had a playground area in the center courtyard—this had been one of its selling points for Cassie. She nudged her son toward the courtyard, and a few moments later he was chasing the puppy around the slippery slide. Cassie sank into one of the swings, and Andrew sat next to her.

"All right," she said a bit grimly. "Let's talk."

Andrew seemed to be searching for the best way to begin. "Hannah's lawyer came back to town this morning," he said at last. "I had a long talk with him. Nothing official yet—we have the reading of the will, and the settling of the estate to get through. Professional courtesy, one lawyer to another...we had quite a good talk, overall. You know how it is.''

''Actually, I don't know how it is,'' Cassie grumbled. ''Andrew, you're being oblique. What is this all about?''

''Well, here's the thing,'' he said, his tone too casual. ''Hannah left you something in her will. More precisely, she left Zak something.''

Cassie had been rocking gently back and forth in the swing, but now she stilled. ''Maybe,'' she said, ''Hannah left him that cookie jar he loved so much. The one she always filled with her chocolate-macadamia cookies.''

''It's a little something more than a cookie jar,'' Andrew said. He paused. And then, ''Hannah left him the guest house.''

Cassie sat very quietly. ''I don't believe it,'' she said. ''A whole entire *house*...''

''Believe it,'' Andrew told her. ''And, in a way, doesn't it make sense? Hannah knew you were saving up for a down payment on a place of your own. She knew it wasn't easy for you. And she knew how much Zak loved the tree house, didn't she? Put it all together, and you get a legacy that really means something.''

Cassie's hands tightened on the swing chains. ''I can hear something in your voice,'' she said.

"There's more to this, isn't there? For example, who's going to be living in the main house?"

Andrew rubbed the back of his neck. "Hannah left the rest of her property to me...and, yes, that includes the main house."

Cassie laughed weakly. "I don't get it. What was Hannah trying to do? She even warned me that I should stay away from you if I ever met you. But it turns out that she's arranged very neatly for the two of us to be neighbors..."

"Not exactly neighbors." Now Andrew's voice was neutral. "Hannah had to know I'd never want to live in that house. She'd have to know that I'd intend to sell, and get back to Texas as soon as possible."

"Of course. What was I thinking?" Very deliberately, Cassie rocked the swing back and forth again. "Well, Andrew, this has all been very interesting. Hannah was a dear, dear person, and this was an extravagant gesture for her to make. Obviously it's given me a lot to think about. But, the truth is, I *have* been saving up for that down payment on my own, and—"

"There's more," Andrew said. "You might as well hear the rest of it."

She gave him a dismayed look. "More?"

He rubbed the back of his neck again, as if trying to get out the kinks. "Hannah left the guest house to Zak...under the condition that I serve as trustee of the property. In essence, I administer all matters relating to the guest house until Zak turns eighteen. At that point, he owns it outright.''

''Stop sounding so much like a damn lawyer,'' Cassie burst out. She glanced guiltily at her son. Zak hadn't seemed to hear her swearing, though. He was spread out on his stomach, chin propped in his hands. He and Arthur appeared to be deep in conversation.

Cassie took a long breath, and tried to speak in an even tone. ''I want you to know something, Andrew. I loved your grandmother dearly. She gave me and Zak a home when we needed it more than anything. But what she did with her will...I can't say that I want any part of it.'' She scrambled up from the swing and went striding around the edge of the play area.

Andrew caught up to her easily. ''When you think about it,'' he said, ''it's the perfect solution for you. You and Zak need a house. My grandmother left you a house.''

''Right. With you in charge of the whole thing.'' She realized she sounded abrasive again, but she couldn't seem to stop herself. She was too worked up. ''What am I supposed to do when I need a plumber six months down the line—call you, and you fly up from Texas to unclog the drains?''

''We'd work out the details,'' he said carefully. ''The point is—''

"The point is," Cassie said, "what kind of game was Hannah playing? She knew how important it was for me not to have a man involved in my affairs—"

"So that's it," Andrew said. "You can't stand a guy holding the purse strings. Especially if the guy is me."

Like everything else associated with her apartment, the play area was small. Cassie had already completed two laps with Andrew, and was starting on a third. She felt like a fool, but she kept marching on.

"Very well," she told Andrew. "I may be a tad sensitive when it comes to male control in my life. I grew up with a father who thought—and still thinks—it's perfectly acceptable to dominate every aspect of my existence. He still believes a man should be in charge of things. For the longest time he refused to admit that my sister, Thea, could run the ranch as well as he could. He's still not fully convinced." Cassie took a deep breath and tried to speak more calmly. "I married a man who turned out to be pretty domineering himself, except *he* didn't have my dad's money smarts. It's taken me the better part of a year to get myself financially on my feet again. But I've done it, without the interference of any man—"

"And you're damn well not going to let another

man get his mitts on your life," Andrew finished up for her. "Did we leave anything out?"

"Now *you're* swearing," Cassie muttered. "It's a good thing Zak is paying utterly no attention to us." She made it to the swings again, and sank down in the one she'd vacated previously. Andrew knelt in front of her, taking her hands and clasping them in his own.

"Cassie, maybe it's not exactly the way you wanted it, but it's still a solution for you and Zak. You'll have a house. A place for the dog. That seems to be pretty high on Zak's wish list right now."

Cassie tried to tug her hands away. "He'll see us."

Andrew kept a firm hold. "Like you said—he's not paying us any attention."

She gazed at Andrew. "We're headed for bigger trouble than ever," she said in a low voice. "Aren't we?"

He didn't say anything to that. He just knelt there holding her hands. And Cassie sat there, never wanting him to let go.

She was in trouble, indeed.

HANNAH'S LAWYER turned out to be not at all what Cassie had expected. She'd envisioned a kind, elderly man with a country law office. Instead, Ron Gascoway was a brisk thirty-five-year-old who worked for one of Billings's larger law firms. Today was the second time Cassie had met with him and Andrew. As before, Mr. Gascoway had proceeded at such breakneck speed that Cassie's mind was a whirl of legal details she couldn't yet begin to sort out.

"Goodbye for now, Ms. Warren," he said, glancing at his watch, his mind clearly on the next appointment. "I'll leave you in Andrew's capable hands." With that, she found herself ushered from the man's office.

"Spare me," Cassie said, punching the elevator button. "'I'll leave you in Andrew's capable hands'...does he even *think* about the way he sounds?"

Andrew loosened his tie. "The guy really gets on your nerves, doesn't he? It's not intentional, I can tell you that much. In lawyerly circles, Ron is known for his diplomacy."

"Ha." Cassie stepped into the elevator. Andrew stepped in beside her. She punched the down button. And Andrew pressed the stop.

"What are you doing?" she demanded.

"Giving myself a few minutes alone with you," he said. And then he took her in his arms and kissed her.

She didn't think...couldn't think. All she could do was feel his warmth, his nearness, the taste of his lips on hers. She clung to him, silently beseeching more. It was a full minute before they broke apart.

Andrew cupped her face gently. "Damn...why can't I keep my hands off you?"

She gazed at him with misery and joy combined. "Don't you think I've wanted it, too?" she whispered. "But Andrew, there still isn't any future for us. You keep talking about going back to Texas. And meanwhile I've got this—this *thing* Hannah left me with. This cockeyed inheritance with *you* in charge."

"So we'll talk about it," Andrew said. "I suppose we could have dinner together, and try to figure it all out."

She wanted to come up with an excuse, but she couldn't use her son. Janice still had her nephew visiting, and that meant Zak would be sleeping over at her house tonight. For all intents and purposes, Cassie was free to go to dinner with Andrew. She drew in her breath.

"Is that a yes?" he murmured, his fingers caressing her cheek.

She closed her eyes tightly. *Say no,* the voice of reason warned inside her. But another voice, a reckless voice, urged her to say *yes...*

She opened her eyes, drawing away from him. "I'll go with you," she said, "but only so we can discuss this whole mess, and decide what to do about it."

"Not the most enthusiastic response I've ever had," he said, "but it'll do." And, with that, he pressed the go button.

TRUST ANDREW TO CHOOSE a restaurant of unusual character. A truly ghastly moose head jutted out from the wall, opposite a truly impressive art deco mural. The waiters wore cowboy boots and Stetsons, but the table linens were a snowy-white damask, the wine goblets made of crystal. The place was trying to be Montana and New York all rolled into one. Apparently the combination had proved successful; the place was also packed.

"You're amazing," Cassie told Andrew. "You don't even live here anymore, but you know exactly where to go, where to eat. It's almost as if you own the town."

"Maybe it owns me." He spoke in an abstracted voice. Cassie studied his expression.

"Come clean, Andrew," she said. "Today, at the lawyer's office, I could tell something was bothering you. Sure, you keep acting like Hannah's bequest to Zak is all fine and wonderful. But it's just that—an act. Something really is bugging you."

He stirred. "Okay, something is bothering me…big time. Not the fact that Hannah left the guest house to Zak. But the rest of her will…the fact that she didn't leave a single thing to my mother. Nothing. Not even a memento. And that makes me feel pretty bad.''

Cassie took a sip of her wine. ''You mentioned once before that Hannah and your mother didn't get along. But that's pretty severe, cutting your daughter out of your will. It just doesn't seem like the Hannah I knew.''

''She did it, though,'' Andrew said with a frown. ''Somehow I have to break the news to my mom. And somehow I have to figure out why it happened.''

Cassie shook her head. ''Andrew, this is all the more reason for me to bow out of all this. How will your mother feel when she learns about the guest house? We knew Hannah such a short while, and yet she ended up remembering us. It doesn't feel right.''

Now Andrew gazed at her intently across the table. ''It won't help my mother if you refuse Hannah's bequest. That's not the answer.''

Cassie didn't have any answers right now. How could she move back into the guest house under these new circumstances? She wouldn't really own the place. It wouldn't actually be hers—or Zak's, not with Andrew in charge. She wouldn't feel right. And yet, young Zak didn't care about fine points of ownership. All he wanted was a home where he could have the puppy of his dreams. Not even a designer dog, just a brown, furry mutt.

The food arrived: radicchio salad, a savory rice pilaf, grilled salmon. Everything was delicious, but all the questions and problems remained. At last Cassie set down her fork.

"What could possibly have happened to make Hannah cut your mother off so harshly?" she asked.

"I know when it all started," he said. "The strain between them. When my father died...his car accident. I was with him that day. I survived. He didn't." The words were stark and unexpected. Cassie reached across the table toward him.

"Andrew, I'm sorry."

He didn't seem to hear her, just went on speaking in an expressionless voice. "Afterward, my mother and I moved in with Hannah. Back then, my mom couldn't afford to support us on our own. I have a feeling that when you and Zak came along, you reminded Hannah of how it had been all those years ago, with my mother and me."

Cassie waited quietly, sensing there was more to come. Finally, Andrew continued.

"It wasn't easy for either my mom or my grandmother," he said. "Back then, my great-grandmother was still living in the guest house. We were in the main house with Hannah, so you had four generations, side by side...room for plenty of friction. But the funny thing is, I can't remember anything specific. I just remember things being uncomfortable and tense, and my mom dreaming of getting a place for the two of us. Finally she did, when I was about twelve.''

Cassie listened attentively. ''And what happened then?''

He lifted his shoulders. ''A fairly ordinary existence, I suppose. I grew up, went away to college in Texas. Stayed in Texas. My mother ended up moving away from Montana, too. End of story.''

It had to be a whole lot more complicated than that, but Cassie didn't press the matter. She could still sense the pain in Andrew.

''We got off the subject,'' he said now. ''We're supposed to talk about you and Zak moving back into the guest house, and getting on with your lives.''

Cassie sighed. ''Andrew, I haven't decided anything yet.''

''You heard what Ron said today,'' he argued. ''Some formalities to take care of, nothing more.''

''Nothing more,'' she echoed skeptically. ''We haven't figured anything out. Such as why Hannah would leave my son a house, but make you the blasted lord and master—''

''I think I know why she did it,'' Andrew said slowly. ''I've been giving it a lot of thought. Hannah kept telling me I needed someone to take care of…a family. And so, making me the trustee of something for Zak, that was her way of giving me a family.''

Cassie shook her head in disbelief. ''A person

can't just create an instant family. Hannah should have known that.''

''Isn't that what she tried to do with you and Zak from the very beginning—create a family that *she* could belong to? I know she was lonely, with both me and my mother gone. So she turned to someone else, and you were that someone.''

Cassie had never thought of it like that. She'd always seen Hannah as the giver. She hadn't realized that perhaps she and Zak had been givers, too.

''Even if you're right,'' she admitted grudgingly, ''that doesn't change things, Andrew. It can't make me and Zak and you into some semblance of a family. And I'm not going to hurt my son by trying. He's already far too attached to you.''

''But this way I would remain in his life,'' Andrew argued.

''Right, like some sort of distant Texan uncle who comes to visit now and then.''

Andrew didn't seem pleased with the image. ''I'm still trying to work things out in my own mind,'' he said. ''Still trying to figure out the parameters.''

Parameters...of course Andrew would use a word like that. A term that signified barriers that needed putting up. Didn't he realize that in a real family, you couldn't simply erect barriers?

But now dessert came—the lightest, creamiest cheesecake. Andrew was treating her royally tonight. He was that kind of man, willing to offer the best his money could buy. Not willing, however, to share his heart.

The night drew on. They lingered over cups of mint coffee, but at last could find no excuse to remain. Andrew drove Cassie home to her apartment. Suddenly it seemed a very important place to her. Who cared if it made her feel claustrophobic on occasion? She paid the rent with money that *she* earned. And she balanced her checkbook and paid her other bills with no one looking over her shoulder...no *trustee*. No man trying to control how she lived.

Andrew escorted her to the door. "Everything was wonderful tonight," she said, knowing that she sounded far too formal. "Dinner...everything. Thank you."

"We didn't solve anything though, did we?"

"No, we didn't," she admitted. "If anything, we only made it more confusing. But it's late, Andrew, and...it's late, that's all."

"So," he murmured, "you're not going to invite me in."

Inviting him in was exactly what she wanted to do. But she knew what would happen if she did. It took all her force of will to deny the longings inside her.

"Andrew, I can't make love to you again. It would only add to the confusion. Don't you see?"

He gazed back at her gravely. "I see, all right. But I still want you, Cassie."

"Good night," she whispered, and slipped inside the door. She closed it and leaned her head against its surface. And then, after a moment, she heard Andrew's footsteps receding.

CHAPTER TWELVE

THE KNOCK AT Cassie's door came late that night, stirring her from a fitful sleep. She sat up in bed and heard it again: imperious and demanding. Her first thought was Andrew. He had come back, even after she had turned him away.

Her heart pounding uncomfortably, she slipped into her robe, pulled the belt tight and went to the living room. She gazed out through the peephole. But she didn't see Andrew standing outside in the porch light. Instead she saw her kid brother, Bobby.

She felt a surge of uncomplicated happiness and welcome. But that was before she opened the door and saw that her brother was undeniably, irrefutably drunk. His gait wavered just a bit as he came into the apartment, and his grin was just a bit lopsided.

"Hi, sis."

"Oh, Bobby," she said under her breath, managing to grab hold of his arm and get him to the couch. He collapsed there in an ungainly heap, but his grin remained debonairly in place. Bobby wasn't an ugly drunk. Just a pathetic one.

"I knew I could count on you, Cass. Knew you'd

be here for me..." His head lolled back on the pillow, and his eyelids drifted shut. Cassie knelt beside him.

"Bobby, you didn't drive here, did you?" she asked urgently. "You don't have a license. And you're drunk. When I think what could have happened—"

"Hitchhiked," Bobby said, enunciating far too carefully. "Already almost killed one best friend. Can't afford to hurt anybody else."

"You're hurting yourself," Cassie whispered.

"Think she cares?" Bobby mumbled back.

Cassie didn't have to ask who "she" was. Megan, of course. The love of Bobby's life, the mother of his child.

"Dammit, Bobby, of course she cares! But every time you pull a stunt like this, she's just more and more convinced that you're not ready for grown-up life." Cassie shook his arm for emphasis. "What are you thinking—don't you realize you need help?"

His eyes opened briefly. "I need you, sis. Had to get away from the ranch...had to get away from everything..."

She shook his arm again. "Getting drunk isn't the answer. It never is. Bobby, you *have* to get help. You can't get sober on your own. Isn't this proof enough?"

He gave that heartbreaking smile of his, the one

that had charmed his three sisters from the time he was a baby. And then his eyes closed again, and he gave a gentle snore.

Tears smarted behind Cassie's eyelids. The emotions her brother evoked were much like those inspired by her son. Except that Zak was all of seven, and Bobby was on the verge of twenty. He should be a man, taking on a man's responsibilities. And certainly he shouldn't be sprawled out stone-cold drunk on Cassie's sofa. She felt intensely grateful that her son wasn't here to witness this.

Bobby shifted restlessly. His legs were too long for the couch, and they hung at awkward angles. He didn't wake, though. Cassie's previous experience told her that he would be out for hours.

She tugged off first one of his boots then the other. Rummaging in the tiny linen closet, she found an afghan and spread it over him. His toes poked out from underneath the shawl, making him look vulnerable.

Knowing that the family would be worried, Cassie picked up the phone and dialed the number of Walking Stones Ranch. Thea answered, sounding just as anxious as Cassie had imagined. She'd been at home in Paradise Corners, but she and Rafe had driven over to the ranch as soon as they'd learned Bobby was missing. Bobby, after all, was still on probation, still expected to perform community service—and still strictly forbidden to drive.

Cassie explained matters in a low, quick voice. "He didn't get behind the wheel of a car, thank goodness. At least we have that much to be grateful for."

Thea said she'd let Jolie know that Bobby was safe, for the night, at least. She'd let their father know, too. Yes, both sisters agreed, the almighty Boss Maxwell really did love his son. He just didn't know how to express it very well.

"I'm at the end of my rope," Thea said unhappily. "I don't know how to help Bobby. I've tried so hard to stop him from self-destructing, and I'm so scared I won't be able to."

"We all feel the same way," Cassie told her. "I'm scared, too."

"Cassie, thanks for calling," Thea said in a soft voice.

"Hey, what are sisters for?" Cassie hung up the phone, knowing that she wasn't very good at expressing love, either. Maybe she was more like her father than she wanted to admit. Now, *there* was an uncomfortable thought.

She took her own afghan and tucked it around her as she settled in the armchair next to Bobby. She was afraid to go back to her bedroom—if she fell asleep there, Bobby might be gone when she woke. Something told her she couldn't afford to let that happen.

And so she would watch over him.

"GOOD MORNING, CASS."

She opened her eyes with a start, then winced as she felt the crick in her back. She'd dozed in the armchair, after all. Now the very first light of morning was beginning to seep through the curtains. She'd left the lamp on all night, though, and she could see her brother clearly. He was sitting up on the couch, rubbing his forehead. No doubt he had a killer headache.

"You're the only one who calls me Cass anymore," she murmured. "Just like Dad's the only one who calls me Cassandra. How is he, by the way?"

If she'd hoped for a neutral topic, she'd picked the wrong one. Bobby's face tightened. "The usual. Disappointed as hell in me."

"Believe it or not, he loves you," Cassie said gently.

"Sure, he thinks we're all grand. Guess that's why you never hang around Walking Stones any longer than you have to."

"Guess you have a point," she retorted, her voice deliberately light.

"So, where's my nephew?" Bobby asked, his own jocularity forced.

"Zak spent the night at Janice's."

"Lucky break," Bobby muttered. "You probably didn't want your son seeing me plastered."

"No one says plastered anymore." She stood up

and walked across to the kitchen. "How about some breakfast? I'll make pancakes."

"You…cooking?" Bobby said in a skeptical tone. "You're scaring me, Cass."

"Relax. I use a mix straight from the box." How she wished this was just the normal, everyday banter of long ago, before Bobby had taken to drinking. And before she'd run away from Walking Stones.

Now she got out a skillet and a mixing bowl. Bobby came to lean in the doorway. Even in his stocking feet, he had the Maxwell rangy height.

"Hey," he said awkwardly, running a hand through his mussed hair. "Thanks for letting me crash here last night. I didn't know where else to go."

"Anytime," she said, still with that strained attempt at lightness. She splashed some milk into the bowl, got the spatula. But then she abandoned this pretense of normalcy.

"Dammit, Bobby, don't you realize how worried we are about you? All of us—including Megan. Especially Megan! It's killing us to see you trying to destroy yourself, over and over—"

"I can get sober," he said, that old bravado in his voice. "I can do it…I *will* do it. But I don't need to go to some damn shrink for it."

She set the spatula down on the counter with a thump. "Listen to yourself," she demanded. "'I can'…'I will.' So what was last night all about?

Feeling sorry for yourself—going on one last bender?''

''Nobody says bender anymore,'' he told her, and then suddenly he abandoned the act, too. He seemed to slump a little. ''Hell, Cassie, don't you think I hate myself?'' he asked miserably. ''When I go to visit Dan, and I see what I did to him, when I talk to Megan, and I hear the disappointment in her voice...don't you think I wish I could be somebody else—*anybody* else?''

''We don't want you to be someone else. We just want you to stop drinking. That would do the trick.'' She started mixing the batter, working matter-of-factly as her brother watched. She knew that Bobby had caused terrible suffering. Dan in a wheelchair, Dan's distraught family threatening to sue for millions...but would any amount of money ever make up for what Bobby had done to his best friend? The thought must torment Bobby all the time. And then Megan, having every reason in the world not to trust Bobby, and Bobby knowing it full well. How Cassie wished she could step back into the past and change the course of her brother's life. How he must wish it, too.

''Need some help?'' he asked now.

''You could get two plates down from the cupboard. And two cups for orange juice. The silverware's in that drawer over there.''

They shared a few moments of companionable

silence, plates clinking as Bobby set them down on the table, the pleasant aroma of butter filling the air as it heated in the skillet. Again the homey activity in the kitchen made Cassie long for simpler moments from their past. But maybe she was just imagining that anything about the Maxwell family had *ever* been simple.

"I wish you could remember Mom the way I do," she said as she ladled the first spoonfuls of batter into the skillet. She hadn't planned to talk about their mother. The words had just come out. Bobby's face got a guarded look.

"I remember some things," he said grudgingly.

"Like what?"

He sat down, propping his elbows on the table. "Like the way she used to play the piano."

Cassie smiled a little. "I loved it when she played. She made up great stories, too. Sometimes instead of reading to us before bed, she'd just weave one of those stories. I could tell she was making it up as she went along, but the details were so vivid. I asked her once why she didn't write the stories down. But she said they were for speaking, not writing. She said sometimes words were magical, just for being spoken."

Bobby didn't say anything for a while. Cassie flipped the pancakes, and when they were ready she slipped one onto Bobby's plate, one onto her own. She spooned the next batch into the skillet.

"Why the trip down memory lane?" her brother said at last.

"I don't know. Maybe I just keep thinking that if Mom had lived, everything would be different. Better."

"Yeah. I wouldn't be a drunk."

"Maybe you wouldn't be," Cassie said calmly. "Maybe she could have stopped whatever made you start. But we'll never know." She flipped the next two pancakes, waited a few moments, and served them up. Sitting down across from Bobby, she poured the syrup and then pushed the jar toward him. "Eat up," she said. "It'll help your head."

He looked unhappy, but he ate.

"Tell me what happened to you last night," she said. "I have a feeling that you'd like to. I can't think of any other reason you'd come all the way up here to Billings."

"Maybe I just wanted to get away," he mumbled.

"Get away from what?"

He set down his fork. Cassie looked into his eyes, and she saw the sadness there. Unspeakable sadness that made her want to reach out to him. But instead she waited.

"I went to see Dan again last night," he said at last, his voice low. "And I saw all over again what I'd done to him. God, I can't even explain what that's like. Knowing that you've ruined somebody's life. Your best friend's life. It's killing me, Cass…"

He bent his head, the anguish in his voice so clear that Cassie felt tears smarting at her eyelids again. But her instincts told her not to say anything, not to try comforting him, just to wait.

"I keep thinking about everything I've destroyed, everyone I've hurt. I don't know if I can take it anymore."

The silence stretched between them, fraught with his pain. But at last Cassie knew it was time to speak. She pushed aside her plate and leaned toward her brother.

"Bobby, have you asked Dan's forgiveness—really asked it? And Megan's, too?"

He kept his head bowed. "I'm not going to take myself off the hook that way. Saying I'm sorry, those are just words. Cheap words."

"No, they're not," Cassie said urgently. "They're words that need saying. Maybe over and over. And Dan deserves the chance to forgive you. Don't punish him. Don't punish Megan, either."

Bobby lifted his head. The anguish was still there in his eyes. "You want an easy answer, Cassie. There isn't one."

"Maybe not. But we can't go back," she told him. "I can't keep wishing Mom were still alive, still here to take care of everything for us. And you can't keep wishing you could go back before that night, before it all happened. We have to go forward now, Bobby...all of us."

Cassie knew what she had to do. Once again she went to the phone. This time she dialed Dr. Gwen's number, catching her still at home at this early hour. Cassie made her request as brief and succinct as possible. Dr. Gwen clearly understood that this was no time for small talk. She, too, was brief and professional and right to the point. A moment later Cassie hung up the receiver. She had a name and a number jotted on a slip of paper. She held out the paper to Bobby.

"This is the name of a very good doctor here in town," she said quietly. "A man who specializes in the treatment of alcoholism. He runs a clinic, in fact." She paused. "You know," she said, "I could be the one to call him. I could set up the appointment, make all the arrangements. But that wouldn't do any good, would it? This has to come from you. Only you."

Bobby stared at the slip of paper in her hand. He didn't make any move to take it. Cassie saw the emotions battling across his face: pride, stubbornness...sorrow. She waited, pleading with him silently to do what was right. Pleading with him to help himself.

At last he stood up. He took the paper from her. A surge of hope went through her, but then just as quickly died. Bobby didn't go to the phone, didn't make the call. Instead he just tucked the slip of paper in his pocket. Then he went to the living room, put on his boots and walked to the door.

"Thanks, Cass," he said, his voice surprisingly gentle. But he let himself out of her apartment without another word.

ANDREW WONDERED when Hannah's rain gutters had last been cleaned. They were filled with dead, damp leaves, mementos of last autumn. He stood on the ladder, took a clump of the leaves in one hand and tossed it to the ground. Arthur pounced on the leaves, spreading them around and then wagging his tail as if pleased with his accomplishment. He was helping to create a rake job, but Andrew didn't mind. He seemed to keep looking for work to do around the place. And he didn't have to look very far—there was always something to add to the list. The house would sell a lot better if it was spruced up just right.

A car turned into the driveway. Cassie's hatchback, the engine sounding very much in need of a tune-up. He climbed down from the ladder and went to meet her. Arthur came bouncing along, too. Cassie was wearing a sleeveless dress that did things for his imagination. This time he took it easy, though. He kept his distance.

Cassie bent down to give the dog a scratch behind the ears. Then she straightened. "Zak is still with Janice and her nephew. Puts me at loose ends, so I thought I'd just drop by, and..." She lifted her shoulders. There was a strained look to her face. "I can't pretend to be casual around you," she muttered. "Why do I even try?" She shook her head. "I'm still trying to figure out what to do. I thought if I could just come and look at the guest house...well, maybe everything would seem clear. But that's ridiculous, isn't it? I lived in this place for almost a year. Do I think I'm going to see something new I haven't seen before? Get some insight that's been escaping me?" She sighed. "You can stop me anytime, Andrew."

"Don't mind me," he said. "I'm not going anywhere."

She gave him a sharp glance. "I'm surprised you've stayed around this long. Isn't Texas calling to you?"

"I still have some work to do around here," he said.

"I see, but couldn't you hire somebody else to do the work for you?"

"I get the feeling," he said, "that you're trying to get rid of me."

She sighed again. "I'm just feeling edgy. Go back to whatever you were doing. I'll just walk around the guest house a little, if it's okay with you."

"The place is yours," he reminded her.

"No, it's *not* mine," she said with a hint of exasperation. "You're the blasted trustee, remember?"

She seemed to think those two words went together. "Blasted" and "trustee." Maybe she was right.

"Something's bothering you," he said. "Maybe something besides me."

"Is it that obvious?" she asked.

"Pretty much."

She made a restless gesture. "My brother showed up at my apartment last night. To make a long story short, he was drunk again. I tried talking some sense into him, but I don't seem to have gotten very far. And I'm just so damn worried about him. And I keep thinking, if I were down at Walking Stones, I could be closer to him. Closer to everyone in my family." She took a deep breath. "It's all very complicated and confusing—and you're the last person I want to burden with this, Andrew."

He thought it over. Cassie had accused him of shutting off his emotions, not sharing them. But maybe she was good at that, too. She already seemed to regret the little she'd said to him today.

"I have something to show you," he said. "I'm glad you stopped by." He went into the house, and came out a moment later with some sketches he'd made.

"They're pretty rough, but they give you an idea," he said. "I reconfigure Hannah's property, put in a new driveway here…that way the guest house will be totally separate from the main house.

You and Zak would have all the privacy you'd need.''

She stared at the sketches. ''Let me get this straight,'' she said. ''You think a new driveway will convince me to move back in?''

''Something like that,'' he said. ''I'm trying to show you that this really can work, Cassie. Look, we put in a fence over here, totally separate yards. Whoever ends up buying the main house won't bother you.''

''You have it all worked out.''

He got the point. ''Okay, so you decide where you want the new fence…the new driveway. I'm not trying to make decisions for you.''

''Andrew, you're being very generous—I realize that.''

Somehow she didn't make it sound like a compliment. He rolled up the sketches. ''I keep getting it wrong with you,'' he said. ''Have you noticed that?''

''Maybe we both keep getting it wrong. Maybe there just isn't any way to get it right, where you and I are concerned.'' She looked regretful. He felt regret, too. It was a lot stronger than he wanted it to be.

''So walk through the guest house,'' he said. ''Take your time. Maybe things really will become clear.''

She didn't appear convinced, but she nodded. "I'll just be a few minutes."

"Take all the time you want." He opened the door for her with his key, watched her disappear inside. The two of them sounded like distant acquaintances, not people who'd shared a night together.

Thinking about that night was definitely not a good idea. So he climbed the ladder and cleaned more leaves from the rain gutter. Dead leaves, remnants of the past, when all around him green foliage of summer spoke of the future. But no future, no past, he'd always told himself. Live in the moment.

Too bad it wasn't as easy as it used to be.

CHAPTER THIRTEEN

THE SALESMAN SLAPPED the bumper of the brand-new, four-wheel-drive, extra-cab truck. "She's a beaut," he pronounced.

Andrew was getting pretty annoyed with the guy, but he walked around the truck one more time. Even the color was right, a silvery blue that would wear well no matter what the Montana season.

He wasn't staying in Montana, though. What did he care if he'd found a vehicle just right for Montana?

Andrew couldn't explain why he'd stopped to browse at this dealership. A new truck was the last thing he needed. His two-year-old Jeep was waiting for him in Dallas. It got the job done.

"What say we step into my office," said the salesman. "Throw a few figures around. I can make you a pretty sweet deal."

The guy was definitely an annoyance, but somehow Andrew found himself sitting down, talking figures. The salesman made a great show of punching numbers into his calculator.

A truck would be a lot more handy than a convertible for carting supplies to Hannah's house. It would really help him with all those odd jobs to fix up the place.

It didn't make sense to buy a truck for a couple of odd jobs. Especially when he'd be leaving Montana so soon. What did he expect to do, drive the truck all the way back to Texas?

"Here's what I can do for you," said the salesman, flashing the calculator at him. It was definitely time to stand up and get out of here.

"I'll take the damn truck," Andrew said.

CASSIE HEARTILY REGRETTED allowing Dr. Gwen to talk her into this. She positioned her golf club, took a swing at the ball in front of her and watched it go sailing past the dragon's mouth and into the "Den of Despair." Miniature golf definitely wasn't her game.

Dr. Gwen aimed at her own ball. It disappeared neatly into the dragon's mouth. "This is fun, isn't it?" she asked with satisfaction.

Cassie glanced around at the whimsical storybook surroundings: a miniature castle, a prancing unicorn, a debonair rabbit in top hat and waistcoat. She wished she could have brought Zak here this afternoon—her son would have loved this place. But he had begged to spend another night at Janice's. He had such a difficult time making friends that Cassie felt grateful he wanted to spend more time with Janice's nephew. On the other hand, maybe Zak just wanted to avoid spending time with *her*. She was, after all, the mean-monster mom who wouldn't let her son have a dog.

"Why so glum?" asked Dr. Gwen. "Are you thinking about Mr. Texas Hunk?"

Cassie flushed as if on cue.

Gwen was giving her altogether too searching a look. "Do tell," she murmured. "Oh, my, you've slept with him, haven't you?"

"Gwen, just leave it alone, all right?"

Dr. Gwen seemed to be having a very good time. She swung her putter at a jaunty angle. "Tell me all about it," she said. "Was it absolutely wonderful?"

Oh, yes, it had been wonderful. The most magical night of Cassie's life. But one night couldn't keep you warm for the rest of your life. A sense of loss swept over her, an ache that spread to every part of her body.

"Oh, my," Gwen repeated.

"Would you stop saying that?" Cassie grumbled. "I'm not going to talk about it. And besides, it's over."

"Why?" Gwen asked bluntly.

"Because...because he's a man who likes to be in charge of everything—and I don't want a man in charge. Because whenever things almost get serious, he reminds me that he's going back to Texas. Because…he doesn't love me." The words slipped out unbidden, and they hurt.

"Do you love him?" Gwen asked after a potent pause.

"Yes," Cassie said. That word came unbidden, too. She knew it was the truth, though, no matter how she'd been trying to avoid it. She loved Andrew Morris. The knowledge made her catch her breath.

"You've got it bad," Gwen said. "I can tell that much. Well, you have only one choice."

"What's that?" Cassie asked warily.

"You have to tell him how you feel."

"Oh, no." Cassie bent down, grabbed her ball and went hurrying to the next obstacle—a lazily spinning windmill. "I can't possibly tell him."

Dr. Gwen trailed after her. "Why not?"

"Because…because he'll just remind me that he's going back to Texas, to his very *single* life."

Gwen smacked her ball and sent it sailing smoothly between the arms of the windmill. Cassie thwacked her ball, and it bounced off a curb and landed out of bounds.

"You're much better than I am at this silly game," she muttered.

"Stop trying to change the subject," said Gwen. "The topic of Mr. Texas Hunk is much more interesting than putting techniques."

"Would you stop calling him that—"

"Well, he *is* a hunk, isn't he?"

This Cassie could not deny. "Let's talk about your love life instead," she said somewhat desperately.

"Honey," Gwen said with mock despair, "what love life? I am having a monumental dry spell. Why else do you think I'm so interested in *your* romantic escapades?"

"They're hardly escapades." Cassie tried one more time to get her ball through the windmill, and then gave up. "You win," she said.

"You're not getting off that easily," Gwen said. "Cassie, you have to tell him. If you don't, you'll always wonder what chances you missed."

Cassie frowned. "Thanks for the advice, but I'll handle this in my own way."

Dr. Gwen was now taking aim at the rabbit in top hat and waistcoat. "I can't just stand by and watch you ruin your life, can I? Guys like Mr. Texas Hunk don't come along every day."

Cassie gritted her teeth. "*Will* you stop calling him that? It seems like everybody's trying to manage me these days. My father. Andrew. And now you... It's too much to take!"

"Yeah, but I'm the one you should listen to," Gwen said with supreme confidence. Her ball neatly found its target. "Hole in one—right in the rabbit's foot. That's good luck, if you ask me. So tell him, Cassie. Tell him how you feel before it's too late. You know I'm right."

Cassie couldn't deny it.

IT WAS THE FIRST TIME Andrew had talked to his mother since he'd arrived in Montana. She'd asked him not to call—said she didn't really want to know anything about Hannah's estate. But now she was the one calling him, under the pretext of asking how he was doing.

"Don't talk to me about your grandmother," she said after the usual hellos. "It's all over and done with…whatever happened."

"Fine," he said.

"So, how are *you* doing?" she asked.

"Fine," he said.

"Please don't be so verbose," she said. "You're talking my ear off."

Katharine Morris didn't know yet that Hannah had cut her out of the will. How could he make idle conversation when he had that on his mind? But he made an effort, anyway.

"Everything's going well here," he said as non-committally as possible. "How's California?"

"The same as it's always been," his mother said, an edge to her voice. "Overcrowded. Overrated."

"But you get to walk on the beach every day," Andrew reminded her.

"Of course."

Two years ago, she'd moved to southern California for a job as a university librarian. After a late start, she'd been pursuing her career wholeheartedly. Andrew was glad for her, but he knew Hannah had been skeptical. She'd been fond of saying that Katharine focused too much on her work—just as Andrew focused too much on *his*. That had been only one source of contention between Hannah and her daughter. They had seemed to have differences of opinion about almost everything. But, even so...cutting her daughter off entirely...what had made Hannah do it?

"Something's wrong, isn't it?" Katharine asked. "Something you're not telling me. Are you all right, Andrew?"

"I'm fine," he said.

"That's the third time you've mentioned it," she said dryly.

He had to tell her. Sooner or later she had to know. But somehow the words just wouldn't come out.

"Maybe I should fly up there," she said. "I haven't been back to Montana in a very long time."

"Not such a good idea," he said.

"Why not?"

He had to tell her. "Okay," he said very reluctantly. "There is something about Hannah you should know—"

"I don't want to hear it," she interrupted. "I didn't call you to talk about Hannah. I just thought

I could fly up there, and we could have a nice visit. I haven't seen you in ages, Andrew.''

Coming to Montana would be the worse thing she could do. No matter what she said, she hadn't put the past behind her.

"So we'll have a visit some other time,'' Andrew told her. "I'll come see you, or you'll come to Dallas. But here…everything's too close.''

There was a long pause. And then, softly, "He died so long ago, Andrew. You couldn't have done anything to save him. You were only a small boy.''

"Right,'' said Andrew, his voice emotionless.

Another pause. And then his mother said decisively, "I'm coming to Montana.'' She hung up before he could tell her, one more time, not to come.

THE PHONE CALL had made him restless, had stirred up too many old memories. Andrew went out to his brand-new, four-wheel-drive, extra-cab truck and climbed in. He drove to the hardware store, slowing to make the turn into the parking lot.

But then, for some reason he couldn't explain, he didn't turn after all. He just kept going. Without thinking about it, without conscious volition, he found himself driving to the other edge of town. And there he came to the stretch of road grooved so deeply into his memory. The road where it had happened…the sharp curve that could catch you unawares if you weren't expecting it.

He pulled off to the verge of the road, parking just before the curve. It was dusk now, the shadows of evening obscuring his vision. But he had his memories. He knew this road all too well.

He had only been nine years old, and yet every moment of that night was so clear to him. Every sound, every sight…

Tires skidding. The useless whine of the brakes. His father's face, ashen white except for that one solitary trickle of blood. So little blood, that had been the surprise. His father's voice, so weak that Andrew had had to lean close to hear it.

Promise me…promise me that you will never tell what really happened…

He hadn't told. He had kept the promise to his father, all these years. No one else had known the truth. Not his mother. Not Hannah. He alone had carried it all this time. His father had asked for that. And you did not deny a dying man. Even a quarter of a century later, you did not deny him.

Andrew turned the key in the ignition, started the engine again. Only then did he realize that his hands were shaking. He waited a moment to steady himself.

There was only one answer. He had to get out of Montana. He had to go back to Dallas, and to the life he'd made for himself.

A life where he could almost forget what had happened the night his father died.

"PLACE NEEDS a lot of work, doesn't it?"

Andrew didn't mind the comment. "I've been doing some of it myself. The new roof...I'm hiring a contractor for that. Contractor for the plumbing, too."

Scott Reynolds gave a thoughtful nod, and they continued their tour through Hannah's house. Reynolds had been sent over by Hannah's lawyer as a potential buyer. Things were moving quickly. Which meant Andrew could hire more contractors, and get back to Texas as soon as he wanted.

"I'll let you know," Reynolds said at last. Andrew recognized that carefully noncommittal tone. The guy was interested in the house, but he didn't want to let on.

"Sure," Andrew said, equally noncommittal. He'd never believed in the hard sell. If one buyer fell through, there'd be another one. Again, he could leave it all in someone else's hands. He didn't have to be here.

He and Reynolds walked outside, where Arthur came bouncing up to greet them. The dog seemed to grow by the hour, but he was still all gangly puppy. And just then a car pulled into the driveway—Cassie's hatchback, still in need of a tune-up. She got out and walked toward them, pausing momentarily to give Arthur the required attention. It was at that moment Andrew realized he didn't care for Reynolds so much. The guy looked Cassie over with interest. Way too much interest.

"Hello," Cassie said.

Andrew couldn't avoid introductions. He made them, and Cassie shook hands with Reynolds. In Andrew's opinion, the guy held on a little too long.

"The scenery around here just got better," Reynolds said. Andrew winced, but Cassie kept an admirably impassive face.

"Are you new to Montana, Mr. Reynolds?" she asked.

"I'm thinking of moving out here from Chicago. I've got the freedom to choose any town I want. Being a software consultant does that for you." He gave what was probably supposed to be an engaging grin.

"I gather you're in the market for a house," Cassie said, glancing from Reynolds to Andrew, her own expression impossible to read.

"I'm looking," said Reynolds, and he gave Cassie another appreciative perusal. It occurred to Andrew that he genuinely didn't like the guy.

"Guess I'll be going," Reynolds said with obvious reluctance. He gave Cassie a final look, then got into his sedan. At last he drove off.

"Well," Cassie said after a moment, her voice oddly strained. "I didn't expect you to be selling the house so soon."

"Nothing's final," Andrew told her. "I'm fielding prospects right now...don't worry about Reynolds. If you don't like him, he's out of the picture.''

Cassie gave him a sardonic glance. "Let me get this straight. Zak and I are supposed to move back into the guest house, and meanwhile you'll handpick our next-door neighbor for us. That *is* considerate, Andrew.''

Somehow this wasn't turning out the way he'd imagined. "Look, I know it really bugs you, the idea that I could have any say over your life. But once the main house is sold—hey, you won't even see me.''

"Right,'' Cassie murmured. "Because you'll be back in Dallas.'' Her voice still sounded odd, as if she was struggling to keep her emotions in check. But then she motioned toward his brand-new truck. "Quite something,'' she said. "A step up from the convertible, that's for sure.''

"Actually,'' Andrew said, "I bought the damn thing.''

"Really,'' Cassie murmured.

"Doesn't make any sense,'' he admitted. "It's a Montana truck, and I'm not staying in Montana.''

Her face got a closed look. "Of course not. So I guess it will have to become a Texas truck.''

"Something like that.''

Cassie turned and walked restlessly across the yard, toward the oak tree at the back. Andrew and Arthur went with her.

"You know," Andrew said, "when I get the property replatted, I'll make sure the tree house stays on your side."

"I'm sure Zak would like that," she said. She stood beneath the tree, gazing up into the branches.

"And look at it this way," he said, "you can be the one to choose your next-door neighbor. When I go back to Dallas, I can even arrange for you to be the one who interviews buyers. Why not?"

"Why not, indeed," Cassie muttered. She swiveled toward him. "So," she said, "you *are* going back to Texas. And it sounds like you're planning on it right away."

"I have a court case coming up," he said. "I can't delay much longer."

"Of course not. What was I expecting..." She took a deep breath, and gazed at him intently. "Andrew, I didn't just drop by today for chitchat. I...I have something to tell you."

"I'm listening," he said.

"What I have to tell you, it's not that easy." She really did seem to be struggling with words. "If you must know, it's something Dr. Gwen advised me to say."

"Dr. Gwen," he repeated. "Is she mad because I never went back to see her? Finger's working fine, though." He'd meant to lighten the mood, but Cassie didn't seem to appreciate his efforts. Now she gave him an exasperated look.

"Maybe Dr. Gwen doesn't know everything," she said. "Maybe I should just ignore her advice."

"I really am listening," Andrew said.

"Somehow I just can't say it out here," Cassie answered quickly. "I don't suppose you have anything to drink? A soda will do."

Now he was really curious, but he didn't press the issue. He led her back to the house, produced an orange soda, and then ushered her into the living room.

"Wow," she said, glancing at the boxes scattered around. "You *have* been busy." Arthur, who had followed them, trotted over to one of the boxes and began gnawing on a corner of it.

"I brought all this stuff down from the attic," he told her. "Hannah's memorabilia. Thought I'd better go through it before my mother gets here."

Cassie seemed very glad for a change of subject. "Your mother—when will she be here?"

"She hasn't given me a date yet. But, knowing her, it'll be soon. Once she decides on something, she goes after it. Hannah used to say she was reckless that way." Andrew grimaced. "Those two really knew how to get to each other. The accusations piled up on both sides. Pigheaded, thoughtless, and, yeah, reckless." He sat down, rummaged in one of the boxes and picked out a paper at random. He scanned it. "Can't let my mother see this one," he said. "It's a letter she wrote to Hannah years ago, after she first moved away from Montana. It's full of anger and hurt feelings. Apparently Hannah had written something in one of her own letters, something about my mom not knowing how to live on her own. Anyway, it never seemed to end between the two of them. But maybe it should end now.''

Cassie sat down across from Andrew. ''Wait a minute. You're trying to censor things for your mother?''

He didn't like the sound of that. ''I'm just trying to spare her more grief. She keeps telling me she doesn't hold any grudges, that she's put the past behind her. So far she hasn't convinced me.''

Cassie shook her head. ''Andrew, don't you see what you're doing? You're trying to control things for your mother. You're trying to protect her. Maybe that's an admirable sentiment, in a way, but it's wrong. If she still has something to work through with Hannah, maybe going through all those boxes is exactly what she needs.''

''Dredging up the past again won't do any good,'' Andrew said.

''Maybe it won't. But, then again, maybe it will,'' Cassie argued. ''The point is, it's not up to you to decide.'' She sipped her soda, but she seemed too restless even for that. She set down the can on the coffee table in front of her. ''You could ask why I'm even getting involved,'' she said. ''It's just that what you're doing with your mother, well, it's what you're trying to do with *me*. Arrange things. Control them. Don't you see how impossible it all is?''

He guessed he didn't see. ''So this is what Dr. Gwen wanted you to tell me,'' he remarked. ''I'm a blasted interfering trustee.''

''No, it's not that at all.'' Cassie stood up, stared at him, then sank back into her chair. ''Oh, damn,'' she whispered. Now she gazed down at her clasped hands.

''I can take it,'' Andrew said. ''Whatever it is.''

She remained silent for a long moment. And then, slowly, she looked at him again. ''I've come to a decision, Andrew,'' she said, her tone suddenly too calm. ''I've been giving it a lot of thought, and feeling utterly confused, but just now it became clear to me. I have to do what's right for Zak. Absolutely nothing else can get in the way. So, I am going to move back into the guest house. And I'm going to let you be a...a blasted trustee. Zak will have a real home. He'll have Arthur, his dream dog. And nothing else matters.''

She didn't sound happy about her decision. She just sounded like someone determined to do what was right. But Andrew couldn't help feeling relieved. With Cassie in the guest house, he'd have a connection to her. Even after he moved back to Dallas, even after he left Montana behind, Cassie would still be in his life, even in some small measure.

That would have to be enough.

CHAPTER FOURTEEN

CASSIE ATE LUNCH at her desk, endless files scattered around her. It seemed that as soon as she helped get one case settled, ten more sprouted. So many children, so much need. She munched desultorily on her usual peanut butter and jelly sandwich, wishing she could do more.

"Hello, Cassie."

There he was, standing in the doorway to her office. Andrew Morris—the man she loved. Her heart pounded, and she could feel her knees going weak even though she was sitting down. Ridiculous. Impossible. Overwhelming. Those were the only words that came to mind. Certainly words had failed her yesterday. She hadn't been able to tell Andrew that she loved him. She hadn't been able to take Dr. Gwen's advice, after all.

Now she just stared at Andrew, knowing what she wanted to do at this moment. She pictured herself standing up, going around the desk and walking right up to him. She saw herself tangling her hands in his dark hair and drawing his head down to hers.

She saw herself kissing him, and kissing him some more, right there in the doorway.

She stayed where she was, barricaded safely behind the desk.

"Hello, Andrew," she managed to say at last. "How's the trustee business? Are you here to tell me something about the guest house? Or maybe you want to refurbish the tree house before we move in." *Stop talking,* she commanded herself. Before she could babble on, she took another bite of peanut butter and jelly.

Andrew came into the office. "Don't worry. I'll let you and Zak do what you want with the tree house. I'm not here to run your life. Instead, I wanted to ask a favor."

"Have a seat. I'm all ears." She tried to sound carefree. "I have another half a sandwich. I'd be glad to share—I'm not as hungry as I'd thought I'd be."

Andrew sat down across from her desk. "I haven't had peanut butter in a long time," he said. "Not since I was about twelve, I guess."

"When you have a kid, you tend to eat kid food. But here, try it. I insist."

He took the proffered sandwich and sampled a few bites. "Hmm...not bad."

"Glad to hear it," she said briskly. "Now, Andrew. What can I do for you?"

He didn't get right to the point, preferring, it

seemed, to study her office carefully. His gaze traveled over the battered filing cabinets in the corner, dust gathering on top. He examined the fake potted plants stuck in another corner, the out-of-date calendar hanging on the wall, the whiteboard scribbled with appointments and case notes.

"Okay," Cassie said. "I know this isn't exactly the executive suite. But it *is* where I spend a great deal of my time—"

"Doesn't look like it," Andrew said. "Looks like you took over from some guy who retired ten years ago, but you never got around to changing the decor."

Cassie picked up the oversize photo of Zak that she kept in a frame on her desk. "This is something personal," she said. "This is something that declares this office as mine."

"One picture," Andrew observed.

She drew her eyebrows together. "Andrew, I assume you *did* come here for a reason."

"Right." He settled back, resting one ankle on his knee. "Here's the upshot. My mother's flying in tonight. She plans to stay a few days. I'd like you to help me keep her entertained."

Cassie gave him a speculative glance. "Entertained...why does that sound like such a loaded term? Let me see, what you really want me to do is help keep her busy so she doesn't think about Hannah—and doesn't try to look in all those boxes."

Andrew gave her a disgruntled glance in return. "Is that so bad?"

"It's wrong," Cassie told him. "I'm sure you're very concerned about your mother, and very considerate of her, but you really shouldn't try to manage her life. And I certainly don't want to be part of your misguided efforts."

"Don't pull any punches," he told her sardonically. "Say exactly what you mean."

She lifted her shoulders. "I think it's wonderful of you to care about your mom. But if you *do* care, just let her come, and do whatever she needs."

"I guess that's a no," Andrew said.

Cassie wished she didn't feel a stirring of guilt. She thought about the fact that she'd received a part of Hannah's inheritance, but Hannah's daughter had received nothing at all. That put her right in the middle of the Morris-family dynamics, like it or not.

"I hope your mother has a good visit here, I really do," she said.

"I think she'd enjoy meeting you," Andrew remarked. "Maybe she didn't get along with Hannah, but the two of them had one thing in common. They both thought I dated the wrong kind of woman."

Cassie frowned at him. "Well, you and I are *not* dating. So I don't see why your mother would possibly want to meet me—"

"The two of you might like each other, that's all."

Cassie drummed her fingers on the desk. "Think about it, Andrew. I'm the woman remembered in Hannah's will. Your mother wasn't remembered…" Her voice trailed off as she watched the expression on Andrew's face. "So," she said, "you haven't even told your mother that much. She doesn't know about the guest house."

"I'm planning to break it to her," Andrew said grudgingly. "In my own time, my own way."

"Aren't you afraid that if I'm around, I'll spill the beans before you're ready?"

"No," Andrew said. "I trust you."

"It's all becoming clear," Cassie said grimly. "You want to use me to deflect attention from Hannah. Maybe you even want your mother to think we're dating, and that would really divert her attention… For crying out loud, Andrew. How far were you planning to go with this?"

He seemed to settle back even more comfortably in the plain wooden chair across from her desk. "Relax," he said. "I don't want you to pretend anything. No lies, no subterfuge. I'll even tell my mother how much you and Zak meant to Hannah."

"No subterfuge," Cassie muttered. "Just an omission of the more important parts of the truth."

"I'll tell her everything—"

"When you think she's ready," Cassie finished for him. "And meanwhile, I'm supposed to soften up your mother with stories of Hannah's kindness to me and Zak, stories to help her see Hannah in a new light?''

"That's good," Andrew said. "I like the sound of that."

Cassie sighed. "Why do you really want me around while your mother's here? At least level with *me*."

He gave her a somber look. "Because I seem to welcome any excuse to be around you, Cassie. I think up reasons to come see you, reasons to have you near me just a little while longer. Bothers the heck out of me, but there it is."

She couldn't speak. All she could do was gaze back at him. She understood exactly what he had said. Because she felt exactly the same way. She kept looking for excuses to be with him, even though she knew that in the end he would break her heart.

At last she gave a slow nod. And at last she found her voice. "I'll do it, Andrew…. I'll be with you."

ANDREW'S MOTHER hadn't stopped once since the beginning of this early-morning hike. Instead she just kept marching ahead of Andrew and Cassie, long black hair flowing out from under her bandanna. She had streaks of gray that she made no attempt to hide, and she wore no makeup to obscure the subtle lines of age on her face. These facts, however, only made her seem younger than her fifty-eight years. She was tall and athletic, and Cassie was not surprised to learn that as a young woman she'd pursued a career as a ballet dancer. A knee injury had sidelined her aspirations, but clearly not her enthusiasm. She marched along now, tossing comments over her shoulder to Andrew and Cassie.

"...I miss the Montana mountains, I really do. California has mountains, of course, but these are the ones that really get your blood pumping...so glad you both decided to join me..." She disappeared around a bend in the trail.

Cassie took a deep breath of the pine-scented air, and gave Andrew a rueful glance. "Don't tell me you were really concerned about keeping her busy," she muttered. "She seems to be running *us* ragged."

"She is, isn't she?" Andrew remarked. He didn't appear to be out of breath in the least, and Cassie found this annoying. She also found annoying that he looked even better than usual today. He wore a khaki shirt with the sleeves rolled up, hiking shorts, hiking boots and hiking socks. Altogether, the effect was potent. He could have easily posed for a mountaineering magazine, and no doubt would be right at home scaling a rock face.

They continued along the trail, and Cassie found her thoughts going to her son. She remembered the slow, disbelieving grin Zak had given her when she'd told him they were moving back to the guest house, and that Arthur would become a part of their lives. The memory of that grin warmed her even now. When Zak had learned that he'd be spending another day with Janice and her nephew, he'd gone off happily, not as if he wanted to escape Cassie. All of this ought to make her feel wonderful—and it did, half the time. The other half she still felt uneasy and confused. What on earth was she doing, letting Andrew become a part of her life? She would be tied to him, even when he went back to Texas.

Andrew glanced at her as they went along. "Must be pretty deep thoughts," he commented.

She refused to let on that she was thinking about him. Andrew seemed about to say something more, but fortunately they had caught up to Katharine. The woman stopped only long enough to take a drink from her water bottle.

"Should have brought my birding glasses," she said. "Did you see that stunning woodpecker over there?"

Cassie, admittedly, had heard a flapping of wings, but the bird had escaped her vision. She wondered, though, if anything escaped Katharine. At different times during the hike, the woman had glanced curiously from Andrew to Cassie and back again. Maybe she hadn't bought Andrew's story that he and Cassie were "just friends." Cassie herself didn't know if they were "just friends." She didn't know *what* they were.

It seemed at least an hour later that Katharine announced "time for a break." If Cassie had worried about Andrew managing his mother, she was rethinking her concern. Right now, it seemed that Katharine was managing Andrew *and* Cassie. Andrew didn't appear to mind, though. Cassie was surprised at his ability to hold back and just let the day happen. It was a new side to him. Before, he'd always seemed a man who needed to be in control.

Katharine sat down on one of the rocks bordering the trail, and fished a bag of granola mix from her backpack. She handed it to Cassie without asking if she wanted any. No matter. Cassie was tired and hungry, and even granola looked appetizing right now. She sat down, too. Andrew leaned against a pine and took a swig from his water bottle. Cassie watched him, then forced her gaze away. She looked at Katharine instead.

"Well," said Andrew's mother, gazing steadily back. "What's your opinion of me? Out with it."

The woman was nothing if not direct. Suddenly Cassie found herself smiling. "I was thinking," she said, "how much you look like Hannah." Maybe it was the wrong thing to say—maybe it was too touchy a subject—but Katharine just nodded matter-of-factly.

"Growing up, it drove me nuts to look like my mother," she said. "I prided myself on being different than her. She was a homebody…I was going to see the world and *be* someone. She liked gardening…I couldn't grow a plant if I tried. The list went on and on. But eventually I found out I was more like her than I'd ever thought possible. That scared me plenty, let me tell you.''

Andrew glanced at his mother as if this latest was news to him. She gazed off into the pines.

''Truth is, when I got married and had a child of my own, I understood some things about Hannah. I understood the pull of family for the very first time. Oh, I still wanted a career of my own, I still wanted to be somebody in the world, but I couldn't imagine *not* having that little boy, or the husband I loved.'' She drew in her breath, as if her own memories had caught her by surprise. ''Except I lost my husband…and everything changed…''

Andrew, for a moment, seemed to go very still. But then he straightened. ''Think I'll walk on ahead a little.'' His voice sounded easy, but there was something beneath it—something that warned of his need to be alone. Cassie watched him go round a turn in the trail and vanish from sight. A heaviness settled inside her.

''Guess I said too much,'' Katharine murmured. ''Guess I took him off guard. I never talk about Hannah with him, Cassie. For some reason I just can't. Don't ask me to explain it. But with you, it seems possible somehow. Maybe because Hannah loved you. She told me that, you know. She wrote to me, and told me about the young woman who had moved into her guest house, and the little boy who reminded her so much of Andrew when he was young.''

Cassie felt disconcerted. ''I thought you and Hannah...I'm sorry, I thought you and she didn't speak.''

''In a way, we didn't,'' Katharine said wryly. ''The phone calls had stopped. That was a mutual decision—I think we were both tired of hanging up on each other. But we continued to write letters. Not very frequently, but still...the last time I heard from her was only a few months before she died. And you know something? I'll always regret that I didn't answer that letter right away. I just let time drift. I told myself I always got too worked up when I sat down to write to my mother. But then, next thing I knew, Andrew called to tell me she was gone.''

''I'm sorry,'' Cassie said gently.

''It was your loss, too, wasn't it?''

''Yes,'' Cassie said. ''And Zak's.''

Katharine slipped off her bandanna, her hair falling free. Cassie liked the fact that she hadn't cut it, hadn't followed the rules that said you couldn't have long hair if you were older.

''I think you're good for my son,'' Katharine said with that unnerving directness.

''Yes, well,'' Cassie fumbled, ''we're not really involved, you see...''

''What are you, then?'' Katharine asked. ''Because I see the way you look at him, and I see what's in your eyes. And I see what's in his eyes, too.''

Cassie decided to revise her opinion. She liked everything about Andrew's mother except this alarming frankness of hers.

''I think Andrew and I have agreed that we *shouldn't* be involved. That it's simply not a good idea. That it's better for both of us just to go our separate ways as much as possible—''

''Get real. All the two of you want is to be together. So if my son is talking about going back to Texas, why isn't he planning to take you with him?''

''Because I don't want to go to Texas!'' She was outright lying. If it meant being with Andrew, she'd go to Texas, all right…she'd go anywhere. But she needed an invitation first.

Katharine studied her, and then gave a rueful laugh. ''Oh, my, I'm doing it again, aren't I? Saying exactly what I'm thinking. That's one of the reasons my mother and I never got along. I always said what was on my mind.''

Cassie's anger died as quickly as it had flared. ''I didn't mean to snap at you,'' she said. ''It's just that, I do love your son, and it's awful knowing he doesn't feel the same way.'' She was appalled that this confession had slipped out. Katharine Morris, however, was the type to inspire confessions.

"Dear me," she said. "I really do see the way he looks at you. Has he said he doesn't love you?"

"Not in so many words," Cassie admitted. "But the way he walked off just now—that's the way he is with *me*. Making very clear that he intends to be alone."

Katharine nodded reluctantly. "Yes, that's Andrew. I wish I could explain it to you, Cassie, but I don't understand everything myself. I just know that after his father died, everything changed for us. It was like someone extinguishing a light, and we couldn't see our way anymore. Hannah tried to help us, but a mother and grown daughter trying to live in the same house can be difficult. With us it was impossible. I'd never done anything practical before. All my dreams about accomplishing something, being someone, they were just dreams. I didn't know the first thing about supporting a child, and truly making my way in the world. Hannah kept pointing that out to me, kept wanting me to depend on her and no one else. And I just kept wanting to escape. And then there was Andrew...nine years old, and the father he worshiped gone—just like that. He closed up inside, refused to let me in. To this day he's still closed off in some essential way. I guess I've just kept hoping that someone will come along, someone who will help him find a path out of his loneliness..."

"I'm not that someone," Cassie said in a low voice.

For several moments, Katharine didn't say anything at all.

"I'm sorry, Cassie," she said at last. "It's too bad I couldn't raise a son who would have the sense to tell the right woman he loves her."

Cassie unexpectedly found herself smiling again. "Tell me," she said, "do all mothers feel guilty about the children they raise? Do they all feel as if they've done something wrong, no matter how hard they try to do a good job?"

Katharine smiled back. "Guilt is one of those wonderful little things about motherhood no one can ever really prepare you for. You just have to go through it yourself."

Cassie bent down to tighten the laces of her boots. "I wish I didn't feel so guilty about Zak," she said. "I spend too much time at work, and not enough with him. That's plenty of guilt right there."

"Do you love your job?" Katharine asked. Trust *her* to cut right to the point.

Cassie straightened, placing both hands on her knees. She thought about it. "I don't know, anymore," she said. "I keep thinking I should. I really do help other people...other families, other kids. But something's missing."

"Joy, perhaps," suggested Katharine.

Joy indeed was precisely what Cassie found missing from her work.

"You scare me," Cassie said. "Are you a mind reader?"

Katharine shrugged. "No, just someone a few years older than you. And don't you dare tell me exactly *how* many years older."

"I wouldn't dream of it," Cassie said.

"Good then." Katharine stood, tying her bandanna again. "Shall we go find my son?"

"Yes," said Cassie.

"You know, Cassie, for what it's worth—I wouldn't mind at all having you as a daughter-in-law."

Cassie gave another smile. "Just now you sounded so much like Hannah. She used to say, in that offhand way of hers, that she wouldn't mind having me as a granddaughter."

"What do you know," Katharine said. "My mom and I had more in common than we thought." And with that, she linked her arm through Cassie's. Together the two of them went up the trail.

CHAPTER FIFTEEN

THIS VISIT WASN'T GOING as Andrew had planned. He'd hoped to keep his mother occupied, hoped to show her a good time without anybody having to delve into painful topics.

He'd hoped, too, that his mother and Cassie would get along. But he certainly hadn't intended for them to get along *this* well. And he hadn't expected the two of them to talk about times past as if entertaining each other with stories.

Take right now, for instance. He was sitting at dinner with the two women. He'd driven them to a restaurant fronting Beartooth Lake, where they had a spectacular view of the water and the mountains rising beyond. With the coming of dusk, lights sparkled on the lake. This vista should have provided a topic of conversation in its own right, but Andrew's mother and Cassie just leaned toward each other across the table, spinning the past into tangible form.

"...I guess that's another thing Hannah and I had in common," Katharine said. "The fact that neither one of us found anybody else. After my father died, Hannah swore she wouldn't live with another man who drove her crazy. It was just her way of saying that she refused to love another man. And after *my* husband died, there was a place nobody else could fill. Now I tell myself that I'm just settled into my very single ways.''

"*Settled* is the last word I'd use," Cassie remarked dryly. "You make my head spin. What was that latest pursuit you mentioned—kickboxing?"

"You should try it sometime, Cassie. Really, you should. It does wonders for a person's soul."

Cassie laughed delightedly. "I'm sure it does."

Andrew realized how tense he'd grown. Was it from sitting for a long time, or from listening to topics he'd rather not hear? Topics like Hannah, and his father…

He'd never heard his mother open up this much before. She'd always been a conversationalist, but certain subjects had remained forbidden. What was going on tonight? Suddenly she seemed able to remember all the good things about Hannah. That was fine and well, but what would happen when Andrew finally had to break the news about the will? She would end up more hurt than ever.

Cassie glanced at him. "Would you like to dance, Andrew?"

His mother's forthright nature seemed to be rubbing off on her. A jazz quintet was playing, and a few couples had moved onto the small dance floor. Andrew took Cassie's hand and drew her into his arms. This activity was more like it. Of course, with his mother watching, he didn't feel the freedom he'd like.

"You've been rather quiet this evening," Cassie said. "I get the distinct impression you wish you hadn't involved me."

"That's not it," he told her. A beautiful woman in his arms, the lake shimmering outside the floor-to-ceiling window…everything should have been perfect.

"So what's the problem?" Cassie asked, a note of concern in her voice. "We're all supposed to be having a good time."

A good time…he wanted that. Had he lost the knack? Or maybe he'd never had it. Maybe, all his life, he'd just gone through the motions of happiness. The thought wasn't a welcome one.

"It's not your fault, Cassie," he told her. "Nobody's fault but my own."

"If you talked about things, it might help," she said gently.

"There's nothing to talk about." Maybe he'd answered too quickly. She gave him a disbelieving look, and slipped out of his arms before the song ended.

LATER THAT NIGHT, Andrew and his mother and Cassie sat in Hannah's living room, drinking coffee and eating the shortbread cookies Andrew had bought at the local grocery. He'd cleaned the place up, carted all those boxes of memories into another room and closed the door on them. Afterward he'd even swept the floor, rearranged the furniture a little. Not that he'd been able to erase his grandmother's imprint. This was Hannah's house, always would be to him.

The two women had managed to keep a conversation going without much help from him, but now it was lagging. Cassie stood and took the plates and cups into the kitchen. A few seconds later came the sound of water splashing in the sink.

"She's the woman for you, Andrew," said his mother. "Are you too stupid to see it?"

He almost smiled. "Don't mince words, Mom."

"Somebody has to shake you out of this—this place you've put yourself in. This solitary confinement."

It didn't sound like a place he wanted to be. "I have friends in Dallas," he said.

"Friends," she repeated skeptically. She gave him a withering look. "If you were smart, Andrew, you'd grab hold of that girl and you'd never let her go. Don't miss your chance with her."

Maybe he already had.

LATER STILL, he took Cassie home to her apartment. At least she wouldn't be living there much longer.

She stood at the door, not inviting him in. "I had

a great time today," she said. "I think your mother did, too. You were the only one, Andrew, who refused to let down your guard."

He didn't know what to say to that. But Cassie seemed to have her own agenda. She put her key in the lock, then turned to face him again.

"Here's the thing," she said with determination. "I never did tell you what Dr. Gwen wanted me to say to you. Somehow I lost my courage. But tonight…being around your mother…she's not the sort to tolerate cowardice. So here goes." Cassie took a deep breath, and then looked at him squarely. "I love you, Andrew."

He gazed back at her. And the image returned to him: solitary confinement. It was as if he actually stood inside his own cell, unable to reach out to Cassie. Unable, even though it was the one thing he wanted.

The silence stretched between them. Cassie looked angry, and then sad.

"I see," she murmured. And then, very deliberately, she stepped into her apartment and shut the door. He heard the lock click into place. And, afterward, silence.

AROUND MIDNIGHT he told his mother the truth. If courage was demanded tonight, he'd make at least one good showing. He sat down and told Katharine about the will.

"I'm sorry," he said.

"It's not really news," she said, her voice brittle. "She threatened this once, in one of our last phone calls. She said that if I didn't care about her, she didn't want me to have anything to remember her by."

Harsh words. Andrew thought of all the differences between his mother and his grandmother. The way Hannah had disapproved of Katharine's drive and independence. The way Katharine had protested Hannah's interference. He could have continued in his mind, cataloging the hurts and slights that had accumulated over the years. But a piece of the puzzle was missing. What had been at the core of their disagreements? What had impelled Hannah to such drastic action?

Only gradually did he realize that his mother was crying. She sat so silently, so still, the tears trickling down her face, her hands clenched in her lap. He hadn't seen her weep since...since the day of his father's funeral, all those years ago.

This wasn't something for which his experience had prepared him. When at last he made an awkward gesture toward her, she flinched.

"Don't try to comfort me, Andrew...please. Just don't. You can't change what happened."

"I'm sorry it hurts," he said.

"Oh, yes," she whispered. "It hurts."

CASSIE HAD FINALLY finished packing. Everything was tucked into the rental trailer hitched to her car. The car itself was piled high with boxes of linens and dishes and books. There was room only for Cassie and Zak.

Zak came out of the apartment with one last pillow. ''Arthur'll be glad to see us,'' he said, but he sounded just a little anxious.

''Of course Arthur will be happy,'' Cassie told him. ''He'll be ecstatic.''

Zak was also carrying his dog magazine and his castle book. He squeezed into the passenger side. She climbed into the driver's seat. ''All set?'' she asked him.

''All set.''

She pulled away from the curb. They were packed to bursting, but in reality a woman with a seven-year-old son should have accumulated far more possessions. However, everything would be different from now on. They'd have a real home. Cassie could take that down-payment money and invest at least some of it in furniture. She could put down roots at last.

That was what she kept telling herself, anyway, all the way to Hannah's house. She slowed to make the turn into the driveway. She saw Andrew waiting for them, his hand raised in greeting.

And then she just kept on driving, her foot bearing down on the gas pedal. Zak stared at her in outrage.

"What about Arthur?" he demanded, tears welling up.

"We'll send for him—I promise." Cassie was amazed at the calmness in her own voice.

"Where are we going?" Zak wailed.

"Home," she told him. "Home to Walking Stones."

ROBERT MAXWELL SR. came down the steps of the ranch house. He studied Cassie's overflowing car and the trailer behind.

"Could have given me a little more notice," he said gruffly. He tilted his hat brim down, no doubt so that Cassie wouldn't see the pleased look softening his eyes. If Andrew Morris didn't know how to express his emotions, Robert Maxwell was even worse. But now he took hold of his grandson's hand. "This little fella looks tuckered out, but maybe he still has enough energy to go visit the horses with me."

Zak nodded, gazing up at his grandfather adoringly. Walking Stones had, for the moment, wiped out the absence of Arthur.

"Beth'll see to your rooms," Robert said to Cassie, still gruff. "Make yourself comfortable."

"Thanks, Dad." In a way, she was grateful for how he was underplaying this scene. Any hint of effusiveness right now might have destroyed her hard-won composure.

But then, on the way to the stables, Robert Sr. turned back to his daughter. "Welcome home, Cassandra," he said in a low voice. And the tears smarted in her eyes.

NEWS SEEMED to travel fast in this part of Montana. Cassie had barely unloaded three boxes from her car when the truck of Paradise Corners's deputy sheriff rolled up. Rafe climbed out—all six feet four inches of him—and took a box right out of Cassie's arms.

"Hey there, little sister," he said.

"Hey there, big brother." She was grateful for Rafe's easy banter, and for his unquestioning welcome. But now Rafe's wife climbed out of the truck, grinning at Cassie from ear to ear. Cassie had a feeling Thea's welcome wasn't going to be quite so unquestioning.

Thea grabbed Cassie in a hug. "I am so glad to see you," she exclaimed. "Beth called, of course, and told us all about this sudden—and utterly fantastic—occurrence. I can't believe it! You really came home."

"I can hardly believe it myself," Cassie muttered.

Thea gave her a hard look, then turned to her husband. "Rafe, my sister and I are going to have a little chat."

He balanced the box of books in one hand and

tipped his hat with the other. "Yes, ma'am," he said with mock seriousness. "I get the message. Confidential chat with sister. I'll just unload the car here." The two of them exchanged a fond look, and then Thea hauled Cassie purposefully across the yard.

"Okay, what gives?" she asked Cassie. "You know I'm delighted to see you, and I can't think of anything better than having you so close by. But what on earth is this about? You know Dad'll drive you crazy."

"I know, but I did it for Zak. This is where he belongs." Cassie wondered if she sounded convincing to her sister. She certainly didn't sound convincing to herself. She tried again, waving her hand to encompass the entire ranch—all one hundred and fifty thousand acres of sage and prairie and wildflower. "Besides, I've missed this. Walking Stones really is home…isn't it?" She hadn't meant to end on a question.

"Oh, boy," said Thea. A breeze ruffled her short dark hair, and her gaze was very intent as she studied Cassie. "You'd better tell me the whole story. Would this have anything to do with a certain Texas hunk name of Andrew Morris?"

"Of course not," Cassie blustered, but then she gave her sister an exasperated glance. "Please don't tell me that Gwen called, and—"

"What did you expect? Of course she told us everything, including something about a night of passion.''

Cassie groaned and covered her face. Thea gently pried her hands away.

"No use hiding," she said. "Not from me and Jolie, anyway. Speaking of whom…''

Sure enough, now another vehicle pulled up next to the truck. This time it was Jolie's Blazer. Cassie's oldest sister soon enveloped her in a hug of her own. And that was what finally did it. Cassie burst into tears.

"Oh, honey," Jolie murmured, patting her on the back. "What did Andrew Morris do to you?''

"Why is everyone so fixated on blasted Andrew Morris?" Cassie said soggily. She accepted the tissue that Thea handed her. It was humiliating to come undone like this in front of her two sisters. For as long as she could remember, she'd tried to appear confident and in control. She was supposed to be the rebellious one, the one who blazed new paths and left her family behind. She certainly wasn't supposed to be the one who bawled like a kid.

One sister on either side, she soon found herself sitting on the porch steps. The massive stone columns of the house rose behind, as if to shelter all three of them. But she had not often thought of the ranch as a shelter. It had been, more than anything, a prison to escape. Yet here she was back again, with her son and all her worldly possessions.

Thea handed her another tissue. Jolie patted her back again. "You can tell us all about it," Jolie said.

"You should," agreed Thea.

"What's to say?" Cassie mumbled into her tissue. "I finally told Andrew that I loved him. He didn't have much to say in return. Make that nothing to say. And, after that...oh, it's a long story, but here I am. I didn't plan on it. Or maybe I did! Maybe it's what I've been planning all along. To be near the two of you—and Bobby—and even that impossible man we call our father." Cassie took a deep, quavering breath. "Do you realize how much I hate this? Blubbering like a fool."

"I know," Thea said in a comforting tone. "There's nothing worse than being a restrained Maxwell, and then suddenly you find yourself letting it all hang out."

"Been there," said Jolie. "It is truly a frightening experience. Years and years of self-control suddenly down the drain. But here's the thing, Cassie. This is what being in love does to you. It turns even us self-disciplined Maxwells into blubbering fools."

Cassie blotted her eyes wearily. "But you and Thea, you both have men who love you in return. And what I have is...nothing..."

"You have us," said Jolie.

"Yes, you certainly do," said Thea. "But before we overdo the family-togetherness thing, maybe we'd better let you take a nice long hot shower. It's bad enough having the two of us overwhelm you. Just wait until tonight, and the big family dinner you won't be able to avoid.''

''This really is going to be some night,'' Jolie said lightly. ''The prodigal sister come home. Don't worry, though—we'll get you through it.''

Cassie wondered when her sisters had become so understanding and so sensitive and so downright wonderful. Maybe they'd changed—softened— when they'd fallen in love. Then again, maybe they'd been that way all along, and she just hadn't known how to see it.

After their mother had died, Cassie hadn't known how to reach out to Jolie and Thea. She'd known only how to rebel, how to run away from her grief and anger. It had taken a lot of growing up, and the birth of Zak, to realize how important family was. ''Thanks, guys,'' she said, blotting her eyes all over again. ''Just…thank you.''

THAT NIGHT EVERYONE gathered around the big din-ing-room table in the ranch house. Rafe and Thea sat next to each other, surreptitiously holding hands under the table, as bad as two teenagers who couldn't get enough of each other. Except of course they weren't teenagers—their love was full-grown. They seemed to be having a wonderful time plan-ning their future together: a family someday, and the house they were building on a sizable piece of Walking Stones property.

Of course, Matt and Jolie sat side by side, too, their own deep love apparent to anyone who cared to notice. Rounding out their family were Lily and Charlie, Matt's children—and Jolie's stepchildren. But *stepmother* just wasn't a strong enough word to capture Jolie's role in the kids' lives. Under her care and love, Lily had blossomed from a shy and awkward girl into a beautiful young woman. She'd also managed to get her diabetes under control, and fairly glowed with health these days. She'd recently had her dark blond hair cut in an attractive bob, and it was shiny and full. And Charlie—well, Charlie was as irrepressible and rambunctious as ever. Tonight he seemed to have taken over young Zak as his special charge—and apparently he was trying to teach Zak how to blow milk bubbles through his nose.

"Charlie," Matt said sternly. "That's enough of that." Charlie subsided, but it seemed some trick with mashed potatoes was in the offing. Matt kept an eye on his son without pressing the issue. What a good father he was, firm yet knowing when to give. Lucky Charlie, to have a dad like Matt. How Cassie wished the same for her own son…

Beth Peace bustled back and forth from kitchen to dining room, constantly ignoring Thea's entreaties to sit down and eat with the rest of them. The housekeeper loved orchestrating these family get-togethers. No doubt she was really in her element now…so many of the Maxwells actually getting along for once. Occasionally Beth joked with her brother, Herman, foreman of Walking Stones. And every now and then she gave a lingering glance to the patriarch of the family—Robert Maxwell Sr. Now and then Robert glanced back, seeming just a bit flustered. Boss Maxwell…*flustered?* Cassie didn't know what to think. Over the years, she and her sisters had speculated about the possibility of something developing between their father and Beth. Certainly they'd seen the way Beth fussed over Robert—the way she'd worked miracles lately getting him to take his heart medications. But, as far as Cassie had been able to tell, Robert treated Beth with nothing more than respect and courtesy. Today she couldn't help wondering, though, if something had changed.

But Robert Sr. was now staring hard at his only son. The two Maxwell men sat across the table from each other, the tension between them almost a palpable thing. What had been the latest run-in between them? Cassie could only imagine.

After dinner, she was the one who took Bobby aside. They went out to the porch together, where they could see the vast Montana sky glittering with stars.

"Even in Billings, you don't get a sky like this," Cassie said.

"That's why you came back...the sky?" Bobby asked her with gentle mockery. He had changed so much over these last months. From what Thea and Jolie said, he spent most of his time working on the ranch, keeping to himself. But the question was...had he changed enough? Cassie couldn't shake the thought of that night such a short time ago, when he'd shown up drunk on her doorstep.

Bobby seemed to read her mind. "If you live here, sis," he said, "what am I going to do when I need to escape to Billings?"

Cassie studied his face in the light spilling from the windows. "I take it you haven't called that doctor yet," she said in a low voice.

He stared straight ahead, gripping the porch railing. "I can do this on my own, Cass."

Her heart ached, but she was very glad for one thing. If nothing else, she was happy to be someplace where she could watch more carefully over her kid brother.

"What about your job?" he asked. "You quit that, too?"

"I'll work something out," she told him. "Maybe I'll commute for a little while—who knows. But the way you phrased that...you make it sound like I quit something else, too."

He shrugged. "Even I get to hear the family gossip. I know there's some guy involved. But that's your business, I figure."

Noise and laughter from the house spilled out to them, too. Here they stood—both of them outsiders in a sense. Bobby, not knowing how to make up for all the pain he had caused. Cassie, home at last but more confused than ever.

What would become of the two of them?

CHAPTER SIXTEEN

CASSIE'S HORSE, a roan gelding named Toby, loped across the northwest pasture. It had been years since Cassie had been in the saddle, and yet she felt as comfortable and at home as if it had been yesterday.

Home. That word kept resounding in her mind. In so many ways, Walking Stones *was* home. Why had she fought the fact for so long?

On the other hand, home implied all kinds of contradictions. Warmth. Coldness. Welcome. Rejection...

For now, though, she just rode. The view was breathtaking: the mountains rising in the distance, the sweep of prairie grass all around, the sage a gentle gray-green, clumps of paintbrush here and there still a bright orangy red. There were clumps, too, of Angus cows, lifting their heads to observe her with mild interest.

Toby pricked up his ears, the sign that he had heard something not audible to Cassie. She twisted in the saddle to look behind her, peering out from under the brim of her hat. And, sure enough, in the distance another rider was approaching. She watched, and as the rider drew nearer, her heart seemed to turn a somersault inside her chest. It was none other than Andrew Morris…the man who didn't love her. And he was riding Snowdrop, the bay mare for whom her father had a special fondness. Robert Sr. never let anyone but himself ride Snowdrop, until now, it seemed.

Andrew came to a halt near her. Toby and Snowdrop greeted each other in the way of horses, with a nudge here and there, an answering snuffle. Cassie didn't give Andrew any greeting at all. She just stared at him. He was like a mirage, a materialization of all her longings.

"What are you doing here?" she managed to say at last.

He cocked his hat—perhaps that, too, borrowed from Robert Sr. "More to the point," he said, "what are you doing here?"

She supposed it was only natural that a man who had lived all those years in Texas would look so good astride a horse, and wearing a cowboy hat. But that didn't help her to marshal her thoughts. They seemed to have scattered like cotton puffs on the wind.

"This is where I belong," she said. "It just took me a while to admit it."

Andrew frowned. "I thought we had a deal. You were going to move into the guest house—I was going to leave you alone."

"You can leave me alone even more if I live out here," she retorted. And then, "Clearly, you've met my father. Either that, or he's about to come after you with a shotgun for absconding with Snowdrop."

"Yeah, I met your dad," Andrew said. "Nice guy."

Cassie narrowed her eyes. "You're being sarcastic, of course."

"No. We hit it off right from the start. Told him I'd come to deliver a dog for his grandson."

Arthur... Cassie had been trying to figure out how she was going to send for the puppy. Maybe she should have known Andrew would see to the task personally. He did so like to be in control of the situation.

"Zak is going to be overjoyed," Cassie said. "Thank you."

"He's already pretty happy. I left him and the dog chasing each other in circles. I'm kind of jealous—one look at Arthur, and Zak forgot I was around."

Just as it should be, Cassie said silently. *My son needs to forget all about you, Andrew Morris. I need to forget, too.*

"I'm sorry you had to come all this way," she said out loud. "It really was generous of you."

"Dammit, Cassie—will you stop thanking me? And maybe you wouldn't mind telling me what this is all about. I thought the last thing you wanted to do was hide out on this ranch."

"I'm not hiding out," she said stiffly. "I'm just doing what's right for Zak." She was still using her son as an excuse, and that made her feel guilty all over again. But it was true, wasn't it? She knew Zak could be happy here...already *was* happy. Even Andrew had seen it.

She urged Toby into a trot, and headed back toward the ranch house. Snowdrop fell into pace beside her—Andrew really was an expert horseman.

"Is there anything you can't do?" she said acidly. "You perform house repairs, you hike, you ride...sure, maybe you don't know much about carburetors, but you *are* an expert lawyer."

"Who said I'm an expert?" he asked with a hint of humor in his voice.

"Your mother, for one. She's as bad as Hannah at singing your praises." Cassie paused. "Has she gone back to California yet?"

"She left yesterday. She didn't want to be around after I told her about Hannah's will."

"Andrew, I wish it could have been different. I'm sorry—"

"You have to know my mom doesn't begrudge you anything, Cassie. She wants you to move into the guest house, too."

Cassie had genuinely liked Katharine. Too bad she'd never get to know her better.

"This is where I belong," Cassie repeated. "For now, at least. Until I can resolve a few things with my family. And until I can build up my house fund a little more.''

''You already have a house,'' Andrew said stubbornly. But Cassie refused to listen. It was a relief to get back to the stables, where she unsaddled Toby. Andrew, of course, followed with Snowdrop. He seemed to know all the things to be done with horses...the unsaddling and the cooling down and even the brushing.

''Did you learn all that in Dallas?'' she asked with a sigh.

''You forget. I lived in Montana until I was eighteen.''

She did have a habit of forgetting that, maybe because Andrew refused to talk a whole lot about himself. Everything reminded her of the way he kept his emotions closed off. Oh, he knew how to touch a woman, and kiss her and make love to her. He certainly knew how to do that. But when it came to the *real* touching, soul to soul...he refused.

Cassie went striding toward the house. ''I'm sure you're in a hurry to get back to Billings,'' she said over her shoulder at him.

''Actually, no. Your father invited me to spend the day.''

Cassie stopped to glare at him. ''And you accepted?''

''Seemed the polite thing to do.'' Andrew sounded so relaxed, so in command. This was too much. *Two* men in her life trying to take control. Maybe she was playing with fire, coming to Walking Stones where every day of her life she'd have to stand up to her dad. Right now it felt impossible to endure *one* day with both Robert Maxwell Sr. and Andrew Morris waltzing around the ranch.

"I'm rescinding the invitation," Cassie said through gritted teeth. "I'd like you to go, Andrew."

He studied her. "Do you really mean that?"

"Of course I mean it," she exclaimed, "or else I wouldn't have said it."

"Okay," he said. "I'll go."

Somehow she didn't feel the satisfaction she'd expected. They walked on and reached the ranch house. Zak came running over to them, Arthur bouncing right at his side.

"Hey, Andrew, Grandpa says you're staying for lunch. And dinner, too. And I just taught Arthur how to roll over. He's very smart."

Andrew glanced over at Cassie. "Well, about lunch. And about dinner—"

Cassie knew when she was defeated. "Of course you're staying," she muttered. "We can't disappoint the grandpa—or the grandson."

EVERYONE IN Cassie's family, it seemed, approved of Andrew Morris. They'd barely just met the man, but they were ready to declare him an unqualified success.

"He really is a hunk," Thea whispered at lunch-time.

"Just as gorgeous as Gwen described him," Jolie pronounced when she took a break from her clinic to drop over and see "Cassie's guy." Robert Sr. and Bobby didn't say much of anything, but somehow, at some point in the afternoon, the two of them sat down with Andrew to discuss the potential lawsuit hanging over Bobby. It was still uncertain whether Dan Aiken would ever walk again. Dan's parents hadn't made the lawsuit official yet, but they were threatening to sue for at least five million dollars. Maybe the only thing stopping them so far was the fact that they'd be going up against the powerful lawyers who represented Robert Maxwell Sr. Cassie could imagine that would be enough to make any-body hesitate. It gave her a sick feeling, knowing the kind of influence her father could wield with scarcely a thought on his part. Power and money...the Maxwells had always possessed too much of those.

But today something of a miracle was happening, Robert and his son were sitting at a table together and actually having a conversation where one of them didn't end up shouting. What kind of magic was Andrew working on them?

Cassie prowled outside, where the cool Montana breeze chased after her. Already there was a promise of fall in the air. In only a week or so, it would be time for Zak to start second grade. He'd be able to go to the school in Paradise Corners. Everything would work out here, surely. If only Cassie could shake that apprehensive feeling deep inside...

Thea came across the yard toward her. As usual she was dressed for work at the ranch, wearing faded jeans and cowboy boots. As she reached Cassie, she slipped off her well-worn leather gloves.

"Where's Andrew?" she asked casually.

"Still charming everyone in sight, I'm sure. Even Beth likes him, and she *never* used to like the guys I brought home."

"You don't sound too pleased," Thea observed.

"How can I be?" Cassie asked discontentedly.

"Because he refuses to utter the L word?" Thea asked, her tone astute. "But I see the way he looks at you, Cassie. The man wants you big time."

Wanting wasn't the same as loving. Cassie felt so restless she thought she'd explode. It would be better when Andrew left. The knowledge of his presence wouldn't taunt her then.

"Are you and Rafe going to spend a quiet evening at home?" Cassie asked, trying to change the subject.

"Nothing doing," Thea said. "We're all congregating over here again. Didn't you know? Everyone wants a look at Andrew, Rafe and Matt included."

Cassie really felt as if she'd explode now. "Is it

always like this around here—no control over your own life? No control even about dinnertime—''

''You knew that before you came back,'' Thea said wryly. ''Cassie, do you really think this move is the best thing for you and Zak? You do have your own house now in Billings. Andrew says—''

''Andrew says a lot of things.'' Everything except the one thing that mattered.

IT SEEMED FOREVER before Andrew came out of the house and joined Cassie. He sat down beside her on the porch steps.

''I don't believe it,'' she told him. ''I really don't. My father gives advice to *lawyers*—he never takes it. Now suddenly he's listening to a man he only met today—a man he doesn't even have on retainer. What did you do to him?''

''Look at it this way,'' Andrew said imperturbably, ''I merely represented an opportunity your dad didn't want to pass up. No doubt he'd been trying to find a way to talk about the lawsuit with your brother—a way that wouldn't ruffle as many feathers as in the past. I'm a lawyer, but I'm a neutral observer—someone who's not representing one side or the other. It was natural that your father would ask me to listen in...as a moderator of sorts.''

''Nothing is that easy,'' Cassie muttered. ''Not where my father is concerned.''

''Maybe it is.''

Cassie thought it over. She had to admit that over the past months, Robert Sr. *had* softened in a couple of ways. After some rough spots, he'd accepted Rafe and Matt into the family...two new sons-in-law. And she couldn't ignore his ongoing gentleness with Zak. Certainly she couldn't ignore the new look on his face whenever he glanced at Beth. An embarrassed but hopeful look...

"Wonders never cease," she said dryly, almost to herself. Then she turned to Andrew. "So, tell me. How much ammunition are the Maxwells going to use in their fight this time?"

Andrew rubbed his jaw. "No ammunition," he said.

Cassie studied him suspiciously. "What happened in there?"

"Nothing that was my doing," Andrew said in a quiet voice. "It's like I told you, Cassie, your father and your brother had been working their way toward this talk for some time. They just needed a little bit of a catalyst to get there. If I supplied the excuse, I'm glad. But the upshot is, your brother doesn't want to contest the lawsuit. In fact, he wants to go to the Aiken family on his own, without any lawyers, and offer them a settlement. A very generous settlement, I might add. He's asking your father to convert his part of the Maxwell inheritance into a trust fund for Dan."

"Wow," Cassie said, letting out her breath.

"That just sounds so...right." She blinked rapidly, dismayed at the tears that came so readily to her these days. But she was proud of her kid brother. Very proud, indeed. Only now she couldn't think of him as a kid anymore. It seemed that Bobby Maxwell had started to grow up at last.

"What did my father have to say?" she asked after a moment.

"He didn't say much of anything. I gather he's a man of few words. He just growled something at the end about no son of his giving up his *entire* inheritance. And then, when the two of them stood, just for a second or two, your father put his hand on your brother's shoulder. That's all."

It was enough.

THE FAMILY GATHERING that evening was just as much of a strain as Cassie had imagined. Unfortunately, *she* seemed to be the only one under strain. Everyone else was having a wonderful time.

Rafe and Matt hit it off with Andrew right away. In fact, while they waited for dinner, the three of them organized an impromptu game of tag football on the lawn. Thea and Jolie joined in, too, their competitive Maxwell streak showing up big time. After a short while a few of the ranch hands were drawn in as well, along with Herman Peace, Beth's brother. Herman, despite his sixty-odd years, gave the other men good measure. And the kids, of course—Zak and Charlie and Lily. Not to mention the animals racing after the ball: one relentless puppy named Arthur, Rafe's amiable bloodhound Jed, another bloodhound known as Leona—Rafe's gift to Thea—and Charlie's little black-and-white powder puff of a dog known ironically as Samson. Cassie played for a bit, too, but then stood on the sidelines, watching. So much noise and laughter...could it be that the old wounds were beginning to heal at last? If so, why did she feel so melancholy?

She wandered inside the house, to the big homey kitchen where Beth was putting the last touches on dinner. Cassie had always loved this room best: the gleaming copper pots hanging from a butcher's rack, Beth's potted geraniums scattered on the window-sills, the ancient cherry-wood sideboard with its collection of mismatched china.

"Smells great," Cassie said. "Want some help?"

Beth stirred the thick vegetable sauce simmering on the stove. "That is possibly the most insincere offer I have ever heard," she said. "You hate to cook, Cassandra Maxwell Warren."

"Don't blame me," Cassie said with a little smile, sliding onto a stool. "It's all your fault. You always made such delicious meals while I was growing up. I couldn't compete with you."

"Flattery," said Beth, shaking her head so that her soft brown hair swung from side to side, "will get you nowhere with me."

"Don't I know it." Cassie propped her elbows on the breakfast bar. "You know, Beth, I'm sorry I was such a pain when I was a teenager. I don't know if I've ever really apologized. All those nights I snuck out of the house, the late nights when I know you must have been so worried…"

"Figured that out, did you?" Beth asked. "I did worry, about all three of you girls. But you turned out pretty well, I think. I like to believe I had a hand in it. And now, if I could just stop worrying about your brother…"

"If we could all stop worrying," Cassie murmured. After a pause, she went on. "You really did raise us, Beth. You were like a mother to us—"

"No, I'd never try to take Helen's place." Beth spoke sharply, and turned away. She got just a little too busy with the cabbage she was chopping on the cutting board.

"Beth," Cassie said. "I'll only say this once so that I don't embarrass you. Everyone in this family would be more than happy if, well, if you and Dad…"

"Stop, already," Beth said, but her brown eyes belied her words and she gave Cassie the briefest look of gratitude. Then she reverted to her usual efficient and no-nonsense self. "If you think your father is going to consider me fondly tonight, think again." She gestured at the vegetable sauce. "No meat. Just tofu."

"You're going to feed him *tofu*—"

"There's a first time for everything," Beth said grimly, "especially when a man's heart is at stake. That stubborn noodlehead known as your dad, well, tonight, he really is getting noodles. The egg-free kind. And a big salad."

"You are a brave woman, Beth Peace," Cassie told her.

"Don't I know it. Now, get back out there and tackle a football."

"I just can't seem to relax," Cassie said. "Bobby's nowhere to be found, and I can't help wondering—"

"He's up in his room," Beth said. "Having a think. Best thing for him right now. Stop using your brother as an excuse, and go romance that young man of yours."

Cassie gazed indignantly at Beth. "Don't *you* start again—"

"Just get out of here, Cassandra Maxwell Warren. Stop lecturing me about *my* love life, and do something about your own."

WHEN IT WAS TIME for dessert that night, Beth produced low-fat cherry cobbler. "Except," she said, "there isn't quite enough to go around. I miscalculated. Cassie, guess you'll have to take your young man into town. You can stop at Grizzly's for some pie."

Cassie frowned at Beth. The woman had never once in her life miscalculated when it came to a recipe. ''Beth—''

''Go along, now.''

Knowing glances traveled around the table. Suddenly it seemed like a very good idea to get away from the overpowering Maxwell clan. Cassie escaped outside with Andrew. The night was cool, and she zipped up her fleece jacket.

''If you don't mind Grizzly's, I don't either,'' she said.

''I liked the way Beth phrased it better,'' Andrew replied.

''Beth,'' Cassie said, ''should stop playing matchmaker.''

''She's a nice lady,'' said Andrew.

''The feeling is mutual, it seems. Everyone in my family approves of you heartily.''

''Everyone,'' said Andrew, ''except you.''

She didn't have any answer for that. She just climbed into Andrew's truck, and let him make the thirty-mile drive into town. The vehicle took the ranch road as if born to it. Cassie stared out into the night, where a million stars sparkled in the vast sky.

''When are you leaving for Texas?'' she asked.

''Soon.'' That one word had such a finality.

''Just can't wait to get away, can you?'' Cassie said.

''I don't want to get away from you, Cassie.'' The

words seemed to come reluctantly, but his voice was just a little husky. A shiver of awareness went through her body. Awareness of Andrew so close to her…

She hunched inside her jacket, even though the truck had a more than capable heater.

"I'm thinking about stopping," Andrew said. "Pulling over, and—"

"Just drive, Andrew," Cassie whispered. "Please." She held her arms tightly against her.

She felt better when they reached town and walked into Grizzly's. She didn't feel so vulnerable here. She'd known this place for as long as she could remember, with its log walls and exposed beams. The owner, Mona Rangel, had spruced it up a bit, though—vivid wildlife prints hanging everywhere, and fresh daisies and violets adorning the tables. Mona herself came to wait on them. She was open and friendly with Andrew…polite but more than a bit reserved with Cassie. Cassie couldn't help thinking that the woman had to resent the Maxwells. She'd been a teacher for twenty years but had lost her job when she'd refused to pass troublemaker Bobby Maxwell out of sixth grade. Mona was just one more casualty of the power Robert Maxwell Sr. had wielded so long in Paradise Corners. Even now, Cassie felt ashamed for her family. No matter that

Mona was now doing very well at Grizzly's. She had suffered wrongfully because of the Maxwells.

Mona delivered two slices of her specialty—rich, flaky blackberry pie. Then she hurried away.

"She didn't seem in the best mood," Andrew remarked.

"It's a long story," Cassie said. "In fact, there are all kinds of stories about Robert Maxwell, and the way he's tried to rule this town. As his kids, we get a lot of fallout. A lot of resentment and anger." Cassie shook her head. "Sometimes the resentment has been downright dangerous. Only a few months ago, Megan Wheeler's father went after Jolie. He'd always blamed my family for the misfortunes in his life, and he ended up turning all his hatred against Jolie." Cassie shivered at the memory. "He went to the cabin where Jolie was living at the time, and he attacked her. He really could have hurt her, but fortunately Matt and Rafe got to her in time."

"Sounds like you're dealing with a whole lot of history," Andrew said. "Makes me realize how much I don't know about you, Cassie. I don't know who Megan is, let alone Megan's father."

She'd always accused Andrew of keeping himself shut off from her. But she'd done the same with him. Suddenly, even though the pie was delicious, she didn't seem to have much appetite left. She set her fork down.

"Megan is—*was*—Bobby's girlfriend. Not to

mention the fact that she's the mother of his baby daughter. Jolie helped her to get a scholarship at Montana State in Bozeman, and she's starting there this fall. Meanwhile she's continuing to work at Jolie's clinic, and she's living with Matt and Jolie…'' Cassie realized that she was rambling on. She had so little time left with Andrew—how much of her life *could* she share? ''Anyway,'' she went on quickly, ''Megan's father has always hated the Maxwells—blames them for losing his ranch—and finding out that his daughter was going to have a Maxwell baby didn't help matters any. When Megan refused to try to get any money from my family, Abe Wheeler really got mad. One thing led to another, Jolie got caught in the middle…you get the idea. Maxwells stir up all kinds of emotion in this town.''

Andrew had a look of unwilling fascination on his face. But he, at least, seemed to suffer no appetite problems—he was polishing off his pie. ''Sounds to me,'' he said, ''like this Abe Wheeler isn't an all-around nice guy.''

''He's not, but that doesn't change the fact that my dad has done some rotten things. You're lucky, Andrew. He could've made *your* life miserable. When Jolie was dating Matt, my father decided that he was just one more man out to get the Maxwell money. In the process, he almost ruined Matt's construction business. I know you came here today, and you charmed everybody and they charmed *you*, but there's a whole lot more to the Maxwells than you realize.''

Andrew finished the last bite of pie. ''Cassie,'' he said, ''why are you telling me this? Are you trying to warn me away?''

She stared at him. ''Maybe. But maybe that's not necessary. Because you've already decided that you're leaving, Andrew. You've already decided that nothing's going to happen between us.''

He just gazed at her across the table, and his look seemed to say too much about desire and loss. Cassie felt the blood heating all through her, felt the heartbeat of her own desire and longing. And then she did something reckless, something she had no business doing. She tossed some bills on the table, enough to pay for the pie and a generous tip. Then she stood, grabbed Andrew's hand and pulled him out the door.

''There's someplace I want to show you,'' she said. And the pulse of longing inside her only grew stronger.

CHAPTER SEVENTEEN

LAST WOMAN PEAK GAVE an impressive view of Paradise Corners. Cassie and Andrew settled on the grass. Far below them, they could see the town lights glimmering, obscured here and there by maple and fir trees. It wasn't really much of a town—a total of twelve square blocks—but Cassie knew every bit of it. She pointed out to Andrew the four church spires that had given the town its name: one on each corner of Main and Church.

"The town kids have a game," she murmured. "A version of tag where you run as fast as you can from one church to the other. You have to touch all four corners of Paradise…that game's been around as long as I can remember. I played it with my sisters, way back before my mother died."

"I guess you really do belong here," Andrew said grudgingly. "Maybe this really is home."

"Maybe." But she hadn't come up here to talk about Paradise Corners. She knew exactly why she'd brought Andrew here…for this. For the moment when he turned to her and cupped her face in his hands, and kissed her. She had missed the taste of

him, the feel of him. And she had never stopped
needing him, not once.

He lowered her to the ground, the grass flattening
beneath them. She held him with all the yearning
and need inside her. All the love...

And then, with a low moan, she twisted away
from him. She sat up, shoulders huddled, head bent.

"Dammit, Andrew," she whispered.

"I want you, Cassie."

The words sounded so compelling. But they
weren't the ones she wanted to hear.

"I love you," she said, her voice raw. "Why...
why can't you love me in return?"

Again he had no answer for her.

"YOU SHOULDN'T HAVE come back," Andrew told
his mother, a few days after his visit to Walking
Stones.

She looked up from the letters and papers spread
out around her on the floor. "When my son starts
telling me what I should and shouldn't do..." she
began with some asperity. But then she just lifted
her shoulders. "I had to come back," she said simply. "I've been running away from Hannah all my
life. Sooner or later I had to stop running, didn't I?"

Andrew wandered around the spare room where
he'd stuffed all of Hannah's memorabilia. Not that
there was much space for wandering. His grandmother's possessions had taken over.

"You weren't supposed to find any of this," he told his mother.

"I poked my head in here on my last visit," she said. "Hannah was never tidy. When I looked in the attic and saw how clean it was, I knew you'd done something sneaky."

He hadn't meant to be sneaky. He'd just meant to protect his mother.

"I keep asking myself," he said, "what really went on between you and Hannah. It couldn't have been just that she liked to bake cookies, and you liked to buy them. Or the fact that you got a master's degree, and she barely finished high school. Differences, yes, but not enough for what happened."

Katharine had been sorting more papers on the floor, but now her hands stilled. She didn't speak for a long moment.

"It was about your father," she said at last. And then she looked at Andrew. "Even from here," she said softly, "I can feel the way you've tensed up. I guess that's why I've never talked about it before—because you couldn't seem to bear it. And I didn't want to remember, either, but it has to be said, Andrew. I should have talked to my mother about it while I still had the chance. But now...I'll talk to you."

He didn't want to hear. It had been a mistake to probe for deeper answers. Almost without realizing it, he moved toward the door.

"No, son." His mother's voice was firm, allowing no argument. He might have been a kid again. But there was the danger...remembering back to when he was a child, a nine-year-old boy.

"Hannah never approved of your father, not from the first moment she met him," Katharine said. "She said he was irresponsible—no, more than that. She said he didn't have good judgment, and never would. She was worried that he would hurt me somehow. I didn't see her concern, of course. I only saw that she rejected my choice. I had a terrible blowup with her. I accused her of turning your grandfather against Neil, too. So Neil and I—we ended up eloping. When we came back to town, I suppose all of us tried to patch things up. Mother tried to be civil to Neil. But nothing was ever quite the same afterward. The usual mother-daughter disagreements began to escalate. Rejection on both sides..."

Neil Morris. That had been his father's name. But Andrew never tried to say it. The name only made his memories all the more vivid. Now he remained by the door, aching to leave...unable to move.

"And then the night came...the night your father died," Katharine went on. "The night you could have died, too. We found out later that he'd been drinking right before he took you in the car. Not a whole lot, just enough to impair his judgment. And that was the terrible irony, don't you see? That

Mother was right all along. Neil didn't always use good judgment.'' Katharine's voice seemed to drain away. She gestured at the papers and letters strewn out before her, many of them turned yellow and brittle with the passage of time. At last she spoke again.

"I hated her after your father died. I was so full of grief and anger that I had to turn on someone. So I turned on her. I thought if only she'd accepted Neil, if only she'd believed in him, then maybe he wouldn't have done that one foolish, terrible thing that killed him. It didn't make any sense, I know, but I had to blame someone. And then I let the years pass, I let the hurt just keep building up...I kept holding on to it. Hannah did the same. And that phone call...I accused her about Neil all over again. And she started crying, and said she wanted to hurt me the way I'd hurt her. She found a way—she cut me off.''

Andrew remained imprisoned by the door. He couldn't do anything to comfort his mother, couldn't speak, couldn't move toward her. He was nine years old again, and it was the night his father had died. As if from a great distance, he heard his mother go on.

"I have to believe somehow that she still loved me. Because, in spite of everything, I still loved *her*. She saved every letter I ever wrote to her. Maybe she saved everything else, too, but I have to believe, Andrew. I have to hold on to something. I can't believe that it all ended in bitterness and anger, and there can never be anything else.''

He still couldn't speak. He couldn't help his mother. Because he was watching it all over again, hearing every sound. The skid of tires, the whine of brakes. His father's face, ashen white, except for that one trickle of blood. His father's voice, very faint. *Promise me...promise me that you will never tell what really happened.*

Yes, his father had been drinking that night. But that wasn't what had killed him.

ZAK AND ARTHUR went racing across the front hall of the ranch house, leaving a trail of mud behind them.

"Zachary!" Cassie called. "Come right back here and clean up after yourself."

Zak skidded to a halt and came morosely back. "Grandpa's waiting for me—"

"And Beth just cleaned this floor. Go get some paper towels from the kitchen."

Robert Maxwell Sr. appeared just then in the doorway from the living room. "I'll send someone else to clean up after Zachary. He and I have an appointment out at the stables."

It's just a little thing, Cassie told herself. *A little mud on the floor. I can let it go this time.*

But she'd been letting too many things go over the past week she'd been at the ranch. Letting her father countermand her instructions to Zak. Letting him interfere with things like bedtime and what Zak ate and whether or not he picked up after himself.

"No, Dad," she said as evenly as possible. "Zak will get some paper towels and clean up the mud."

Robert Sr. faced her across the hallway. "I know what I'm doing with Zachary," he said in the rumbling voice that meant he was working up a head of steam. "I watch over him as if he were my own son. But you're away all day, Cassandra."

"I can't quit my job," she said tiredly. "Not yet, anyway." The long commute back and forth to Billings had been sapping all her energy, and taking far too much time away from Zak, she knew. But at least her son was with family while she was gone.

Except that family could cause all kinds of problems.

"Zak, go get the paper towels," Cassie told her son. Zak stood for a moment, glancing wide-eyed from his mother to his grandfather. But then he darted toward the kitchen, Arthur close behind. Cassie faced Robert again.

"Zak needs consistency," she said. "He needs to know there are consequences for his actions—"

"So he's a little sloppy," Robert said dismissively. "A Maxwell trademark."

"There are a lot of Maxwell trademarks I'm not happy with," Cassie retorted. "Such as thinking that other people will clean up after you. Hasn't that been the problem all along with Bobby? We spoiled him rotten, let him believe he could do anything he liked, and someone else would take care of the mess.''

''You mean *I* spoiled him.'' Robert was beginning to breathe hard, his face turning red. ''Just come out and say it. You think *I'm* the one to blame for all my son's problems.''

''We're all to blame, Dad. Just calm down—''

He went to the stairs and thumped the newel post. ''I damn well don't need to calm down. This is still my house, isn't it? And if I have another chance to raise a Maxwell boy—to do things right this time—I'm damn well not going to give up on it!''

Cassie was truly alarmed at the raspy sound of her father's breathing, but she couldn't afford to let the last comment pass. ''*I'm* raising Zak,'' she said quietly. ''You're his grandfather. And if you don't calm down right now, I'm going to call Jolie and have her come over to take a look at you.''

Robert Maxwell Sr. swore again. He was truly an impressive figure, towering there by the stairs, his reddish hair showing only those few strands of white. But he was also a man with a serious heart condition.

''Dad, just sit down. I'm calling Jolie right now.'' She went to the phone, and started punching in her sister's number at the clinic.

''All I want is another chance. That's all,'' Robert

said. And then, his gait heavy, he began climbing the stairs.

EARLY THE NEXT MORNING, Cassie met her sisters for a summit at Jolie's clinic. Jolie's roster was full for the day, but the first patient had yet to arrive. By now, Cassie should have been well on her way to Billings, but after yesterday's run-in with her dad, she'd decided to take the day off. Robert Sr. might be the most exasperating father a girl could have, but he *was* her father, and he did have congestive heart failure. She was worried about him. She could see the worry in her sisters' faces, too.

"I called Beth just before you guys got here," Jolie informed Cassie and Thea. "Dad had as good a night as can be expected. What worries me is the recurring edema. I think he's been pulling a fast one on Beth—not taking all his pills the way he should. We'll just have to watch him. Thank goodness you called me yesterday, Cassie. Thank goodness you were there, period."

Cassie sank into a chair in Jolie's waiting room. The surroundings should have been conducive to happiness and peacefulness. Jolie's decor was charming, the walls painted a light, creamy color, the inviting rural prints adding splashes of brighter color. But Cassie didn't feel happy or peaceful. She just felt tired and anxious.

"Every time I try to make the right decision for

Zak, things seem to end up even worse. Now I have even more problems than before. Dad's spoiling Zak, and it reminds me of how he spoiled Bobby. And me being there…clearly it's not good for Dad's health. I don't know what to do.''

"Don't blame yourself," Thea told her, settling into another chair. "It's Dad's nature to get worked up. If it hadn't been you, it would have been something else.''

Jolie pulled up a chair so she could sit between her sisters. All three of them were turned so they could look out the window at Paradise Corners. Jolie propped her feet on the sill.

"Honey," she said, "unfortunately, when you're trying to run away from the man you love, you just make more complications for yourself.''

Cassie scowled at her. "I told the man I loved him—*twice*. What else am I supposed to do?"

"I don't know," Jolie confessed. "But it doesn't change the fact that you *are* running away from Andrew Morris.''

"I feel like you're trying to run my life all over again," Cassie grumbled.

"Well, we know you have issues about being managed," Thea said teasingly. "In fact, if there's one thing that can be said about Cassandra Maxwell Warren, it's the fact that she absolutely *hates* to be managed.''

"All right, all right," Cassie said. "You've made

your point. I suppose Dr. Gwen has been on the phone to you again.''

"That,'' said Jolie, "and the fact that we grew up with you…remember?''

"How I do remember,'' Cassie murmured. She glanced at her sisters. "You know, it's really nice to be with both of you like this,'' she said awkwardly.

"You mean we're not sniping at each other or nursing hurt feelings?'' Jolie said wryly. "Yeah, it is nice. Wonder what finally happened to make us all take off the boxing gloves.''

"Let me see,'' said Cassie. "Rafe happened. And then Matt happened.''

"Oh, so it's the men in our lives,'' Thea said gravely. "Before *they* came along, we were absolute monsters.''

"You know that's not what I meant,'' Cassie protested. "It's just that, well, being in love does give you a new perspective, doesn't it? Even if it breaks your heart, it teaches you what's important. It's made me realize how necessary Mom was to Dad. How necessary she was to all of us. And when she died…I guess this family fell apart a little.''

"Make that a lot,'' Jolie murmured. "We all lost our way. It's taken us years and years to begin to heal.''

"But we *are* healing, aren't we?'' Thea asked.

"Yes,'' said Cassie. "We are.''

All three sisters linked hands for a moment. That was how they were sitting when Jolie's nurse, Irene, came breezing into the office. Irene gave them a cheerful good-morning, as if she was quite accustomed to the Maxwell sisters getting all sentimental. Then, a few moments later, Megan opened the office door, wheeling in a stroller. This event only created more sentimentality: all three Maxwell sisters gathering to admire their young niece, Melissa Jo.

Melissa was only a few months old, but she was already a beauty. She had her mother's dark auburn hair, arranged in downy curls. And she had Bobby's intense eyes…the eyes Bobby had inherited from his own mother. Cassie gazed at this baby, and saw generations' worth of hope and love. She knew why people kept having babies…you needed a wealth of hope in this life. You needed new beginnings. She knelt before Melissa, allowing her niece to take hold of her finger.

"You are truly something, Melissa," she said.

"I second that," Thea said.

"Motion approved," said Jolie. The three sisters smiled at each other. Megan smiled, too.

"My daughter's going to end up thinking she's the princess of Paradise Corners."

"Hmm…a princess in Paradise," said Thea. "I like the sound of that."

Megan's smiled faded. "Except Melissa and I

won't be here much longer," she said. "We'll be in Bozeman."

"Where you'll be going to school for that business degree, and loving every minute of it," Jolie said briskly. "And of course you'll come back for lots of visits."

"Of course," said Megan, regaining confidence. How she had changed from the shy, frightened young girl who had once adored Bobby Maxwell. She really did have confidence now, an aura of strength and courage.

"I'll get to work," Megan said now, pushing the stroller over to the playpen set up in a corner of the office. She lifted Melissa into it, settled the baby with some toys, and then turned on the office computer.

Meanwhile, Jolie shrugged into her white lab coat. "Guess I'd better get to work, too," she said.

"Guess I'd better head for the ranch," Thea said. "That new mare is about to foal, and I want to be there when she does. I'll grab a lift with you, Cassie, if you're headed back now."

"Yes," Cassie answered. "I'm going to spend some time with Zak *and* his granddad. Hopefully this time I won't cause a catastrophe."

Yet, as the three sisters prepared to go about their day, someone else walked into the clinic: their brother, Bobby Maxwell, tall and handsome and very serious. Megan drew in her breath and sprang up from the computer. She gave Bobby a cool glance.

"I'll just go back and do some organizing," she said, heading toward the examination rooms.

"Don't go—I'd like you to hear this, too, Megan," Bobby said altogether too formally. "I have something I want all of you to know." But first he went over to his daughter. He knelt by the playpen for a moment, gazing somberly at Melissa. Then he straightened and faced his sisters—and the girl he loved.

"I just wanted to tell you that I'm on my way to Billings," he said. "To the doctor Cassie told me about. I've already made the appointment." Now his eyes were focused only on Megan. "Last night I had a beer in my hand," he told her. "I was going to drink it. I kept telling myself that it was the only thing that ever made me feel good. But then I thought about you, Meg, and I stopped. That's all. I stopped. And I'm going to find somebody who can help me."

Bobby went to each of his sisters in turn and gave them a bear hug. "Thanks," he told them. "Just…thanks."

"One of us will drive you in," Cassie said, her voice clogged with more of those annoying tears.

"No," Bobby said. "Nothing personal, but I don't think I should do this with any Maxwells around. Bill's driving me," and he gestured outside to the battered green pickup that belonged to one of Walking Stones's ranch hands.

"You'll be fine with Bill," Jolie said, looking suspiciously misty-eyed herself. But Thea didn't make any effort to hide her feelings.

"Oh, Bobby," she said, and enveloped him in another hug, letting the tears roll down her cheeks.

Megan had been watching all this with a guarded expression. Bobby stood in front of her without making any move to touch her.

"For what it's worth, Meg, I do love you. I'll never stop. I know I've been a jerk, the worst kind, but I do love you...and Melissa. Goodbye." He turned, went out the door and clattered down the steps to Bill's waiting pickup.

Megan remained frozen for another moment, myriad emotions etched across her face. But then she, too, dashed out the door.

"Bobby...Bobby, wait!"

She caught up to him beside the pickup. Cassie, Thea and Jolie knew no shame now. All three of them crowded at the window to watch. They saw their brother and Megan talking very intently to each other. And then they saw Bobby gather Megan up in his arms, twirling her around joyfully.

"Let's show some decency," Jolie chided her sisters. "Let's give them a little privacy." And so the Maxwell sisters turned their backs to the window. But all three of them were grinning from ear to ear.

CHAPTER EIGHTEEN

ANDREW'S OFFICE afforded a vista of Dallas sky-scrapers. It was a stunning view, his clients often told him. He was a lucky man, they also told him. Successful law practice, view from the top. What more could a guy ask?

So why was it that all he could think of was the view from a certain mountaintop overlooking the town of Paradise Corners, Montana? A mountaintop where he'd held Cassie Warren in his arms, and where he'd said goodbye to her, too.

His secretary buzzed him. "Mr. Dolan called to say he'll be half an hour late for his appointment."

Another half an hour to himself. Maybe he'd get some work done. Or maybe he'd just sit here some more and think about views.

"By the way, Andrew," his secretary said over the intercom, "it really is good to have you back."

"Thanks, Fran." She always knew how to say the right thing, but he suspected that she'd enjoyed having him out of the office. She'd been able to take off early, have a little time to herself. Fran was a woman who understood her priorities. He envied her that.

He swiveled in his chair and stared out the window. It was the best window money could buy, made from double-paned glass that filtered out the sun but still allowed you to enjoy the view.

He wondered what Cassie was doing right now. He pictured her on the ranch. Now that he'd been to Walking Stones, he had a lot more insight into what made her tick. She'd grown up with all the wealth and power of her father, and then she'd done everything she could to stand on her own two feet. No wonder she wouldn't tolerate any hint of a man taking control of her life.

Andrew glanced at his watch, surprised to see that only five minutes had passed. He had another good twenty-five before Dolan showed. Walking restlessly around his office, he saw all the order and control he had established for his own life: the dust-free file cabinets where everything was arranged precisely from A to Z, the potted plants that Fran watered and cared for so he didn't have to worry about them, the modular sofa where he could stretch out when he was working late and didn't want to bother going home. Because there was nothing—and no one—for him to go home to.

He went to his phone and punched the intercom button. ''Fran,'' he said.

"Here, boss," she answered in her best military voice.

"Call Dolan on his cell phone and cancel the appointment. And, Fran—"

"Yes, boss?"

"Take some more time off," he told her.

ZAK SHRUGGED. "I don't have to," he said.

"Of course you have to take your vitamins."

"Grandpa doesn't take *his* pills," Zak said. "He flushes them down the toilet."

The guilty party entered the kitchen just as Zak spoke. Cassie gave her father a worried frown.

"Dad, is this true—you're still not taking your medication?"

Robert Sr. looked chagrined. "How can I not take it, with Beth standing over me all the time and threatening to stuff the damn pills down my throat?"

"Obviously you're still managing to get around her." Cassie studied her father. His complexion didn't look as healthy as it should; it was blotchy in places. Robert had once appeared to be all muscle, but now there was a puffiness to his skin. And the way he struggled with his breathing more and more…

"Don't call your sister," Robert growled. "The last thing I need is a doctor."

"A doctor is the first thing you need," Cassie retorted. "When are you ever going to listen to us?

Don't you realize we want you around for a long time to come—'' She bit off the words as soon as she saw the frightened look on Zak's face. ''Grandpa is going to be just fine,'' she told her son. ''Go out and play with Arthur.''

Zak hesitated, but then dashed outside.

''He's already lost too many people in his life,'' Cassie told her father. ''Don't make him lose one more, especially one as important as you.''

''That boy means everything to me,'' Robert said gruffly. ''Do you think I'd do anything to hurt him?''

''Not intentionally, no,'' Cassie said. ''But you're neglecting your own health. You look at Zak, and you see youth and promise, and you figure you're going to ignore any sign of age or weakness in yourself.''

Robert scowled. ''Think you know everything, don't you?''

''I know enough.'' Cassie poured a cup of Beth's delicious coffee, sipped it, but then set it down. ''Dad,'' she said quietly, ''it was wrong for me to come back here. Turns out I *have* been running away. From Andrew mostly, but maybe even from my own fears about being a good mother. I thought if I came back, and surrounded Zak with family, I'd make everything right again. But it hasn't happened. You *are* spoiling him, you know. And actually that is a grandfather's prerogative. But by moving back here, I've cast you into the father role. It was wrong of me. You're not Zak's dad. You can't take that place for him.''

Robert stared at her. She could tell he was getting steamed again, and that was the last thing she wanted. The Maxwell temper was altogether too volatile.

''Zak needs me,'' Robert said. ''He needs me more than once every three or four weeks. I can give him stability. A real home—''

''No,'' Cassie said, trying to keep her voice from shaking. ''I'm the one who has to do that. Not you.''

''I don't want to argue with you, Cassandra, but you've done a rotten job so far,'' he told her. The words hurt. They hurt deeply, but Cassie lifted her chin and gazed steadily back at her dad.

''Maybe I have done a rotten job,'' she said. ''I've carted Zak from one place to the next, never knowing where to settle down. But it's time for that to change.''

''This is the place for you to settle,'' Robert said. And, in spite of the harshness of his voice, there was also a pleading in his hazel eyes. That almost got to her…the silent entreaty. She'd never known Robert Maxwell Sr. to beg for anything in his life. Yes, it almost got to her.

But the time for running and hiding was over.

LATE THAT NIGHT, Cassie let herself into Hannah's guest house. Her house, she amended. Hers and

Zak's. She'd gotten the key from Hannah's lawyer, and now it was just a matter of making a home here. Of course, she'd have to send for all their things from the ranch, but she and Zak were finally going to settle down. Hannah had given them a chance to establish roots of their own, and Cassie was no longer going to refuse that chance. As far as having Andrew Morris as a trustee—well, she would deal with that later.

Zak gave a hiccup, fresh tears trickling down his face. He clutched Arthur in his arms as if the puppy was his only comfort in the world. Watching her disconsolate son, Cassie felt a twist of pain so intense that she had to draw in her breath. But she couldn't waver—not anymore. She knew, at last, that she was truly doing the right thing for Zak.

"You can call Grandpa in the morning," she said. "You can tell him how much you miss him, and how much you look forward to seeing him on our next visit to the ranch."

Zak buried his face in Arthur's fur. His voice came muffled. "What if Grandpa...what if something happens and we're not *there*..."

Cassie's heart ached all the more. Zak was so young, yet he carried the same worry she did. She knelt in front of her son and gathered him in her arms, puppy and all.

"Tell you what," she murmured. "When you call

Grandpa in the morning, you tell him exactly how you feel, and that we're counting on him to take his medicine because we love him. That way you'll be doing something to help him.''

Zak lifted his head cautiously. ''Maybe he'll listen to *me*.''

''You know, I think he just might.''

Zak looked relieved. He yawned sleepily, the tears on his face beginning to dry. Now Cassie got him settled in bed, the puppy flopped out beside him. She didn't have any sheets to put on the mattress, but no matter. All those details could come later. Zak fell asleep almost at once, his hand curled around the dog. Soon both boy and dog were snoring gently. Cassie tiptoed out of the room and down the stairs.

A knock at the door made her start. She peered out the window, and saw Andrew standing there. Her heart leaped. She had to give herself a second or two to compose herself, and then she opened the door.

''Didn't expect to see you, of all people,'' she remarked. ''Last I heard, you were back in Dallas.''

He looked as good as ever…that dark hair, those darker eyes, the broad shoulders in a Texas Rangers T-shirt.

''Mind if I come in?'' he said. He sounded oddly distracted.

She opened the door farther and ushered him inside. "Fortunately, Hannah's furniture is still here. Otherwise, Zak and Arthur would be sleeping on the floor, and…" She realized she was babbling again. She had a habit of doing that around Andrew.

"Last I heard," he said, "you were at the ranch."

"Not anymore. You were right," she said simply. "This is home for Zak and me."

"I'm glad." He said the words in an automatic tone.

"What's wrong, Andrew?" She searched his face, and saw the strain in his expression. She also saw the haunted look in his eyes. "Something *is* wrong," she exclaimed. "Andrew, what is it?"

He couldn't seem to sit still. He wandered into the living room, then into the kitchen. Cassie followed him. He sank into a chair, propped his elbows on the table and rubbed his temples.

Cassie knelt beside him. "Please tell me," she whispered.

He lifted his head and gazed at her. His eyes were still haunted. "I can't keep the promise anymore," he said. "I've tried…for twenty-five years I did what my father asked. But I can't do it anymore, Cassie. I'm so damn tired…"

She took both his hands in hers. "Tell me," she said.

He bowed his head once more. "The night my father died…the night of his accident…he'd been drinking. Not a whole lot, though. And maybe if he'd just climbed into the car, and we'd made the drive as usual…nothing would have happened. He would have arrived home safe. He'd still be alive today. But he said he was going to teach me how to drive. He let me hold the wheel, and put my foot on the gas pedal. I was sitting right next to him, and we were both driving the car. I thought it was great. I felt so damn grown-up. But then…we came around that corner, and another car was riding the yellow line. I swerved—or maybe my dad grabbed hold of the wheel, I don't know—and I don't know what my foot was doing. Maybe I was pressing down on the gas when it should have been the brake—only I thought I heard the whine of the brakes—" Andrew's voice caught.

Cassie reached up and wrapped her arms fiercely around him. "It wasn't your fault, Andrew. It wasn't…"

"He said that, too, right before he died. He said it wasn't my fault. But he made me promise not to tell anybody what really happened. Not even my mother, not even Hannah…because he didn't want me blamed. And then he died. He died while I was holding him, before anybody else could get there."

Cassie held Andrew all the more fiercely. With that promise, his father had exacted years of suffering and silence. He had imprisoned his own son, when he had wanted to do exactly the opposite.

"It wasn't your fault," she whispered again, not

letting go. But, even as she embraced the man she loved, it seemed to her that he was miles distant from her.

Maybe the damage of that promise could never be undone.

CASSIE SAT IN HER OFFICE, surrounded by case files. But she wasn't paying attention to them. Instead she had a notepad in front of her, and she was scribbling furiously. She glanced up just in time to see Jolie coming through the door. Cassie studied her in surprise.

"What are you doing here?" she asked. "I mean, it's great to see you. Really. I just didn't expect..."

"Thought I'd drop by, see how you were doing." Jolie sounded altogether too nonchalant, and Cassie wasn't buying it for a second. She leaned back in her chair.

"Let me see, you have a medical practice in Paradise Corners that is really picking up speed. You have almost more patients than you can handle these days. You also have a daughter going through all the awful and awesome throes of adolescence. Not to mention a son who can't go three minutes without knocking over a can of paint or getting into some other type of trouble. *And* not to mention a husband you're besotted with. However, you just happened to have a spare day, so you drove up to see me. Sounds perfectly reasonable, I'll agree."

Jolie was clearly trying to ignore her. She leaned over and examined the scribbled words on Cassie's notepad.

"Your handwriting's terrible," she said. "You should have been the doctor, not me."

Cassie allowed a momentary detour. "I'm brainstorming, if you must know," she said. "I'm trying to figure out what to do with my life when I quit my job."

"You actually *quit?* That's fantastic, Cassie. I know how much stress this job puts you under."

Cassie glanced all the more suspiciously at her sister. Jolie was really forcing it more than usual today. "No, I haven't given my notice yet," she said. "But I'm going to, as soon as I decide on my next career path."

"I see... What's it going to be?" asked Jolie.

"I don't know yet. That's why I'm brainstorming," Cassie explained patiently. "It's something Dr. Gwen suggested. She seems to have an idea for everything. She told me to free-associate, and write everything that came to mind. My dreams, my hopes, my fantasies. No holds barred."

"Any leads yet?" Jolie asked, sounding genuinely interested at last.

Cassie scanned her sheet. "So far, I love working with children. I love sports. Maybe I was meant to be a soccer coach...and yes, this bit here says I absolutely hate to be managed. Which gives me the distinct impression that I should be self-employed.''

''Well, I could have told you that.'' Jolie sat down in the plain wooden chair across from Cassie's desk. ''Gwen does come up with some novel ideas. I wish I'd tried to get to know her better when we were growing up. I was so afraid to let anybody get close to me. That was my way of dealing with being a Maxwell.''

Cassie shook her head. ''Jolie, I know you didn't come all the way up here to tell me how much you appreciate Dr. Gwen. What gives?''

Jolie looked very uncomfortable. ''It made perfect sense for me to drive up to Billings. I wanted to see how Bobby was doing, after all.''

Cassie nodded slowly. Bobby had not only made an appointment to see the doctor recommended by Gwen, he'd checked himself into the clinic run by the man. However, no family contact had been allowed the first few days. Cassie understood that; she realized that in problems of addiction, the whole family played a complex role. It was entirely possible that at a later date, all the Maxwells would be called in for counseling with Bobby. She tried to picture her difficult, cantankerous father in such a scenario, and almost winced. No matter how much progress had been made, the Maxwells still had a long way to go.

''Did you get to see Bobby?'' Cassie asked now.

Jolie shook her head. "That didn't seem like such a good idea. I figured he needed some space. But I called the clinic, and I was able to ask about him. And apparently he's doing fine so far. Just fine."

Cassie dared to hope that all *would* be well with their brother. Now he had Megan and his daughter waiting for him when he finished his treatment. She took comfort in that, but she sensed that she still hadn't gotten to the bottom of Jolie's visit.

"I'm sure you could have called the clinic from Paradise Corners," she said. "You didn't drive all the way up here for *that*. Stop stalling, Jolie. What's going on?"

Jolie had a pained look now. "Cassie...Thea and I discussed the possibility that maybe both of us should come up here to break the news. But then I told her no, it was better if just one of us came. I'm the doctor...I'm used to delivering difficult news, but I didn't know it would be this hard."

Fear clutched at Cassie, an icy feeling of dread. "What's happened? Is it Dad—"

"In a manner of speaking, yes." Jolie took a deep breath. "Cassie, I'm sorry, but he's initiated proceedings to file for custody. He wants Zak."

At first Cassie didn't believe she'd heard right. All she could do was stare at her sister, but that icy feeling continued to spread through her.

"You must be joking—"

"I wish I was. Dad's impossible, but this time

he's really gone too far. We've all been furious with him, we've all tried to talk him out of it, but he's already contacted his lawyers.''

Cassie was shaking as if with a fever. *My son,* she thought. *All that Maxwell power poised to take my son from me... How could my own father do this to me?* She felt faint. And that was something else she wondered—how could her body weaken so, when she needed to jump out of this chair right now and go defend her son? Defend him from his grandfather...

Jolie came around the desk and expertly prodded Cassie's head downward. ''You'll feel better in a minute or two,'' she said. ''Just take a deep breath.''

Steadied now, Cassie raised her head. Jolie took hold of her hand and held it comfortingly.

''We'll solve this together,'' she assured Cassie. ''The whole family will stand against Dad. In a way, this is so damn typical of him. When he decided that he was going to run Matt out of town, just in case Matt was a gold digger, I tell you, I've never been so mad in my life. And now *this.*''

Cassie kept hold of Jolie's hand, afraid that if she let go she'd really faint this time. ''I've heard of cases like this,'' she said, her throat tight. ''Even had one come through the office—grandparents suing for custody, charging their daughter with being an unfit mother.'' Her own words sent ice through her. *Unfit mother...*

"We'll fight it together," Jolie repeated. "That's the difference now, Cassie. We'll all help each other, and support each other—and we'll figure out what on earth our father is trying to do."

Cassie needed to hear all this. But she needed to do something else, too. She finally let go of Jolie's hand, picked up the phone and began punching a number.

"Who are you calling?" Jolie asked.

"My own lawyer. He may not love me, but he *is* damn good. And right now, I need the best lawyer there is."

CHAPTER NINETEEN

THE NEXT DAY, Cassie met with her lawyer at the community center where Zak took his swimming class. She wasn't about to let her son out of her sight if she could help it. If that meant taking off work early so she could spend time with him, so be it. Her boss wasn't happy, but Zak was infinitely more important than any boss in the world.

Cassie and Andrew sat in the bleachers in front of the pool. She watched as Zak paddled around awkwardly. There could be no denying—he wasn't very good at this. But wasn't that the whole point of swimming class? You learned. You got better. And, from what she could see here, plenty of the other kids weren't very good at swimming, either. Zak had lots of company. When he came to the side of the pool, red hair plastered against his forehead, she saw him talk briefly to another little boy. Maybe that was a sign of friendship.

"I'm glad I didn't give in," she told Andrew. "I'm glad I didn't let Zak quit this class. I think he's coming along just fine."

"I think so, too," said Andrew. "Cassie, about the talk I had with your dad—"

"You can tell me in a few minutes. Right now I just want to enjoy the sight of my son." She knew she was delaying, much the same way Jolie had delayed yesterday. It was a defense mechanism, a method for pretending that nothing really terrible had happened.

She and Andrew watched Zak in silence. There was plenty of noise around them, though: the shouts and laughter of the kids, magnified by the water and the concrete. At last Cassie stole a glance at Andrew. Maybe she was imagining it, but there seemed a peacefulness about him now. His eyes no longer seemed haunted by the past. And yet, he still kept to himself. He still seemed shut off from her. Sorrow filled her. Suddenly she felt overburdened by everything that had happened. It would be better to know right now what her father had said to Andrew.

"Please tell me," she murmured.

"He's stubborn," Andrew said. "He insists this is the best thing for Zak. He says he can devote all the time and attention that Zak needs. But clearly there's something else going on. My opinion? It's your father's way of saying he's sorry about everything that happened with your brother, and that he really *does* want a second chance."

"He has a funny way of showing it," Cassie muttered.

"Here's the rest of my professional opinion," Andrew said. "This isn't a matter for lawyers, Cassie. You need to go down there and talk to your dad."

"I can't! After what he's done, how can I possibly?"

"All the more reason," Andrew said. "He's doing this because he doesn't know any other way. All his life, he's wielded power. It's what he knows. Subtler ways of expressing himself have escaped him."

Cassie thought about going to the ranch again. She couldn't think of anything she would hate more. How could she even look at her father right now? And yet, she'd do anything for Zak.

Her cell phone rang. She fished it out of her purse and answered. As she listened to Thea's frantic voice, her fingers tightened on the phone.

"Yes," she said. "Yes, I'll get to the hospital in Bozeman as soon as I can." With trembling fingers, she closed the phone and then turned to Andrew. "It's my father," she said. "He's had a massive heart attack. This time things are so bad they don't think…they don't think he's going to make it."

ROBERT MAXWELL SR. LOOKED very frail in the hospital bed. He didn't look like the tall, imposing man who had ruled Walking Stones for decades. Instead he just looked…sick.

It had now been some hours since his attack, and his prognosis was still uncertain. But he was awake, and coherent, and demanding to see his children.

"If I'm on my deathbed," he grumbled to one of the nurses, "I damn well am going to have my last say."

Cassie, Thea and Jolie glanced at each other. Maybe it was a good sign that he still had so much spirit. But it was awful seeing him like this, a tube running into his nose, a heart monitor beside his bed. Cassie stared at the screen. The irregular blips frightened her. Maybe she was furious at her dad right now, maybe she could barely stand the thought of talking to him—but she wanted him alive.

"Where's Bobby?" he murmured, his voice hoarse.

"He's on his way," Thea assured him. "I spoke to the doctor at the clinic in Billings, explained everything. He's releasing Bobby temporarily so he can get down here. In fact, one of the staff members at the clinic is driving Bobby. They're good people at that place. Now, don't try to say anything else. Save your strength."

"I'm saying what needs to be said. Cassandra?"

Cassie moved closer to the side of the bed. "I'm here," she said.

"You hate me, don't you?" His hazel eyes were very alert.

"No, of course I don't—"

"Tell the truth, Cassandra. Now is not the time for prevaricating."

"All right," she said in a wavering voice. "Sometimes I do hate you. But I love you, too—"

"Don't get all mushy on me," he growled. He reached out and clasped her hand, his grip surprisingly strong. "Cassie...I don't want to take Zak away from you."

"Then why—"

"Dammit, I just don't want you to take him away from *me*. I don't want to lose him. I don't want to lose any of you." Something truly amazing happened now. A tear trickled out of the corner of almighty Robert Maxwell's eye. He was...*crying*.

"Oh, Dad..." Cassie leaned her forehead against the side of the bed. "I don't want to take Zak away from you. I want him to have his grandpa for years and years to come. I want you to be an old man of ninety, giving everybody grief."

"That's what I want, too," said Thea.

"So do I," said Jolie.

All three sisters gathered around their father. The tears continued to seep out of his eyes.

"Dammit," he said. "I haven't cried since... since Helen."

"We didn't even know you cried then," Jolie murmured.

"I didn't want you to know. I wanted to be strong for you..."

"We needed somebody strong," said Thea.

"I didn't know what to do after your mother died." His voice had grown fainter. Jolie glanced at the heart monitor and nodded silently. They would let him talk.

"I tried my best," he murmured. "But girls...I didn't know how to raise girls. I thought I knew what to do with Bobby...but I failed there, too."

The Maxwell patriarch, admitting failure. That was something terribly new also.

"We all turned out pretty well, don't you think?" Cassie asked him. "You must have done something right."

"Something...I wish..." He sighed, his eyelids drifting shut. Cassie wanted to shake him, to tell him that he couldn't go. *You can't leave now, not when you're finally telling us that you care. We have so much lost time to make up for...*

Just then, Bobby came into the room. As he approached the hospital bed, his face was white. "Is he...?"

Robert Sr. opened his eyes and scowled at his only son. "I'm still alive, if that's what you mean."

Relief flashed across Bobby's face. "Glad to hear it," he said. "We happen to...love you."

"Lord," Robert said with a hint of the old bellow. "What are they doing to you in that damn clinic? Teaching you to emote?"

"Something like that." Bobby grinned.

"Dammit all, I love you, too!" He glared at each of his children in turn. "Bobby, get one of those nurses in here," he said then. "Tell them to crank the bed up—I'm not going to lie here like a beached salmon."

"I'll do it, Dad," Jolie said, carefully turning the bed handle.

"I'm trying on a new name for size," Bobby remarked.

"Dammit," Robert growled, "that confounded clinic is getting you to change your name, too? What's it going to be—Merry Sunshine?"

"I was thinking more on the lines of Robert Jr."

Robert Sr. closed his eyes. "I like the sound of that," he said gruffly. "I like it fine."

FIRST METHODIST CHURCH in Paradise Corners, Montana, had never looked more festive. White and gold streamers lined all the pews, and the stained-glass windows sparkled. The bride standing with her mother at the very back of the church sparkled, too. Her dark auburn hair was caught up beneath a lacy veil, and her floor-length gown shimmered as she moved. She clutched a bouquet of miniature white roses in both hands.

"I'm so nervous," she said. "What if I trip or something?"

"I'll catch you in my wheelchair," said Robert

Maxwell Sr. "That'll be a sight—me carting my son's bride up the aisle."

"Don't forget I'll be pushing you," said Thea. "I can get going pretty fast."

"Thanks for giving me away, Mr. Maxwell," said Megan. A shadow fell across her face. Her own dad was behind bars and undergoing psychiatric therapy. Maybe he'd been a terrible father to Megan and her sister, abusing them physically on more than one occasion, but still...she was probably wishing everything could have been different.

"Sometimes," Cassie said, "you just have to go on. You have to stop wishing for things the way you'd like them to be." She saw the sympathetic glances her sisters gave her. They, no doubt, knew she was thinking of Andrew.

"Let's get this show on the road," said Robert Sr. "I want to see my son married before my granddaughter has her *own* wedding."

Jolie held baby Melissa in her arms. "We've got some time yet before we have to worry about this one. You're still trying to control everything, aren't you, Dad?"

"Of course I am," he muttered. "Just wait until I get out of this damn wheelchair—then you'll all be sorry."

For now, Robert's wheelchair was having quite an effect on the citizens of Paradise Corners. Apparently it made Boss Maxwell seem more accessi-

ble. All morning people had been coming up to him,
stopping by just for a chat. In the past, no one had
dared to subject Robert Maxwell Sr. to small talk.

The wedding march had started, the music swell-
ing joyously throughout the church. And now the
wedding party proceeded down the aisle: Jolie's
stepdaughter, Lily, and Megan's sister, Lisa, were
the flower girls, while the matron of honor, Jolie,
carried baby Melissa. Bridesmaids Cassie and Racey
came along, too. Before Bobby's accident, Racey
Taylor had been Megan's best friend. But she'd also
been—still was, in fact—Dan Aiken's girlfriend.
Her grief over Dan's injuries had turned to anger
against Bobby and Megan. At last, though, it seemed
as if all the wounds from that terrible night were
beginning to heal. Megan and Racey were friends
again—and Racey was as misty-eyed as the rest of
the wedding party. Even the two ring bearers, Zak
and Charlie, seemed a bit overwhelmed by the occasion. There had been a brief panic earlier, when
Charlie had momentarily lost one of the rings. But
now, both gold wedding bands were perched on the
velvet pillows where they belonged.

Megan came floating down the aisle between
Robert Sr. and her own mother. Bridesmaid Thea,
despite her threat, rolled the wheelchair along at a
sedate pace. At the altar, Robert Jr. waited with his
three best men—Rafe and Matt, and Dan Aiken.
Dan and Robert Jr. had made their peace. They were

best friends, just as before… No, not entirely as before. Their friendship had a depth and strength now. It had been tested, and it had survived. Dan might be in his own wheelchair for the rest of his life—no one could tell for certain. But proceedings were under way to help him as much as possible; a good part of Bobby's inheritance would be used to set up a trust fund for Dan. This fact seemed to have given Bobby an added hopefulness.

Meanwhile, Robert Jr. was gazing only at his fiancée. Robert Sr. did the honors of giving her away, and Thea wheeled him next to the pew where Beth sat. Beth reached over and straightened his tie. He grumbled at her. Beth was going to have her hands full, but she seemed equal to the task. She looked lovely today, in a blue gown and a little blue hat. Everyone was present and accounted for…everyone except Andrew, of course.

The reception took place at Four Pines Lodge, a suitably elegant venue. Robert Sr. had spared no expense, having hired a twenty-piece orchestra for the occasion. Cassie watched all the couples take to the dance floor: Robert Jr. and Megan, Rafe and Thea, Matt and Jolie. Racey even wheeled Dan onto the floor, the two of them smiling gently at each other as Racey moved the chair to the music. Well, *Cassie* would dance with Zak. She might even take ten-year-old Charlie for a whirl.

"This must be our waltz," Andrew's voice said from behind her.

Cassie swiveled so fast she almost dumped her fruit punch all over Andrew's tuxedo. Her heart was beating so fast she thought she might have to call Jolie over for some medical attention.

"Dammit, Andrew," she said at last. "What are *you* doing here?"

"You sound just like your dad," he said. He looked wonderful in a tuxedo. Wonderful and impossible...

"I love you, Cassie," he murmured. "It's taken me a long time to say those words. So long, in fact, that I'd better get everything out at once. Will you marry me?"

She set down her punch with an unsteady hand. Then she gazed into his eyes and realized that she no longer saw the haunted look there. Instead all she saw was...love.

Part of her still didn't dare to believe. "You can't do this to me," she said shakily. "You can't just come in here and expect that I'll go into your arms and say yes." But that's exactly what she did. She went straight into his arms. And "Yes," she said. "Yes!"

He held her close, the two of them swaying to the music. "I love you," he repeated, his voice low and husky. "I love you with all my heart. I want to spend my life with you, and then some. I guess I just had to forgive myself before I could tell you so.''

''Andrew, you don't have anything to forgive yourself for.''

They swayed together some more, but what they were doing could scarcely qualify as a dance. It might even be considered scandalous.

''Andrew,'' Cassie murmured, ''I think we really *should* waltz.''

He drew her onto the dance floor. ''I've got my truck parked outside,'' he said. ''A Montana truck. Figure I can do some lawyering around here.''

''Andrew, Texas is just fine—''

''So is Montana,'' he told her, and drew her closer. Thea and Jolie gave Cassie glances that were altogether too smug. *See,* they seemed to say. *See what happens when you fall in love.*

Joy…that was what happened.

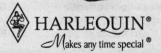

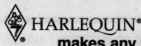

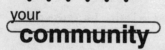

If you enjoyed what you just read,
then we've got an offer you can't resist!

Take 2 bestselling love stories FREE!

Plus get a FREE surprise gift!

Clip this page and mail it to Harlequin Reader Service®

IN U.S.A.	IN CANADA
3010 Walden Ave.	P.O. Box 609
P.O. Box 1867	Fort Erie, Ontario
Buffalo, N.Y. 14240-1867	L2A 5X3

YES! Please send me 2 free Harlequin Superromance® novels and my free surprise gift. After receiving them, if I don't wish to receive anymore, I can return the shipping statement marked cancel. If I don't cancel, I will receive 6 brand-new novels every month, before they're available in stores. In the U.S.A., bill me at the bargain price of $4.05 plus 25¢ shipping and handling per book and applicable sales tax, if any*. In Canada, bill me at the bargain price of $4.46 plus 25¢ shipping and handling per book and applicable taxes**. That's the complete price, and a saving of at least 10% off the cover prices—what a great deal! I understand that accepting the 2 free books and gift places me under no obligation ever to buy any books. I can always return a shipment and cancel at any time. Even if I never buy another book from Harlequin, the 2 free books and gift are mine to keep forever.

135 HEN DFNA
336 HEN DFNC

Name	(PLEASE PRINT)	
Address	Apt.#	
City	State/Prov.	Zip/Postal Code

* Terms and prices subject to change without notice. Sales tax applicable in N.Y.
** Canadian residents will be charged applicable provincial taxes and GST.
  All orders subject to approval. Offer limited to one per household and not valid to
  current Harlequin Superromance® subscribers.
® is a registered trademark of Harlequin Enterprises Limited.

SUP01   ©1998 Harlequin Enterprises Limited

*H*ugh Blake,
soon to become stepfather to
the Maitland clan, has produced three
high-performing offspring of his own. But
at the rate they're going, they're never going to
make him a grandpa!

There's *Suzanne*, a work-obsessed CEO whose Christmas spirit
could use a little topping up....

And *Thomas*, a lawyer whose ability to hold on to the woman
he loves is evaporating by the minute....

And *Diane*, a teacher so dedicated to her teenage students she
hasn't noticed she's put her own life on hold.

But there's a Christmas wake-up call in store
for the Blake siblings. Love *and* Christmas miracles
are in store for all three!

Maitland Maternity
Christmas

A collection from three of Harlequin's favorite authors

Muriel Jensen
Judy Christenberry
&Tina Leonard

Look for it in November 2001.

CALL THE ONES YOU LOVE OVER THE HOLIDAYS!

Save $25 off future book purchases when you buy any four Harlequin® or Silhouette® books in October, November and December 2001,

PLUS

receive a phone card good for 15 minutes of long-distance calls to anyone you want in North America!

WHAT AN INCREDIBLE DEAL!

Just fill out this form and attach 4 proofs of purchase (cash register receipts) from October, November and December 2001 books, and Harlequin Books will send you a coupon booklet worth a total savings of $25 off future purchases of Harlequin® and Silhouette® books, AND a 15-minute phone card to call the ones you love, anywhere in North America.

Please send this form, along with your cash register receipts as proofs of purchase, to:
In the USA: Harlequin Books, P.O. Box 9057, Buffalo, NY 14269-9057
In Canada: Harlequin Books, P.O. Box 622, Fort Erie, Ontario L2A 5X3
Cash register receipts must be dated no later than December 31, 2001.
Limit of 1 coupon booklet and phone card per household.
Please allow 4-6 weeks for delivery.

**I accept your offer! Enclosed are 4 proofs of purchase.
Please send me my coupon booklet
and a 15-minute phone card:**

Name: _____

Address: _____ City: _____

State/Prov.: _____ Zip/Postal Code: _____

Account Number (if available): _____

---

097 KJB DAGL
PHQ4013